Twisted
Heart

REBECCA GOWERS is the author of *The Swamp of Death* (Hamish Hamilton), the true story of a fatal showdown between a late Victorian con man and a corrupt detective, shortlisted in 2004 for a CWA Gold Dagger award. Her first novel, *When to Walk* (Canongate), was longlisted for the Orange Broadband Prize for Fiction in 2007.

Also by Rebecca Gowers

Fiction
When to Walk

Non-fiction
The Swamp of Death

The Twisted Heart

REBECCA GOWERS

CANONGATE

Edinburgh · London · New York · Melbourne

CHAPTER 1

There was an hour of learning steps, then an hour of social dancing. Kit learned the steps but she didn't stay for the dancing.

The hall, property of St Christopher's, was more cramped and more decrepit than she had pictured it. Just to get in you had to edge round stacks of unmatched plastic chairs. The street-side windows were filled with wire glass. The walls were littered with Sellotape, tin tacks, the dog-ends of near-illegible notes: *do not DO NOT* boiling wa—Thursdays *Every Time BUT*. The plasterwork, too, was a mess. In another part of the world half the plaster damage might have been taken for bullet holes. Or perhaps this was another part of the world? Even the air carried the dead-alive smell of split sewerage cut with bleach products. Kit felt near illegible herself as she paced the beautiful, old, battered, softly sprung floor.

She had wavered, up in her little attic bedroom in the late summer gloom, thinking, Friday evening, should she go out and dance, or flick on the lights and settle down to some work? She had failed to imagine at all accurately what she'd be in for, the dirty wire glass, wrecked plaster, eau-de-Nil paint, a maladjusted sound system, not that any of this really mattered. The moment the class had begun she'd ceased to register these things, and had instead succumbed to the rote enthusiasm of the endlessly yelling instructor, 'That's it, people, *passion!*—one *two,* three *four*; come *on*, come *on*; let's *see,* you *move*—hips!, TWO, three *four*. Excellent, nice—TWO, three *four*; and *left*, and—WHAP! Nice there, better—whap *whap*, whap *whap*; like *this,* like THIS! Girls?—cooee, you all right, mate?—three FOUR; keep *up*, keep *up*; and *next* and LEFT and *hips!*, and LEFT and—'

*

Kit, once she'd chosen to go dancing, had discovered as she walked along to the bus stop that it was warmer outside than in. She had got herself to the hall, all the way across town, but that had only been the start of things because, having shown up for the Beginners try-out session, she had found that it was full. Full? It hadn't even occurred to her this was possible.

The instructor had shouted, at Kit and others, the surplus gaggle of them, that they could either try again, 'Okay, next week Thursday', or could wait an hour, come back and try Intermediate.

Once more, Kit had found herself wavering. Intermediate? How hard was *that* likely to be? Would she be able to hack it, more or less? Would it be worth the wait of an hour? And if she waited, tried, and found it too difficult, then what?

She teetered on the verge of abandoning her project. She could have caught a bus back into town never to return, and she'd considered this. But, stepping out of the hall onto the pavement, she had spotted a café opposite through a break in the traffic, had, seizing the moment, run through the traffic without especially thinking about it, over the road and into the café, Pams Cafe, had bought herself a sandwich and a cup of tea and—there she had found herself with an hour and nothing much to do.

That was what had happened, not planned or anything.

Of course, her dash through the break in the traffic, had she misjudged it just a little, whap *whap*, whap *whap*, she could have been killed. And that would have been it.

Kit had picked this particular dance club mostly on account of its being run out of a hall up the nearest hill in East Oxford; not a hill, more a slope really—St Christopher's Social Dance Club, an easy stroll from the estates lying on the inner outskirts, as she conceived it, of the roughest edge of town. What she'd fancied to herself, when she had happened upon a flyer advertising the class, had been beginner dancers dancing up the hill, twirling like deranged weathervanes on a level with the tops of the city's ghoulish spires. This much she had pictured, set within a church hall that had not, in her imagination, appeared war-damaged.

Instead of any of which, here she was at a table in a comfortless East Oxford café with a cheese-pickle sandwich and a large cup of tea. The only work-related material she had with her was the notebook that she kept in her bag. She got it out and flipped through the pages: brief comments on a seminar from the end of the previous term, 'Electricity and the Imagination', heard it all before. Notes from *The Times* on the Bermondsey cholera outbreak, 1849, 'N.B. several witnesses in the Manning murder case died of cholera before they could give evidence'—amusing at a distance, she reflected; though, amusing? Notes in rough for the first lesson she'd given Orson:

> O. TWIST. Plot—Dickens begins it in instalments starting Feb. 1837. Almost certainly initially intended as just a few episodes, 'The Parish Boy's Progress', social satire—only then? does Dickens decide to upgrade it to a full-blown criminal-romance serial novel. N.B. includes a brutal prostitute-murder, Nancy bludgeoned to death in her bedroom by her pimp, Sikes and—

Kit was bored. She flicked backwards through the pages, stopping randomly at a list she'd scribbled months earlier, names of various criminal suspects mentioned in the memoirs of John Wilson Murray, a late nineteenth-century Ontario detective: 'Hunker Chisholm, Knotty O'Brian, Senator Voorhees, Young Billy Nay, Nettie Slack, Napper Nichols, Poke Soles, counterfeiter, or "shover of the queer". Polly Ripple, Meta Cherry, Baldy Drinkwater, Ebenezer Ward'— was 'Meta' a real name? Yes, certainly it was.

After half an hour Kit bought a second cup of tea. Intermediate-level dancing—perhaps, come to think of it, it was preferable to fail where there was no hope of succeeding, i.e., perhaps Intermediate would be less embarrassing than Beginners, not more so. Well, so what? The principal point was to avoid meeting anyone she knew, because all Kit was really after was to lose herself in some steps, a form of loss for which, in her view, anonymity was a prerequisite. She glanced over the road and thought, bloody hell, and wondered, what am I doing here in this shabby little café?

Answer: she was reading, or trying to.

Kit tried to read. On the page facing the name list she had recorded the outlines of a couple of Detective Murray's cases. In one he had posed as a comatose dosser under a bench, simulating unconsciousness in order to eavesdrop on a gang of firemen who were suspected of setting fires for profit. The firemen, in turn, had seized this opportunity to urinate all over him. Pissing arsonists, Kit thought. She found she had also copied out—mainly, she deduced, because the line was in metre—Murray's description, p. 73, of the effect on a farmer's wife of being forced to confess to murder: 'Her eyes were like those of an ox in whose throat the butcher's knife has been buried.' And then, God, below this, yes, here were notes, sentences Kit had patiently transcribed one after another, concerning the case of Jessie Keith, a young girl—a real young girl, these were real cases—Jessie Keith, who had gone missing near Listowel, Ontario, on October 19th, 1894:

> The party hunting beyond the Keith home came upon the pieces of a body lying in the woods. Newly turned earth showed them where the parts had been buried. Other portions were spread out while others had been tossed into the brush. Tightly wrapped around the neck was a white petticoat, soaked crimson. The head was uncovered and the pretty face of Jessie Keith was revealed. The girl had been disembowelled and carved into pieces.

Kit bent closer to the page. In almost hieroglyphic scrawl her notes indicated that the hunting party had been able to find, and had roughly reassembled, some two-thirds only of Jessie Keith's body. Detective Murray had been called in, and had tracked down a locally escaped lunatic called Almeda Chattelle; and no doubt it was the warped lucidity of this madman's explanations that had led to his being found fully responsible for the crime. To Kit, though, re-reading Chatelle's remarks, he seemed about as insane as it was possible for a single human being to be. He had spoken with ostensible distress about the moment at which he had taken the pretty girl, of how it had come over him 'like a flash':

> 'I grabbed her around the waist and carried her to the woods. She screamed and dug her heels into the ground, so I tied the white skirt around her neck. She still struggled, so I took out my knife and I cut her across this way and then down this way, and I threw away the parts of her I did not wish, and the parts I liked I treated considerately, and later I buried them under a tree. I was not unkind to the parts I liked.'

The parts I liked I treated considerately, and later—later? *The parts I liked I*—I was *not unkind* to the parts I—

Kit, repelled, allowed her gaze to leap up from the page and was confronted by the sight of people spilling elatedly from the hall. Beginners try-out was over. Her pulse started to race, she snapped her notebook shut, rose like an automaton to her feet.

There was an hour of learning steps, then an hour of social dancing. And the learning part was fine. It was great. In sum, it engaged Kit completely without being so hard she couldn't do it.

The instructor started off with a flurry of points. 'Bit of

a crowd in, extras from Beginners, please, chaps, ladies, this side, that side. I know, I know. We'll learn the steps in groups. Ghost partners for now, call it a refresher lesson; sorry, folks. Next week—Beginners will be Thursdays from next week, not Fridays, *do not forget*—it's in at the deep end for you new people, it's—aren't we popular!'

But the shouting, where it actually mattered, was a case simply of, 'Right, girls this side, blokes that side'. The term 'ghost partners', meanwhile, was as much as to say that they would all be dancing alone.

Kit observed at once, immediately, that she was the tallest person there, and so was relieved about the pairing business. Being paired off, or worse still, failing to be paired off, was what she had most dreaded about the entire exercise. If only she had known this wasn't going to happen, or not straight away—phantom partners, 'ghost position', arms circling no one—how much better she might have endured her slow and fretful hour of waiting. You goof, she said to herself repeatedly, as she paced the sprung floorboards and waited to begin.

Even the dancing wasn't at all what she had expected. The instant they started Kit found herself exhilaratedly stamping in formation with the other girls. The boys, men, danced in a block to the side of them, a different dance, the complement, obviously, to their own; *Polly Ripple* one side, *Senator Voorhees* the other—'whap *whap*, whap *whap*; like *this,* like *THIS.* Girls?—cooee, you all right, mate?—three *FOUR*; keep *up*, keep *up*; and *next* and *LEFT* and *hips!*, and *LEFT* and—' And the fact that numbers of people found it difficult led

7

to incidental chaos, but this exhilarated Kit too. It lifted her spirits. It was—'whap *whap*, whap *whap*'—exhilarating simply to be exhilarated; not at all what she had been picturing when she'd sat motionless on her bed. She had imagined a much more floaty experience. The mob aspect felt—'yes *yes*'—like preparation for a war. It was therefore no doubt somewhat debasing, she thought vacantly; though if so, it was definitely debasing in an uplifting-feeling way—if that wasn't, oh brilliant!—what being debased *meant*.

After a while, Kit consciously began to take stock, noticed the glimpses of shimmer on her side of the hall, these girls dressier than the Beginner crowd had been, more serious, the ones who could do it, pearl-spangled skirts, sequins, gloss, their more pronounced movements leading to after-tremors of glint—'and *left*, and *back*, and *three*, and *turn*'—their hair though, in the main, impeccably unmoving. Kit wasn't dressed right, but she hadn't expected she would be, not even for Beginners; this distinction she had swallowed in advance—'yes *yes*. That's it, people, *passion!*—one *two*, three *four*; come *on*, come *on*; let's *see*, you *move—hips!*, TWO, three *four*. Excellent, nice—TWO, three *four*; and *left*, and—WHAP! Nice there; good you!—better—'

Kit tried to stop thinking. And for a while, it was everything she had wished it to be, and she lost herself in the steps. Yet as minute succeeded minute, she came slowly back to herself, realising that if she was happy to be implicit in a gang, this pleasure by no means fully offset the awkwardness of managing such steps alone. With her body she felt keenly the lack of a partner. She hankered for his missing balance—force?—lilt? It was disordering to be unsupported. Especially her top half felt adrift. With her feet, the steps, the formation stamping, the experience was fun. But her top half keened to be held.

She grasped that the first hour was done only when the instructor shouted, 'Ten minutes,' before adding with a saucy wink that after this they'd be able to pair themselves off or not as they pleased, as it fell out.

Kit walked over and propped herself up against the pockmarked wall, closing her eyes as small defence against a sudden but not surprising fit of light-headedness. Most people had shuffled towards the back to drink water they'd brought with them. The noise of those who knew each other or were just friendly covered the silence of those who didn't or weren't—a mash of sound that receded crazily fast as Kit bent, crouched, slid floorwards, head tipped between her knees, afraid she might be pitching into a faint.

When she had sufficiently recovered—it was only a few seconds, and she was used to the brief descent of this somehow razorish fog—she hauled herself back up onto her feet and passed amongst the others, shaken still, but aware of their ironical comments, their complaints, their readjusting of garments and fanning of faces. Kit went to her bag, picked it up, looked inside it for no accountable reason, and then quietly, downheartedly, slipped away.

It hadn't been like any dance club she had ever heard about or seen represented on screen, or, indeed, dreamed of.

On the contrary, the place had felt borderline hostile, not to mention its being so badly organised. There were all sorts of reasons to leave, yet the one most acceptable to her, irritatingly enough, was the fact that she had been the tallest person there; not by much, but even so.

She had noticed it at once, and had had the duration of the first hour to get over it. Easy to say that it couldn't have mattered less. In some part of her mind she *had* said this to herself, for an hour.

Then she'd left.

Outside on the hall steps, Kit shivered. It was cooler now and her own heat was largely expended. She decided to salvage the evening by fitting in a short stint at the library. Pams Cafe, where in virtual solitude she had sat out the previous hour of her life for the price of a sandwich and two cups of tea, had transformed itself into the strip-lit refuge of four, five, six huddled figures.

Kit walked up the street, drooped against the bus stop and stared back at them, and it came to her abruptly that of everyone on the Ontario-criminals name list, it was Jessie Keith, a child one day cut into pieces and then in some appalling fashion raped, who had best exemplified the name, *Meta Cherry*. In the act of forming this thought—too late, that is—Kit wished her mind would leave words alone where words didn't serve.

The scene through the café window, plus the window itself, scattered over with special offers handwritten on dayglo stars, looked like a black-and-white photograph, 'Useless People at Twilight', that happened to have come out in colour.

Who were they all, Kit wondered, these wasters? She stared at them, annoyed, until two of them started to laugh, at which she was pierced by a sense of her own loneliness. Oh yes, she thought, more annoyed still, and isn't this just exactly the kind of moment where you're supposed to ask, 'What is life for?'

While she was busy replying to herself that this was a question she was unqualified to address, she was startled by a hand on her arm, 'You off then?' She—a man had taken hold of her, nondescript, tough, thin, Kit only peripherally looked at him—crop-haired, a not-quite-youngish man.

He let go.

Kit said, 'I'm just catching the bus,' and looked back at the café, at the laughing people inside it, at the sun-bleached, illustrated menu, green and orange dayglo stars. She looked around at the street, at the world, at the rest of the world, at a cyclist, a graffitied dustbin, a kid opposite who—

'You're okay, are you?'

—a kid opposite who was walking along with odd, stiff, jolly, deliberate steps.

The man hesitated then tried again. 'Were you thinking of coming back next week?'

Not now, I'm not, thought Kit, though she hadn't been planning to anyway.

'I was hoping I might get a chance to dance with you,' he said. 'You were—you didn't want to try out with a partner?'

Kit felt got at. She was a definite pip taller than him. She drew herself up. She muttered, 'I don't know, I have to be off.' As she had just left the hall, wasn't that pretty obvious?

'Might you make it next time, do you think?' he asked.

'If I can,' she said, gracelessly.

'Joe,' he said, and held out the hand with which he had notionally detained her.

She shook hands—how could she not?—and seemed to remember hearing that blind people judged the beauty of strangers by the feel of their hands. What did his hand feel like? He was nondescript, tough. His hand was nondescript, tough. It meant nothing to her. What might her hand feel like, come to think of it, to him? Nothing, also?

'Kit,' she replied.

'Kit?'

'*Kit*,' she said, more distinctly. Perhaps he wasn't nondescript after all. Tough though, yes. There was about him a certain—what? He caught her eye, smiled and turned away, and walked away back towards the hall.

On the short return bus ride down the hill to town, Kit felt furious. She often thought about joining this or that club, society, about attending events, getting out, meeting people. She would think about it, would revolve the idea in her mind, would feel she had understood whatever it was she wished to understand, and would then proceed to remain at home. The scheme of a dance club, of really going to one—the fact that she had done it had been an exception.

Now, trailing along in the traffic past the drearily colourful little Cowley Road shops, murals, tawdry and decayed; now, sitting on the bus in a bad mood, it felt to Kit as though she had left the dance class expressly to avoid, as he had said he was called, *Joe*; though the fact was, she hadn't known he existed until after she'd got outside. She wished she had walked back down into town, he wouldn't have caught up with her then; but she had wanted, and did want, to fit in time at the library, and it was late.

For an instant what felt like another hand settled lightly on her head, the gesture of a priest. But it turned out to be the elbow of a young man who, as he walked past her seat, paused to get the zip up on his jacket. Kit shook herself, faintly disgusted.

She had left the club because she'd been too tall, and because she'd had the sense that depression was gathering, not within her exactly, but at the edges of the experience. She had had the powerful sense that if she didn't get out while the going was good, it would cease to be good; that the going barely *was* good, in fact—was pretty weird, you might say—but that the thing was still at a stage where it would be possible to think about it afterwards as having been good, maybe, viewed in retrospect; the stamping, for example, humorous. She could still be funny about it speaking to someone who hadn't been there, about the self-regarding boys and the girls with their glue-hard hair—if she chose, and had anyone to speak *to*.

Had she stayed, however, she didn't doubt that she would very soon have reached the point where going to a dance club would have seemed like something she should have known from the start was a mistake, a girl like her, going to a dance club off up out eastwards from town. It almost felt like a mistake now, either despite her having been asked back, or because of it—because he, so-called *Joe*, had made her wonder really why she had gone: Joe. He had looked capable; but capable of what, she had no idea.

When the bus reached the High Street, Kit walked along the aisle from the back to the middle exit, stooping to pick up a wallet-sized zip bag that lay on the floor. Ahead, the Queen Street stop was already blocked by several other buses, so Kit's driver pulled up short. Kit made a hasty offer of the bag to the nearest passenger, a woman, who took it from her in confusion. 'Oh my God,' she said, then, 'Thanks. You're a star.'

The driver bent round to see what was happening. Kit scowled back at him.

As she ran over the High Street she said to herself, you're a star. *You're a star!*

She loped up the Old Bodleian Library's main staircase two steps at a time. These steps always felt wrong to her. She assumed their dimensions had been worked out so far in the past that even tall people had been short then. At any rate, one step at a time reduced her to mincing her way up, while two required an over-long stretch, and what she considered uncouth athleticism.

Happily, going down was different. Unless she was positively unwell, Kit liked to rush down this staircase one step at a time as fast as possible, giving her a buzz akin to riffling her thumb through a 900-page paperback.

She had ordered for herself, on a whim, two different editions of the novel *Eugene Aram*, based on the life of a real murderer, and written by Dickens's friend, Bulwer

Lytton. She also expected to find waiting in her name a clutch of W. S. Hayward's so-so erotic novels. These Kit had ordered from the library's low-frequency storage dump in case there was any merit in recommending them to her sole student, Orson McMurphy, whose name, she now realised, made him sound rather like a late nineteenth-century Ontario cattle thief.

Kit slipped through the swing doors of the upper reading room and attempted to walk noiselessly across its exasperating cork floor. She didn't want to draw attention to herself, not that it was any big deal. Who spent their Friday nights in the library before the start of a new academic year? Outcasts and lunatics, was her answer to this question, or more bracingly, those with nothing better to do.

She strolled light-footed past the ranks of vast work tables, towards the issue desks, about to have to retrieve a stack of mid-Victorian erotica, oh dear. She had long since stopped needing to give the librarians her name. They recognised her as 'Farr, Christine Iris', and would hand her her books in silence. The regular librarians, Kit thought, were like barmaids to her mind, with the upper reading room her favourite mental watering hole. What'll it be tonight? I'll take a half of Bulwer Lytton with a low-grade erotica chaser, thanks. And what did the librarians care? They didn't care. Would they even know what the books were? Presumably not. Nevertheless, *The Soiled Dove*, *Skittles in Paris*, *Anonyma*.

The reading room was calm and warm, peaceful, concentrated, enclosed by the vision of nightfall. The great windows glittered where light from the ceiling lamps reflected off the insides of the panes. Kit took seat 103 and stared out through the glass at the looming roofline of huge, ancient buildings, each one caught in its own dense dose of sickish electric glare.

She was back in a good mood because she had questions in her head that intrigued her to which she was about to find out a few answers. What a blessing so much of the trash she wished to consult had survived the purges of well-informed librarians long ago. *The Soiled Dove*, though, 1865, oh God, she thought.

It proved to be a pathetic story. The Honourable Plaistow Cunninghame liked to arrange fake wedding ceremonies for himself, performed by his good friend Black, and would then debauch his latest supposed bride for as long as she amused him—so far, so hackneyed. His career had reportedly begun with the apple-cheeked, country-girl type, figured in the person of Dolly Dimsdale; but at the novel's start he could be found upgrading to the sweet-natured and well-bred, though inadequately protected heroine, Laura Merrivale. How enchanting when she remarks, 'Papa says I am playful.'

Kit whisked her way through three hundred pages of wickedness to the point where Cunninghame, in a contrary and drink-sozzled fit, had been reduced to hurling himself out of an upper-storey window, with the conclusive result, the next sentence, that his 'brains bespattered the roadway'. And a couple of pages after *that*, there was Laura Merrivale frozen to death on a bench in the Mall at half past three in the morning. Tough for both of them, but quite a thrill for the reader.

Hayward's last word on the subject, which Kit scribbled down in her notebook, was, 'Life exposes those who enjoy it to many vicissitudes.' In brackets, she added childishly, 'On the other hand, life's just wonderful for those who don't enjoy it, right?' There was one other quote, regarding the Honourable Plaistow Cunninghame, that she couldn't resist: 'He had commenced his holocaust to the Moloch of lust when he was very young, for he was naturally depraved and vicious.'

Kit rolled this phrase luxuriously around her mind. A middle-aged man squeaked across the cork tiles behind her, a reader coughed, a couple of people murmured a greeting. How many of them, she wondered, were contemplating in their blood some small contribution, quite soon—that night preferably—towards their own little holocaust to the Moloch of lust?

And so immediately did she form a reply to this question, if not quite an answer, that she found herself mouthing, 'You take your chances.' Kit glanced sideways, having talked to herself, to see whether anyone was perhaps observing her, around or over the wooden screen fixed along the centre of her table. What her eyes finally met, however, was the reading room clock. She didn't want to be chased out when the place closed for the night. No more time for Skittles and Anonyma, with their merry vales and dim dales—the erotics of deluded consent. It was more urgent that she press on with Bulwer Lytton and his attempts to justify exploiting in fiction the case of an infamous, true-life murderer.

She opened the earlier edition of his novel, 1831, and read the preface at speed. Eugene Aram, though he had, yes, been a killer, had also been a scholarly gentleman, hence neither a 'vulgar ruffian', nor a 'profligate knave'. In other words, Aram had been no dismal, commonplace, *ordinary* murderer, but an intriguing 'anomaly', fine, well, nothing new in that argument.

Kit slowed her pace, read properly, compared the earlier with the later preface, jotted down a few notes, felt an abrupt burst of fatigue, jumped up, handed her books back in, and wondered, ashamed, what Hayward would have made of the name, 'Fanny Price'. As she skimmed down the Bodleian stairs, she recalled the frame of mind she'd been in coming up them and thought, this is a silly existence I'm leading—which was fine so long as she didn't care.

Which led her to ask herself, as she quit the library, what the point was to caring, about anything? For example, why had Joe, if that was really his name, smiled at her on parting? It hadn't felt fair, somehow, the fact that he had smiled as he turned away.

It was dark outside. Kit crossed Broad Street, briefly slewing the axis of her shoulders so that she would pass untouched through a group of revellers, drinkers, loud voices, along to St Giles and beyond, up the Woodstock Road—pale, late-blooming roses glimmering in a front garden—strode at her usual swift pace as soon as this was possible, quarter of an hour to where she lived in a tiny room on the top floor of what had once been a substantial mansion.

It still was a mansion in its brickwork, but the building had been crudely converted years before into graduate lodgings. Kit took it that her own room had originally been quarters for a suffering maid or two. Below her, on the family floors, other residents of the house had scored a drawing room, a parlour, a visitor's room, what have you.

Kit slipped up to the attic flat, surplus married quarters awaiting renovation, and went into her own room. She shut the door behind her—not a confirmed habit—and began to dance with herself the fastest dance she'd learned in class, though she did this in a quiet, hoppish way; quiet, so that if he was in, she didn't disturb the boy who lived beneath her; hoppish, because strewn across her floor there lay a mass of papers and books.

Hoppishly she twirled, her arms curved out in front of her, in ghost position, imagining being held. And if nothing else, she *was* being held, by her thoughts.

After a few such solitary minutes, Kit took a leap to her desk chair, landing with a gleeful thump on her bottom. 'Zip, zip, zip!' she cried. She switched on her computer and set to, copying out scribbles from her notebook:

N.B. 1831 preface to *Eugene Aram* = Bulwer defends having tampered with the 'historical' record on the grounds that his alterations constitute moral improvements: 'With the facts on which the tale of EUGENE ARAM is founded, I have exercised the common and fair licence of writers of fiction.' But nine years later, after being attacked for writing on such a dubious topic in the first place, he produces a new preface = 'Did I want any other answer to the animad-versions of commonplace criticism, it might be sufficient to say that what the historian relates, the novelist has little right to disdain.'

Meaning what? In 1831, if Bulwer's version was moral, that trumped the need to be factual, but in 1840, if it was factual, that released him from the requirement to be moral? Yes? No?

Kit tried for about ten seconds to work out whether or not these positions were mutually exclusive. Anyway, rubbish, she thought. Weren't the murder details, true or false, intended principally to be entertaining? Of course they were. She abandoned the subject in order to construct a new reading list for Orson. It had been amongst a heap of flyers on a shelf below the pigeon holes in Orson's lodging block, before she'd been given his email address, that she had found the leaflet that advertised the St Christopher's Social Dance Club. It was *your* fault I went, she thought, mentally addressing Orson in words.

He had done his *Oliver Twist* essay for her in week one of his course. Week two, this week, he'd done a second essay, on lawyers' clerks. Now Kit wanted him to think about the alluring character of the woman detective in nineteenth-century British police fiction. 'Orson: Week Three', she tapped, 'Reading + Questions to Bear in Mind'.

Some time past eleven, exhausted and growing dull, Kit creaked up onto her feet and went to the kitchen. The moment the idea of supper struck her, she wanted to eat; but as she was still deep in mulling over facets of her work—facts, stories, murder—she experienced a blur of disappointment when she discovered Michaela, who had the other room in the flat, perched on the kitchen table with a chocolate biscuit. Still, another human being to talk to.

'Been out?'

'Library,' said Kit.

'Do I smell?' Michaela pushed a stray crumb into her mouth with the back of her hand.

'Not from here.'

'Good. Look at us,' Michaela waved her half-biscuit expansively, 'Friday night. Bloody useless.'

Kit girded herself. 'Ah, but *beforehand*, you'll be amazed to hear, I went out dancing.'

'I completely don't believe you. Where? I mean, seriously?'

'I went to a club—yes, "seriously"—over in East Oxford. Not what you think, a club in the sense of learning how to do—a kind of a mix-up of styles, I don't know, Latin steps and different kind of things like that. It was really funny.'

'Kit, I'm amazed. Good girl. Good work! I would've never believed it. And those dance clubs. I mean, it's so uncool it's almost cool again.' Michaela shook another biscuit out of an expensive-looking tube. 'Any blokes?'

'I'd have expected you to ask me that first.' Kit leant on the fridge, a small, student-grade appliance. She put her elbow on top of it and rested her hip against her hand. 'Strangely enough, I did get this bloke wanting to know if I'd be going back next week. But it was a trial thing, the class I mean, and I wasn't even in the right level, although it was okay actually, I coped. But, basically, I don't think I'm going again.' She shrugged with false cheer, slopped over further and opened the fridge to assess her supply of one-person food containers and packets. Already she was in a state of regret that she'd mentioned the dancing merely for the thrill of giving Michaela a surprise. She was happy to be a witness to Michaela's own ups and downs, indeed somewhat relished the details, but was herself by habit reticent.

'I didn't know you danced in, like, a properly got-together way,' said Michaela.

'I can't claim it was proper; but my father sent me to ballet lessons as a kid. He wanted me to learn to walk tall, which worked, I have to admit, although I used to loathe it—' coleslaw, garlic bagel, fudge yogurt, '—wriggling about with a crowd of midgets in pink tutus, and all I had was a black leotard—ask my mother. Fucking hell. And anyway—' couscous with sweetcorn and red pepper, two days over its sell-by date, 'anyway, I spent half my time lying on the floor next to the piano because of nose bleeds. But he said, "If you slouch, it'll make you look even taller." He thinks no one's going to marry me. There was this pair of ancient dinner ladies at my primary school who used to say, "You could be a Bluebell Girl when you grow up." Have you heard of them, Bluebell Girls?—a particular sort of six-foot, Parisian stripper.'

'Talking of slouching,' said Michaela, 'you know Mr Fleet who does maintenance stuff round by the back bicycle lock-ups in college?'

'Mr Fleet, yes.'

'He came up to me this afternoon and started talking about his wife. So what was I supposed to do? He starts telling me about how he thinks she's stopped loving him, and he says, "My wife doesn't kiss me properly any more. She only kisses me like this." And he says, "Look, I'll show you." And I'm thinking, crap, he's going to kiss me. By the way—no, sorry—no—'

'What?'

'No, doesn't matter. So, yes, he takes my hand and sort of—kind of flutters his mouth just over it, just—I—I mean, Kit, it was one of the sexiest things that's happened to me in ages.'

'Well, well,' said Kit with a guttural purr.

'Yes, I know. And now I can't work out where to leave my bike.'

'How about—the back bicycle lock-ups in college?'

'I'd rather drink a pint of piss.'

'I thought you enjoyed it.'

'Pay attention, *Farr*. I didn't say I enjoyed it.'

'All the same, Mr Fleet.'

'Give up,' said Michaela.

Kit assembled a plate of mixed leftovers and began to eat standing.

'Was he fit?' Michaela asked. 'Fanciable?'

'Who? No. That is, God knows, I don't know. Anyway, I'm not going back.'

'Come on, why not? Seriously, you're both into dancing, right? Why not?'

'I didn't go to this thing because I like dancing. I wanted to dance—' Kit choked on a mouthful of dankly chilly supermarket quiche, '—to, you know, excuse me, get lost in it, kind of—' the wet pastry was proving horrible to get down, she had to swallow three times, 'sorry—to enjoy being a bit out of it, you know? Like why I go to the

23

cinema all the time. It was meant to be the same thing, just with more burn.'

'How many times this week?'

'What, the cinema?'

'Yes.'

'Oh. Every day? Except today, actually.'

'Honestly. Should I be worried?'

'I don't know. The death tally is in the order of, well, God, seven named characters, plus a pogrom, yes, plus a comical, multi-vehicle pile up with explosions, plus a bit of the First World War in the trenches, yet again, bore, bore.'

Michaela looked disapproving. 'Just tell me this,' she said, 'is there any reason *not* to go for him, that you know of?'

Kit didn't answer—didn't, couldn't, wouldn't. She sat down at the table as Michaela slid off it. Michaela didn't leave, though. She started to make them both cocoas, with Kit's milk, Kit noticed.

'Anyway, it wasn't a date, it was just a question, and I didn't say yes.'

'Don't bother,' replied Michaela, 'I don't even want to hear. It's a date and I'm on your case.' She stood there looking grumpy until the roiling milk almost flooded across the rim of the saucepan, whereupon she swiped it expertly from the gas, placing one overfull cocoa mug on the table by Kit's plate of fridge food, and taking the other with her away out of the kitchen.

'Up yours,' Kit murmured.

After she'd eaten, Kit ran herself a bath, got in, and lay submerged, apart from her face, in the near-scalding water.

She breathed in the steam. It swirled as she drew on it, blew into it, drew on it, blew into it. Her ears were under. She could hear her heart thumping, and the slow, pulsed flair of her blood as it whirred in her veins. From an early age she had suffered bouts of faintness when getting up too fast, standing still for too long, dancing, shuffling round under-ventilated museums. Sometimes she grew faint simply from lying prostrate in a scalding—

Kit pushed herself up fast, curved up and round, water sloshing everywhere, up into a sitting position, bent her body forwards and over, clutched her legs, rested her head—her eye sockets—on her knees, and forced herself to breathe heavily and slowly through her nose, afraid she might vomit in the water.

When this disorderly spell had subsided, which swiftly it did, and she was able to sit up straight again, she found herself mesmerised by two black arcs of eyeliner on her knee caps. A shiver of mental connections caused her to wonder whether she would ever succeed in making Orson stare at her, as Detective Murray might have done, with a gaze like that of an ox in whose throat the butcher's knife has been buried.

Kit had been unable to resist putting Hayward's erotic novels on Orson's reading list, not that she wanted to confuse him. He was supposed to be mugging up on the undercover woman police detective in Victorian literature, and Hayward, in addition to being a prominent member of a porn-writing syndicate, had been the first English author of any note to include such a figure in his work.

Given that detectives in this period were widely thought of as virtual criminals themselves, and thus a disgraceful reflection on any government that employed them; and given that no women were officially acknowledged on the British police payroll until 1919, Kit wanted Orson to consider whether there hadn't, in the 1860s, been something so titillating about the notion of a secret woman detective, that it made sense for a pornographer to have been the first to enshrine one in print.

Though hinting at this possibility in 'Questions to Bear in Mind', Kit had decided to leave the word 'transgressive' to Orson. She bet herself he wouldn't be able to resist, the bet being that if Orson dropped 'transgressive' into his essay, she would buy herself a fancy new pair of knickers.

The butcher's knife—her thoughts returned to her notebook; to Detective Murray's memoir. She visualised her own crabbed scribbles. She herself had been pissed on, well, metaphorically, who could say how many times? Metaphorically, being pissed on was an integral part of human existence. *Metaphorically*, the mass of human beings was drenched in urine. Literally, though, she had been pissed on once, aged about fifteen. It hadn't been an act of affection, and she had been forced to try to sort herself out afterwards in the miniature sink of a converted, peach-décor, suburban boxroom toilet, an event so at odds with her own sense of herself, whatever that was, that she had since banished it pretty well completely from her mind. Once in a while though, the memory would leap back out at her. She recalled it now for the first time in two or three years.

*

Kit's brief phases of nausea, speckled vision and panicky light-headedness she assumed to be a by-product of her blood having to get itself round a long-distance circulatory system. As she sat in the bath—still too hot under the water, but from the waist upwards chilling—her thoughts went into muddled orbit. Who is this bastard, anyway—Joe? Joe *who*? Why the smile? What does he want with me? She took her flannel to the eyeliner on her knees, then attempted to clean the black smears off her flannel, before washing her face and hoisting herself out of the bath.

The attic flat had been divided up in a curious fashion, with the kitchen smaller than the bathroom; while the bathroom had the top floor's most generous window, but neither curtains nor a blind. Except in high summer, however, the panes would quickly steam up when hot water was running, enough to satisfy the most bashful individual, before the condensation would fuse into drops and fall in runnels down the glass. Some of the hot water that you ran for your bath floated off to sheet the uncurtained window, a ridiculously improbable arrangement; but convenient, Kit always thought.

She had forgotten to leave her towel on the rubber-mesh bath mat, and made a jolty dash to the little stool against the far wall where she'd dumped it with her clothes and pyjamas. Late September, the days were still reasonably warm, but not so the nights. She swerved to avoid a daddy-long-legs, tangled up in a ball of dust and hair, that was berserkly whirligigging round the floor, but her attempt to free it led to her pulling off a wing. When she then executed it, folded in a square of loo paper, the body audibly popped.

Kit was now cold to her bones, and slightly distressed. She dried herself fast and put her jumper back on over her night gear.

She returned to her room, and this time didn't dance, hoppishly or otherwise, but sat on her bed, defeated. When she had gone back inside the church hall after her stint at Pams Cafe, she had unthinkingly checked for any men taller than herself. There had been none. But if there had been lots, or just a couple, then what? Then—nothing in particular.

All the same, the fact was that from that point on she had only inattentively observed any of the people around her, and only a few of them; and those only because they'd been hopeless at dancing, or extra good, or had looked unlikely for one reason or another. Men, women, she had fleetingly watched the odd person, but with little interest.

Joe, Kit hadn't noticed. She was flattered, in a way, that he had noticed her; but not that flattered.

She tried to think how old he had been, and came up with a decade-long span from early thirties to early forties. Either he was rising forty, she thought, but had a boyishness to him that made him appear younger, or he *was* younger, but he'd been through it a bit and life had weathered him. His hair he'd had cut very short. His clothes and name told her nothing. Many kinds of men might wear such clothes and bear his name.

She began to debate with herself quite how negligible the height difference between them had been, and when this got tedious, tried to remember his voice—low, straightforward, from somewhere in the middle of things. It hadn't been local to East Oxford, though he had seemed hard enough. She thought about it. Really, he had looked, if thin, as though, should he wish to, he could beat a person to a pulp. But why should he wish to, and anyway, so what? Perhaps he—

Kit chided herself for thinking about any of this at all. What did it matter? Jessie Keith, *I cut her across this way and then down this way, and I threw away the parts of her I—*

She sat on her bed, defeated. What do I care? she asked herself. He had had a certain air, something about him. She didn't know what, some sort of watchfulness.

By the time she'd got properly into bed, under the covers, Kit couldn't remember how tall he had been, how old, what he had looked like, what impression he had given her: nothing. If required, for unimaginable reasons, to pick him out in a crowd, would she actually be capable of recognising him now? She didn't feel at all sure she would. Then again, she wasn't going back, so what the hell?

It took next to no time lying in bed for her to become consciously unhappy. In a book, she thought, her decision not to go back to the dance club would be the hilarious prelude to her going back to the dance club. But not even in her worst nightmares did she behave like a girl from a hilarious book.

CHAPTER 2

A couple of days after the dance club, at the weekend, Sunday, Kit saw an elderly lady on Broad Street who appeared to be texting someone. Until, as Kit drew closer, she realised that the old bird was fumbling with her glasses case.

Kit was haunted by this error. She had been working hard, sleeping badly, getting up weary in the mornings. On the Tuesday she had lost her debit card and had had to cancel it and order a new one: maddening. In fact, all week, for long stretches of daytime hours, she had felt muddled and despondent, not to mention at night. At least on the Thursday, Orson had turned in a reasonable essay. That was good. Michaela had been being her usual self.

Early on the Friday, while Kit was still in bed, eyes closed, up in her little room, she heard through her open window the throaty honking calls of migrant geese. She pictured them, the entire flock-load, as a single great, low-slung wing only just skimming the city's crowded rooftops, though somehow their crying made the air above sound empty and endless.

It was a damp day. Michaela shuffled into the kitchen in her dressing gown, stood in the doorway and said, 'I'm not being rude, but I can lend you just the best skirt, and I mean you do know haemorrhoid cream's an anti-inflammatory so it would totally get rid of the bags under your eyes. *Yes*,' she said, seemingly to forestall dissent, 'the usual way of doing it mostly *is* cucumber slices. But I mean, *cucumber slices.*' The thought of cucumber slices rendered her temporarily speechless.

Kit remained silent. She had been dividing the last of a jar of cherry jam between two pieces of toast, but paused, knife aloft—they both paused—as the boys a floor down started to whoop at each other, '—your dirty *brain* data you dumbfuck *runt*wank'—sneering, insults, of a jokey kind, maybe, '*fuckwad*'.

Michaela lost interest. 'Honestly, it's true.'

'I believe you,' said Kit, starting to eat her toast, 'but you must be crazy if you think I'm putting—yuk—haemorrhoid cream anywhere near my *face*, Michaela? I don't mind if my eyes look tired. They look tired because I'm tired. No big deal. I'm wearing a perfectly good skirt already, and I never said I was going anyway. I specifically said I'm not going, assuming you're on about the dance club here? I'm *not going*. Please can I have my breakfast without you getting at me.'

Michaela bent down to glance under the table. 'You're not wearing the one you're wearing now?'

'Listen, I'm not *going* anywhere. And what's wrong with it, anyway? And by the way, this is what I wore last time, as it happens, so you know.'

Michaela turned away to refill the kettle. 'What's wrong with it, seriously, is that it's too long and it's too, just, black.'

'Yes, and?' said Kit. 'What difference is it to you?'

Michaela flipped the kettle's on-switch, then left the room, calling, 'Wait right there.'

Kit liked her skirt. The cloth was fine Italian wool. She had recently bought it in a charity shop. Only after getting home had she noticed the moth holes near the hem, which perhaps explained the fate of a garment that must have cost its original owner one or two hundred pounds. Well, the holes meant nothing to Kit. She was above moth holes. Who judged a girl by moth holes, in this day and age? What was lovely about the skirt was the lazy, opulent ripple to the way it moved.

Michaela returned holding out, not a skirt, but a dress.

'What?' said Kit.

'Try it on.'

'Okay, I'll try it later.'

'Try it on now. I want to see what—oh, Kit, you caught the message downstairs about the washing machine?'

'Yes.'

'Surprise surprise.'

'I know, "as soon as possible". *Right*.'

'I know, *ha ha*. The nearest laundrette is, where? Jericho, Summertown? I wasn't sure.'

Kit, on reflection, taking in how bizarre Michaela's dress was, found that she, too, quite fancied seeing how she looked in it. It was sleeveless, tightly cinched at the waist, had a full skirt to the knee, and was made from pale blue, possibly waxed cotton. To this extent it was almost prim; but not only was the fabric decorated all over with photographically detailed, life-sized renderings of fruit—peaches, pineapples, pawpaws, figs—these fruits looked as though they had been attacked by a maniac with a machete, giving a wonderful effect of colour, while imparting no less powerfully the impression of carnage.

'What is this, some kind of po-mo joke kind of thing?' Kit began to shuffle out of her clothes.

'Hey, at least your knickers are cute,' said Michaela. 'I like the little lacy bit over your hm-hm.' As the kettle began to boil, she busied herself putting together a bowl of cereal with added bran, and a cup of green tea.

Kit shoved her skirt, jumper and tee shirt onto her chair, from where they immediately slid in a heap to the floor. Then she zipped up the dress's side zip.

Michaela looked round and sighed. 'That's so depressing to think you fit that when you're about a foot taller than me. Look at you. You look amazing. I mean, honestly, if I looked that good.'

Despite herself, Kit gave a quick twirl.

'About tonight,' Michaela shifted her breakfast to the table and sat down at last, and Kit sat down too, dressed for cocktails, picking up her own clothes from the floor and stuffing them onto her lap. 'I mean, sure,' said Michaela, 'sure, you feel shy and everything, I assume. But, just for a second, Kit, tell me this. If you went, what's the best thing you could imagine getting out of it?'

'Like what?' said Kit warily. 'Meaning, he turns out to be—?'

'He turns out to be—' Michaela lifted her hands up all a-tremble, and cast a look heavenwards, her face a picture of lunatic reverence.

Kit started to bite through her now-floppy, second slice

34

of toast and cherry jam. 'I suppose the best, best-case outcome would be—if I clicked with him, you mean?—not being by myself quite so much. Just not *quite* so much of the time, you know?'

'And why?' asked Michaela. 'I mean, cool. But, *really* why, as far as you're concerned, besides sex and it's all right you don't have to tell me.'

Kit baulked at this question, unsure what Michaela was after, then slowed to consider it properly. She finished her toast. 'I guess it would be quite nice when I'm angry to have someone there.'

Michaela frowned. 'Angry about what? What do you get angry about?'

'What's it to you? I get angry about the fact that I'm by myself.'

'But what are you saying? If you had someone there?'

'Fine. Well, if I had someone there, that I cared about, I suppose I'd have other reasons to be angry.'

'Like what? You aren't making sense.'

'Listen,' Kit growled, 'my *life* makes me angry.'

Shit this! she thought, and tried to discipline herself by summoning up the moment—what, an hour back?—in bed, the calling of the geese, the first migrants of autumn, their anxious crying in the air.

Michaela barked out a laugh. 'By the way, Kit, if you're going to wear that dress you need to pay heed to your armpits.'

Armpits? Kit was growing cold. She stared across the table. 'Have you noticed,' she said, 'depilation, how basically in this day and age a girl is faced with presenting herself as either an infant or an animal? I mean, is there anything in between, as it's interpreted in the here and now? Because, in the abstract I'd certainly opt to be an animal, but in practice I find myself keeping on trying to be like a child.'

'I get; but sincerely, don't let it worry you,' said Michaela. 'Honestly, there's better things to worry about. If you're going to start worrying on that level, I'm not sure I can help.'

'Well, fuck off then,' said Kit with a lighter heart, 'because I don't want any help.'

'Okay, I'll fuck off,' said Michaela. And she did.

Kit, super-efficient, emailed Orson his new reading list—it had hitherto been the last thing she did on a Friday, not the first—then wrote all morning, still dressed in the fruit-besplattered frock, but with her jumper on over the top. At noon, though, she took the whole lot off and put on warmer clothes, a pair of black trousers, a tee shirt and a thicker jumper, and went to the cinema, the Phoenix, to see *Nil By Mouth* in a lunchtime series, 'Best of British' retrospective. When the film was over, she strode back to her little room greatly enlivened by the experience—to no end whatso-ever—slept for a while, awoke confused, saw fine rain out of the window and remembered that she had a journal on reserve at the Bodleian—needed to go and read a particu-lar article. Besides, she wanted to get back out in the open again even if it was raining. If the piece she planned to consult left her bored witless, she thought, if it left her really bored—really terribly bored—it would remain a tech-nical possibility that she could run back down the Bodleian staircase, jump on a bus on the High Street, and make it in time for the dance club, Friday, though she was hardly dressed for it now, in trousers and so on.

Well anyway, she thought, at least she had done Orson's reading list for the week, a condensed history of British policing in the nineteenth century '= get the background straight'; articles by Dickens's contemporaries deriding his interest in detectives; Dickens's own 1850s articles for his journal, *Household Words*, in which he interviewed and wrote about London's new detectives '= pay special attention to Detective Charles Field (portrayed as Inspector Bucket in *Bleak House*)', plus, 'Questions to Bear in Mind = how sophisticated as literary narratives are the genuine case accounts?' etc., etc.—plenty for dear Orson to get his teeth into.

As for herself, she was now going to go and read this article, whose title she had stumbled on while preparing the list for Orson, an article too detailed for his studies, and probably of no direct value to hers, but who could say? It purported to give the facts behind various of the real detective cases that Dickens had dished up, in distorted form, in *Household Words*: seemed worth a punt. No doubt his detective informants had exaggerated their own cleverness to him. Yes well, okay. So her fate, Kit reflected, come time for the dance class, would depend upon how telling these discrepancies were.

She packed her work bag, took a bagel out of the fridge, filled it with butter, peanut butter, cheese and a suspect lettuce leaf, then made her way, eating, down the stairs, to the front door, out and down the front steps and over the gravel drive, where, abruptly—confused—she was forced to re-regulate her understanding, because there was no rain. Nor was the gravel wet. Nor was there even much smell of recent wet.

She came to a halt, thought back. On waking from her nap, her vision had been swimey and blurred. Out of her little window she had glimpsed a thin falling in the air. Now she grasped that it must have been her own insufficient and troubled sleep, filtered through bleary eyes, that had conjured the illusion of rain. There *was* no rain. She was discomposed by this fact, set against her recent belief, knowledge, to the contrary.

So much for knowledge, she thought. Kit started walking again. She had also known, believed, for a whole week, that she wouldn't be returning to Intermediate. Yet, as the hour of the second dance class approached, she found herself thinking that it would be pitiful not to go.

Volume 83, *The Dickensian*, Kit took it over to seat 103, happily vacant, and sat down to read, not expecting much. And to her disappointment—after all, she had been expecting *something*—she found the essay cursory and barely helpful. The crime case it examined most thoroughly concerned the unsolved 1838 murder of a prostitute, Eliza Grimwood, in a slum beside the Thames at Waterloo. A decade or so later, Dickens had been keen to get the inside story on a killing that was still notorious. Charles Field, who couldn't pretend his work as principal police investigator had been anything other than a failure, had described for Dickens being challenged by complex false leads—

complex but also imaginary, so the article stated. Kit was already fighting impatience as she reached the concluding sentences, in which the author made two points. First, that Dickens had had a particular interest in the victim, Eliza Grimwood, alluding to her more than once in his later writings. Second, that the details of her murder had been too sordid for him to be able to reproduce them in a family journal like *Household Words*.

Too sordid, how—exactly? Kit felt annoyed. Wasn't it the differences between the *Household Words* accounts and the true facts of the various cases that this article had promised to reveal? As she slumped back in her chair, in close proximity to thousands, millions of printed words, Kit thought about summoning up, out of all those many millions, some small number of hundreds that might make the question clearer.

But was there really much excuse to take the thing further? Surely not. How exhaustive did a person's thesis research need to be? And, more particularly, what did Kit need with the details of another case of brutal slaughter? Wasn't Jessie Keith's death horror enough for one hoppish mind? It was. Whatever had made Eliza Grimwood's murder sordid, it was no business of Kit's. She had masses of real work to do.

In typical fashion, she snapped the journal shut, with what turned out to be an unfortunately loud bang, and, sensing that the day was on the wane, was up on her feet at once, packing her bag. She glanced at the clock, twenty-five minutes to go, took her reading material back to the issue desk, and recognised—that she was playing a shady game with herself; that although her mind might be hesitating, her feet weren't.

Kit ran down the stairs, out into the early evening, over to the High Street. Only when she was installed on a warm bus did she begin to breathe again properly, and it came to her straight away that Joe might also have been a novice, why not?—shunted, like her, as overspill into the previous week's Intermediate class—in which case, perhaps he wouldn't be there today, Friday, given that the regular Beginner class had been set for Thursdays. If he had shown up for this week's Beginners, he would have missed her, a view of things that filled Kit with a tentative feeling of relief.

And why was *she* going to Intermediate? she wondered. But she knew why. She had found she was good enough to cope with it, was the answer, so why do anything else? She had learned dance steps for years as a child, and was quick about new ones. Once on the bus, it was as though she had always planned to go back. St Christopher's was probably the worst dance club in Oxford, but for her it now had one thing over all the others, namely that she knew what she was in for. She felt cross with herself for being in trousers. She should have put her skirt back on. Presumably this week they would be working in pairs from the start, but in trousers, when someone swirled her around, she would be graceful only in so far as her limbs were graceful, no rippling skirt. Never mind, she thought bravely. It doesn't matter. Someone there will whirl me round regardless.

*

She got off the bus in haste, but decelerated to the trudge of the condemned when she saw, up ahead, Joe, bathed in the sodium glare of a street lamp, his arm draped over the railings at the entrance to the hall. She saw him and became immediately self-conscious about when to catch his eye, when to greet him.

As soon as he saw her, though, he straightened up and began to walk her way. In turn, she politely smiled. He didn't smile back. He was better looking than she had remembered, more present, and not as short as she'd been thinking: a sensible height. She got a grip on herself.

'I have a request,' he said, and rotated deftly on his heel to accompany her back towards the hall.

Kit pulled a surprised face at him, for jumping the gun. '*Hello*,' she said, and said it, she felt, with poise.

'Hello,' he replied, '*Kit*. You're late.'

He sounded as though he might have said more. 'Sorry,' she replied. She thought, fuck. Her spirits fell a little. 'So, yes,' she said, 'you have a request?'

They made their way round the jumbled stacks of chairs in the entrance. The instructor was at a table by the inner door. 'I'll pay,' said Joe. Kit protested, but only for form's sake, because she didn't wish to negotiate with him, and he was already handing over a note as he said it. She had forgotten quite how bad the air smelled in the hall. It caught her in the throat.

There was quite a crowd. She and Joe went to the back together to dump their coats and bags, then stayed there like guests marooned together at a party.

'A request?' Kit repeated, raising her voice above the hubbub.

Joe got his mobile out of his pocket, switched it off and shoved it into his shoulder pack, then straightened up and looked right at her. In a voice that she registered as appealingly low and warm, he said, 'You do the boy's half.'

Her thoughts seemed to drain. The hubbub receded. The lights appeared a shade brighter, the smell more difficult. She swallowed hard, disgusted. She didn't doubt she had heard him correctly. She had heard, no point requesting him to say it again.

As witnesses to accidents mouth, 'No, no, no', so Kit, eyes lowered, breathed her silent reply.

'I beg your pardon?' Joe leant closer.

'I'm the boy?' she whispered.

'The boy. That's what I'm asking you—yes. Only if you want. You have the nerve, right?' He grinned. 'I trust you. Be a man. What have you got to lose?' He grinned, it looked to Kit, wolfishly.

There was a blast of music from the scratchy sound system.

'What, because—what?—because I'm tall?' she asked, with much sarcasm. Not me, *please*, she begged, begging the fetid air. When I came all this way, she thought. I was *happy*, she thought. *No, no, no*, she thought.

The instructor yelled, 'Okay, people!' The talk dwindled to nothing; the commands began as, felicitously, Joe murmured in Kit's ear, 'Because you're outstanding'—and that was it: 'Right!—*ONE*, and *two*, and *HIPS*, and *four*; and—' Kit stood, stalled, upset, faltering, '—*SMOOTH*, and *yes*, and *three*, and *four*; and—' somehow or other, Joe had her take him in her arms, '*ONE*, and *two*, and *three*, and *four*—' got her holding him, they started, '—*YES*, and *yes*,

42

and *good*, and *turn*—' and the physical effort of leading him was so instantly extreme, required such concentration, that Kit was locked into the job of it at once, her anguish palpable to her, but secondary—'*two*, and *three*, and TURN; and *left*, and *back*, and *three*, and TURN; and—'

And it was exhausting, each minute a sort of torment. This will come to an end, Kit said to herself over and over, as though it incredibly might not. She fought to stay alert to everything, beat, space, pulse, fatigue, sweat—alarmingly, control of another person, '—GIRLS *one*, and *two*, and THREE, and *yes*; and—'

To begin with, the instructor distinguished between 'followers' and 'leaders'. After this, though, Kit was horribly aware that it was 'girls' for the followers, and any number of designations for the rest: 'gents', 'gentlemen', 'fellas', 'guys', 'boys', 'lads', 'chaps', '*you lot*': 'Come on, *you lot*, show her who's boss, make her do what *you* want. And *oops*, and *two*, and *three*, and *four*; come *on*, come *on*—come on, lads!—come *on*; and—' Kit was the boy. She was the boy. Bad in every way, though only after a while did it come to her that—'*two*, and *three*, and *four*—' that after a collective deep breath of the tainted air, the real girls dancing alongside and about her were evincing apathetic contempt.

I am being anathematised, Kit thought. Her mind, already stricken, narrowed down further. 'Yes *yes*, and *yes*, and *yes*, and *yes*—' She—'*yes*'—was being anathematised, 'yes *yes*, and *yes*—' if the boys, at least, for their own reasons, were less brutal. From one or other of them, as the minutes ground on, she received a flying nod, a smile, at points of maximum exertion, or if they bumped. And with these exchanges, Kit's gratitude was close to being more than she could bear.

Joe, meanwhile, gave her no obvious encouragement. Maybe this made things easier, after a fashion. All the same, the more he trusted himself to her, the more deeply she resented it. They were well matched for ability, but not for strength. 'And *go*, and *go*, and *go*, and *GO*.' This, too, will come to an end, she thought.

There was one other irregular couple. Kit did eventually spot a pair of men. No girls paired up, though there was an excess of them in the class, a floating superfluity whose individual members the instructor switched in and out. When, from time to time, the call went up, 'Change your partners', Kit and Joe didn't respond, and no one tried to make them. They were left to themselves, unswitchable.

This switching business, there were occasional clipped flare-ups in the hall. And didn't numbers of the girls look like Slavic sex workers? Yes, they did—Kit's idea of a Slavic sex worker, anyway. Perhaps, if I weren't a stranger here myself, she thought numbly—but there was no continuation to this line—'*go*, and *go*, and *go*, and *go*—'

At the same time as she learned the steps, she grew ever more knackered, not that Joe wasn't restrained in how he depended on her. She would have depended on him far more. Even so, it required an act of immense surrender on her part to marshal the strength to make their pairing work—'and *two*, and *three*, and *TURN*; and *left*, and *back*, and *three*, and *TURN*; and—'

So they danced—it was dancing. They danced. The

minutes crawled: they danced. The minutes crawled. Kit endured—everything. But only after a terrible long stretch of time did pride cause her to lift herself up, to put her entire will into their pairing, just as fatigue started to give her almost a high.

This will come to an end, she said to herself, the words devoid, now, of meaning. From which point, slowly, slowly, their bodily understanding grew subtler, until Kit's feelings of shame—her *feelings*—fell away.

At the ten-minute break after the first hour, before the social dancing began, when the dancers gave in to forms of collapse, Kit was unsurprised that sickly blotches swirled across her vision. She closed her eyes tight, took rapid, shallow breaths and murmured, 'I don't think—'

'You're—' Joe's voice drifted from her. Her knees gave slightly. He grabbed her by the arm, she could smell him, moved her backwards a few paces gripping her tightly. He led.

'Here,' he said, close in by her, hand around her upper arm, she was whirling in the dark, 'here, wait, wait—hang on—' she felt something solid hit the back of her legs, 'okay, sit. You're okay, sit down. You're okay.' So she did, and slammed into a chair seat halfway on her journey to the floor. Involuntarily her eyes flew open but the room was spinning so fast that she at once shut them again. A bottle was pressed into her hands. She tempered her breathing, water. Blindly, she drank.

*

Same old shit: too much work, not enough sleep. After an indeterminate pause, Kit wiped her face with her left hand, shivered and opened her eyes again, room normal. A few more breaths and her equilibrium returned. She was light-headed though, and felt sick.

Joe crouched down beside her. 'You okay?'

'Yes,' she murmured, 'I am. But I don't think I can carry on, you know?'

'No.'

'I'm okay, but I think I'm going to stop now. This happens to me, don't worry. It's okay. You stay,' she said, and got up and put the bottle down behind her on the chair, and moved away from him along the wall to retrieve her things.

Outside on the hall steps in the dirty fresh air, Kit, pausing to adjust to the drop in temperature, was interested, through a wave of desolation, was interested far inside herself, that Joe had asked so much of her. It was chilly now and threatening to rain; or at least, however cold it was, she hadn't the strength to withstand it.

She jumped when he materialised beside her, pulling on his jacket. 'Sorry it ended like that, but thank you,' he said. 'You were great. I admit, you surprised me.' He tried in vain to win a response from her. 'Come on,' he said, 'it wasn't so bad, was it? You were excellent.' His voice softened. 'Do you need to sit down again? I was going to ask if I could buy you dinner.'

Kit walked dumbly forwards, just straight forwards, until she found herself at the edge of the pavement. Joe came up on the bus-stop side of her. To catch a bus, she would have to pass round behind him. She stood on the kerb trying to marshal her thoughts. It was cold. She was shivering. It wasn't perhaps freezing, but she was cold.

'Anyway—' she said, and left the word to loiter in the air between them.

Anyway, she repeated to herself, flinching in shock as the massive side of a haulage lorry passed a few yards in front of her face, its slogan skidding across her view, the stink of its exhaust in her nostrils.

'—to sit down,' said Joe. He took her upper arm once more and led her through the traffic, over the road, into the fug of Pams Cafe, of course, guided her to a chair at one of the two window tables.

'Do you drink tea?' he asked. 'You're shaking. I think it might be a good idea.'

She stared at him, then at the grubby white back-sides of the dayglo stars taped to the window glass beside her.

'Hey.' He took her bag off her shoulder for her. 'One minute,' he said.

'I was in here yesterday,' Joe pushed a cup of tea towards her and a plate with a paper napkin and a sandwich on it, 'in case you turned up for Beginners, not that I thought—I sat in here for half an hour after the class began, in case.'

'That's funny,' said Kit.

'I'm glad you think so.'

'No, no,' she tried to pull herself together, felt totally sapped, 'I'm saying I came in here myself, last week, when the try-out session was full,' she took a deep breath, 'had exactly this, cheese sandwich and a cup of tea, sat for a whole hour.' Her remarks seemed to float out of her.

'You were great,' he said again. 'Thank you.'

Thank you? It wasn't enough.

Now that she was parked back in the warm with a cup of tea, it seemed to Kit as though she might never be able to stand up again.

She felt so humiliated, so contemptible, and so defence-lessly pleased at being tended to a little, even by the person who had humiliated her, that her eyes momentarily swam. She had believed she was going to the class ready for anything, but what had happened was sufficiently offensive to her that she was forced to acknowledge this hadn't been true. For one thing, she had not envisaged needing to master, so completely, the steps, because she had imagined that some other person would be guiding her as she drifted mostly backwards. For another—

'What made you decide to go to this particular club?' she heard herself ask, retreating into dullness.

Joe perceptibly paused, then replied, 'Actually, the person I expected to meet last week proposed it. You?'

'Chance.'

'You live near here?'

'No. You?'

'No, I don't.' His eyes flickered briefly as he seemed to consider this prospect. 'Eat the sandwich,' he said, and then said, 'I'm surprised you didn't pick a studenty dance class in town.'

'Being I'm a student?'

'Aren't you?'

'Yes, no,' she bit off a dryish mouthful of bread and cheese, 'that's correct. Which is to say, I'm a graduate.' She didn't add, 'You?' First, she had no instinct as to what he might be. Second, she was still absorbing the information that he had approached her the previous week only after having been stood up by someone else.

To her alarm, sandwich in hand, she began to cry.

For a long time Kit couldn't stop. Nor, for this reason, could she swallow the bite she'd taken out of the sandwich. Joe sat opposite her, calm.

When at last she'd got a hold on herself, she wiped her eyes along the back of her sleeve, encountering as she did so the gaze of a man as he looked in through the café window.

He's looking at me because I'm crying, and he's wondering why I'm crying, she thought—or, she thought, as he disappeared from view, he did wonder it, just for a second. Dimly she remembered herself to have seen, it felt quite recent, a woman crying in the street. Daytime, where, Cornmarket? Yes, she remembered the incident, not recent at all. A lady in a headscarf, hand to cheek, distraught, ages ago. A young man had intervened.

'All right?' said Joe.

'I mean, did you see how they looked at us—at me,' said Kit, her voice rising petulantly. 'The last thing, the last thing in the *world*—when I made myself go to a dance place; to end up being the man, strangely enough that was the *last* thing in the *world* I ever would have wanted. I didn't even know it was an *option*. You—'

She got herself in hand. 'Sorry,' she said blankly, 'I've had it.'

How wonderful, she thought, if I could magically click my fingers and find myself sitting in a bath, in a near-faint, shimmering but blitzed, on a slow clock, hidden away from the world, with clean sheets waiting, warm blankets, a decent pillow.

'And you know, sod them, sod everything,' Joe was saying. He sounded, not heated, but not indifferent either. 'You don't exactly belong around here. I hoped you'd have the nerve to be unorthodox. I wasn't sure, though. You go somewhere properly cosmopolitan, no one would have cared. It started out, the tango, for example, immigrant workers in Argentina—it had to be men dancing with men because, whatever women there were, they weren't allowed out by their fathers, unless you're talking a bordello—'

Kit struggled to follow what he was saying.

'—and it wasn't considered effete, not at all. You learned to be a better dancer that way.' He gestured impatiently. 'And you know what? Nowadays, if you go to the right cities, not in *England*,'—he sounded so dismissive—'it's understood that it's a sign a man is, I don't know, strong, if he dances the following part; like he's daring the world to say something, like those gangsters who carry pink-dyed chihuahuas. It's understood that you can only behave like that if you're ready to kill anyone who disrespects you. Lo and behold, the symbols of effeminacy are inverted and become signs of aggression.'

Kit, in a drained sort of way, was as much amazed by the

50

fact of this speech as by its content—Joe, not so likely after all, she reflected, to be, say, a garage hand. 'You don't think that was what was going on with those two men in class?' she asked.

He shook his head. 'Just now, you mean? No, no. Where do you think you are? No, those two? They're gay.'

Kit sagged again, almost too tired to speak. She said, 'You know them? They were good.'

'I know who they are.'

Their conversation lapsed. Kit continued methodically to eat, washing down each dry mouthful with tea. She remembered when it had been her looking in at the people in Pams Cafe, looking in at the wasters, whom she had envied.

'So what did make you come up here?' Joe asked.

'I wanted to be carried away,' she said reproachfully.

'So did I.'

Kit was discomfited by the expression on his face. 'I hoped it might be, you know, mesmerising,' she said, trying to explain. 'I like to be mesmerised. Actually,' she added, on thinking about it, 'in a way, I was. I don't sleep very much so I try to do other sleepish kind of things, or brain-dead, you know?'

'And what other techniques do you have for going about this interesting pursuit?'

She checked, but he didn't appear to be mocking her. Who else in the world, she thought, cared enough to ask her this question?

'Oh, well, books, obviously,' she said, 'and going to the cinema all the time, and I guess listening to certain music, preferably loud; and I do five times as much work as I strictly

51

need to, that's probably the main thing; and I like beauty parlours, and, I don't know, various things. The main one is probably walking. I feel like I'm at rights when I'm on foot, letting my thoughts work on their own. I dream about being somewhere so flat I could walk for miles with my eyes closed. When I'm indoors, to me that's not exactly at home, or safe indoors, what have you, that's the in-between bit between being myself walking along outside.' She wasn't sure that what she had just said was quite accurate; nor could she think why she was speaking like this to a stranger, unless it was for the very reason that he didn't know better.

'Beauty parlours?' he said.

'Well—' Kit smiled. They had slipped into conversation. It was odd, but okay. 'At the hairdresser's,' she said, 'or having your face done, or even your nails, whatever, which I only have once, it allows you to lose yourself completely. I don't think anything while I'm having my hair cut, or if you're lying there in a back room wrapped in hot towels and stuff. It's pleasantly tactile, but,' she took a breath for a second, then carried on, '—I don't lie there thinking, oh yes, that's a great idea for my next chapter: when I get out of here, I must scribble it down. It isn't like that. It's just *nothing*.'

'You could—well, yes. No.'

'What?'

'No, I was going to say something stupid. What music? I'm trying very hard to think what you might listen to.'

'Diamanda Galás?'

'Christ.'

'You know who I'm talking about?'

'I do, but I think it qualifies as left field, all the same.'

Kit felt inconsequentially miffed. She hadn't listened to Diamanda Galás for well over a year.

'You have these beauty treatments often?' Joe asked.

'Sadly, no. But if I were rich, ta-da, I'd spend all my time conked out in a beauty parlour, just lounging around.' Kit smiled again to show she didn't mean it, though she could have wished she did; that it would be just fine to surrender herself to a life of indulgence and extreme mental neglect.

'Who needs sleep anyway?' said Joe, with friendly absurdity.

'Have you ever heard of Gurdjieff?'

'Who?'

'It's nothing, don't worry. I thought I'd ask. He helped kill Katherine Mansfield because he didn't believe in sleep and she had TB. It's not important. He was a famous Russian charlatan—Russian, I think. I can't remember. He had this colony where people had to mow the lawn and no one was allowed any sleep. What do you do?'

'I work for the university.'

That was all he said, but he said it in a tone to cast a pall over them both. Kit felt diminished by the picture of him in some mid-ranking, central admin post, and wondered now whether he mightn't automatically be looking down on her as a lackadaisical student, if his job happened to be dedicated, in some tedious way, to keeping her sort going.

'Not by any chance mowing lawns?' she said, in the hopes he might find this funny.

His eyes did crinkle. It made him look kind. The end of

one of his eyebrows was missing, she noticed. 'Now that you seem a bit better,' he said, 'you wouldn't like to come back to my place and let me make you something decent to eat? I live off the Woodstock Road, up near Summertown?'

'Oh,' she said, 'I go that direction too.'

They barely spoke. They took a bus as far as the High Street, then walked through the city darkness. The rain that had threatened didn't fall. In time, the shaky feeling faded out of Kit's legs. As they went along, she was half-saying, in her head, the entire way, *no*; but half a 'no' was tacitly much like a 'yes'.

Joe ushered her into a large brick house, up the neglected communal staircase, up to the top, where they stepped through his front door into an extraordinarily sleek flat, all chrome and dulled colours and expensive fittings, surely not the abode of a person in a mid-grade admin job. He turned the heating on. Kit was startled by the money implicit in everything she saw. It was also all disconcertingly tidy. She tried to guess whether his spells of maximum boredom took place here, when he was at home, or whether they happened elsewhere, away from home.

'Glass of wine?' he said.

He's making this easier for me, she thought. What am I doing here? Do I have to do this?—to both of which questions the answers were straightforward. It had been about a year, more than a year, since a man she found catchingly attractive had tried to sleep with her. That was what she was doing there, edged into his cold, glittery kitchen, feeling, on the one hand, hollow, and on the other, almost excited. I find him attractive? she enquired of herself; but it was a silly question. Going to his flat was admitting it by default.

And did she have to do this? Of course not.

She didn't expect him to ask, exactly. They both drank a little, still standing up. He was staring at her hands but didn't appear to see them. 'I'm sorry I upset you,' he said.

She wondered why he hadn't said it before; glanced sideways at herself in a large, ornate, antique mirror that hung on the kitchen wall. 'I know what they were all—' she said. 'Just because I was the boy, because I had control of you, it didn't mean—and I was the only girl in trousers, and they obviously all thought I was—'

'What does it matter?' he said.

She looked back at him, saw that his gaze had become more focused. In another of his felicitous turns of phrase, delivered so that there was no possibility of her misunderstanding him, he asked softly, 'Would it be good if we put things straight between us?'

Kit drank her wine down like water. The longer she stood before him, the more she felt vanquished.

'Hey, I'm not going to jump you,' he said, with a funny look.

'You already jumped me,' she replied.

This is going to ruin everything, she thought—though what *everything*? And so what if it did? How would that be different from usual? She felt nervously vague as she made a maladroit gesture of agreement.

'Was that a yes?' he asked, his lesser eyebrow raised.

Ah, the brink, she said to herself facetiously. What luck

Orson had put 'transgressive' in his essay. Hurrah for pretty knickers and the lacy bit over her hm-hm.

'I don't have any protection,' she muttered—and thought, against anything.

'Don't worry,' said Joe.

'Don't worry—you've got it covered?' she asked, wanting clarification.

'Yes,' he said, providing clarification.

So much talk. *You've got it covered*—dismaying, the phrase that had volunteered itself.

Joe smiled at her again, another kind look. For a brief moment, she believed he was letting her go; but an atmosphere of surrender propelled them onwards.

Perched on his bed, Kit noticed what an evil colour the sky was, its louring clouds underlit by the street glare from across Oxford. She had been brought up to believe, somehow proof against the common run of her thoughts, that it was unseemly to sleep with a man you hardly knew. And then, once her career in this regard had begun, once she in fact *did* start sleeping with men she hardly knew, she found that any vestiges of seemliness felt perversely the more important. It was too unpleasant, too awful somehow, to have to say to a man you hardly knew, 'Not like that, like this', so she never did, not even when, by some people's standards, she was being assaulted.

She accepted that this was all very ridiculous, mad even. Nevertheless, she conducted such sexual encounters in a manner both superficial and disengaged, taking comfort from the thought that if she felt disappointed, it followed that she couldn't have given up, and must still be hoping for better. She wasn't always disappointed, either. Casual sex she considered a contradiction in terms, but pointless sex, she didn't. Sex for her was generally an unsimulated fiction; however, sometimes it seemed to work.

As she lay there bathed in the ugly light that seeped through the bedroom window, Kit found that, although ordering herself not to do this, she was unstoppably chanting, in her mind: *the parts he likes he treats considerately*, he is *not unkind to the parts he likes*. And being inexperienced in the matter of saying, 'not like that, like this'—she took it. He had said they would put things straight between them, so she let him and she took it.

Whatever they both thought they were up to, it was over fast. As Kit reorganised herself in Joe's bathroom, she felt restless relief. She still couldn't tell really what she made of him, or why she was there, why on earth she'd acquiesced. But what she did know, with baleful certainty, was that she hadn't been much fun, and that it was all over, and that that was it.

It wasn't that you couldn't fake pleasure, she reflected, seating herself on the loo and trying to manage a trickle of pee not too loud. Supposedly that was the single greatest advantage women had over men, the ability to fake it, as much as you liked. But faking pleasure was one thing— even, obscurely, faking it to yourself—that was one thing. Having a stranger inside you was another, and not a business over which you could be very much deluded.

She wiped herself, pulled up her knickers, she didn't like them any more, washed her hands, dried her hands, put on her trousers, put her shoes on, flushed the loo, glanced round the bathroom to check it wasn't disarranged—it was possibly the neatest bathroom she had ever been in—then looked in the mirror and saw in the glass her freakishly lit-up face.

She had planned to go straight home, but he was waiting for her. He said, 'Let me cook you something.'

'You don't have to.'

'I don't *have* to. Would you like an omelette, salad? I have some great olives. Or are you tired? You need to sleep?'

Kit stared down at her feet.

'Anchovies?' he said. 'Fresh herbs?'

'Okay, all right.'

'And I have some great bread.'

'Okay.'

'Right. More wine?'

'Sure.'

Well now, she thought, surprised, pulling out a chair from the kitchen table, which caused a cold scraping noise on the tiles—well now, at least I get a free meal out of this; kind of *expensively* free, but in a free kind of way.

She sat limply and watched. He was careful, when he cracked the eggs, to get the shells straight in the bin. When an olive fell off the spoon onto the counter where he was working, he wiped up after it at once. He arranged the bread in a pan in torn slices to warm it in the oven, but tore the loaf carefully over the sink. He hadn't been like this in bed.

As someone who wore skirts with moth holes, Kit was unimpressed.

He turned abruptly. 'Okay?'

'Could I have some water?'

'Glass in there,' he said, gesturing with an elbow at a wall cupboard. 'It'll have to be tap, I'm afraid. I don't drink water so I don't ever buy it.'

'You don't drink water?'

'I don't know, probably a glass every couple of weeks.'

'You had a bottle at the dance session,' said Kit.

'That was given to you by a friend of mine.'

She was oddly dismayed by this answer. He'd had a friend there? Boy, girl? Who on earth?

'I don't sleep well either,' said Joe, tripping her thoughts another way.

'Oh.'

He laid mats down on the table: mats for the plates, a mat for the salad, two trivets, a silver salt cellar, Georgian—Kit's grandfather had had one the same. 'Some nights I feel like there's hardly any point in going to bed unless there's someone else there,' he said. 'Obviously you sleep so you're in a fit state for the next day, but why give up on the day you're in just to ensure the next one, when there's absolutely nothing to choose between them?'

'Don't you simply get tired?' she asked.

'No. Well, yes, I do. But, like you maybe, I find it hard to fall asleep whether I'm tired or not. Alone, I find it hard to fall asleep.'

Don't keep saying that, she thought.

'Sometimes I go to bed,' he said, 'and then I get up again

59

and go out walking, you know, three, four in the morning—and fast; fast.'

'You do walk quickly, I noticed,' she said. 'It's pleasant to me, personally speaking, as someone with a long stride.' She didn't mention it, but often, when she walked alone, she sang.

'No, but I'm talking *fast*,' he said, 'because then, when I'm going down all these streets and they're empty, and the greater part of Oxford's population is unconscious—although, you'd be surprised how many invitations I've received at four o'clock in the morning—' He lost his thread. He was filling up her wine glass again, but she'd had enough. She was asking herself, not for the first time, how it was possible to kiss a person you didn't really know; or rather, what that kiss exactly *was*.

Their talk turned, in dilatory fashion, to politics, the arts, subjects of the day, matters over which they had, if any, uninvolving influence: student misbehaviour, the city's rat population, disasters in China. They despatched several of these topics between them as Joe cooked, before Kit said, 'What about your work? I mean, about your work—what is it exactly that you do? You didn't say.'

'Don't ask.'

He omitted to turn round this time, nor did he speak with emphasis, yet it was clear to her that he meant it: *don't ask*.

Perhaps he's a vivisectionist, she thought.

'You?' he said.

'Oh,' Kit pulled a loopy, apologetic face, which, with his back turned, he didn't see, 'well, I hate to say it, but *my* work is fantastically interesting and I don't mind in the least being asked.'

'Go on then.'

'I—' How to begin? She blundered about in her mind trying to formulate the right first sentence. It wasn't as though she hadn't answered this question before.

'Give me a précis.'

'You sure?'

He glanced round at her. 'Give me a précis, woman.'

Kit said nothing.

'Very well, what discipline are you in, and what are you working on at the moment?'

She breathed in deep. 'DPhil in English, nineteenth century. The past couple of weeks I've been tackling my introduction, which I rather bypassed at the start. Roughly speaking, I'm looking at the use made in their work by some of the more substantial Victorian writers of real crimes, bearing in mind the complicating factor that, in their way of looking at it, you could legitimately draw distinctions between factual truth and, as they conceived it, higher moral truths; but also bearing in mind that, increasingly, from the 1830s onwards, writers were prepared to use quite recent real crimes in their novels, so that where they changed the details, their original readers couldn't avoid comparing the fictionalised result with a more accurate version they would remember from the newspapers—something we miss out on, reading these books now. Added to which, detectives were considered corrupt back then, yet they were seeking the truth, a little like these authors themselves, in a way. In fact, the first police detective unit in England, 1842, was a clandestine operation—the government kept its existence secret from the public.'

'It did?'

'For fear of massive disapproval. Just for starters, people thought it was terribly wrong for detectives to be in plain clothes. This wasn't playing fair. It was deemed un-Christian, kind of thing.' Kit leant back in her chair and laid her hands down flat on the table. 'Well, bore, bore,' she said.

'Don't go. Food's ready.' Joe put a plate on her place mat, remembered napkins, pepper, bowls for the salad.

'Start,' he said, cooking his own omelette.

'Blimey.' Kit tucked in, eating fast. It was the best meal she'd had in ages as well as the smartest, and she was deeply hungry.

'So. So you're working on Victorian true-crime detective fiction, is that right?'

'Admirably concise, yes; and n.b., police detectives only. This is delicious, by the way. Yes, and I'm teaching for the first time. I have my first-ever pupil. You won't believe this, but he's called Orson.'

'Orson?'

'Orson McMurphy.'

'Which college?'

'None. He's in digs with some outfit called Milkweed Hall or whatever. No, I'm kidding. But the small print of the thing is that he's studying *in* Oxford, not *at* it, although considering all the people who teach the courses do appear to be *at* Oxford, I suppose it isn't a complete con. I don't know. He's American, from some expensive little Liberal Arts place in the Midwest. I don't think anybody's taught him much before—well—but he's sharp. It's interesting. Basically, he said he wanted to write a piece on early detective literature, so they dug me out to help, and I persuaded him, for my own convenience, to focus on *Bleak House*.'

'Why's that?' Joe sat down opposite her with his own food.

Kit suddenly *really* wanted to go. She'd had enough. She had walked, talked, drunk with, gone to bed with, and broken bread with this man. She had shattered herself dancing with him backwards. It was enough. Who was he? She would have talked about his work, except he'd twice told her not to, and she was too tired to parry or think up some other gambit.

She struggled to finish her food, before retrieving his question from the back of her mind and responding mechanically, 'It's the first great English example. It has a detective in it who's based on a real detective called Charles Field, and it also has other, recognised detective stand-ins—a lawyer's clerk; the detective's wife. In England, before detectives-proper existed, along with humble police inspectors you also had lawyers' clerks and insurance men as functionally the detective class. Actually, Dickens started out as a lawyer's clerk, but not in a good way. Still, that's by the by. What I'm doing for Orson is a more or less Dickens-and-detectives thing, starting with *Oliver Twist*, and blah, blah, blah. I teach him on Thursdays, then I email him his next reading list on the Friday, after I've chatted to him in the tutorial to find out how he thinks he wants to slant things next—makes him feel he has input.' She smiled to herself. 'I was instructed to involve him in the process.'

'Right. And *Oliver Twist*? That fits in how?'

For a split second this question pleased Kit, the fact that Joe was interested enough to ask—or was prepared to pretend, in plausible style, to be interested. *Nobody* was interested. She continued to smile, while saying diffidently, and sounding, she thought, about ninety, 'Oh, I won't go on.'

He responded with a believable noise of dissent.

What to do? Kit sighed. Truly, she wanted to leave now. But there sat this person she hardly knew, waiting for her to speak. 'Okay,' she said, not quite patiently, '*Oliver Twist*, Dickens started it the beginning of 1837, before the detective department existed; we're talking the year Queen Victoria came to the throne. He originally conceived it as just a few instalments of pretty blunt polemic about the poor, and only afterwards had this brainwave to bump it out into a full-length, crime-novel-romance thing. If you take the plot apart, it really doesn't work well at all. But he couldn't revise the opening as it was already in print, which left him with crazy narrative problems to unravel; plus he'd landed himself with this goody-goody, orphan-waif hero to carry a whole book. But he hashed up a longer plot regardless, and—so, yes, it's incredibly violent in parts, and all the crimes in it effectively solve themselves without police work, that's the basic point. What I'm saying is, *Oliver Twist* was simply so Orson could draw fruitful comparisons across from the start of Dickens's career to *Bleak House*, which was 1853, in the middle.' She looked Joe in the eye and said, a little insolently, 'Get?'

'Put like that, I do.' He offered her apples, biscuits and cheese, coffee; but Kit refused them all.

'Speaking of work, honestly—' She stood up and pushed her chair back in under the table, walked out of the kitchen to the little hallway, put on her coat—Joe followed her, and helped her—she picked up her bag and heard herself say, 'Thank you for a lovely meal, I really must be off.' It occurred to her that this was ludicrous from someone who'd done what she had that evening. Nevertheless, her assemblage of words succeeded in rendering the moment sufficiently formal that it felt as though they might almost shake hands.

'Well—thank you,' said Joe; and then, leaning on the phrase slightly, he said it again, 'Thank you.'

Kit nodded and was already through the door when he added, 'You're all right? Should I see you home? I don't know where you—'

She glanced back at him and waved westwards. 'I only live the other side of the Woodstock Road. I'm fine. Thanks.' And before he could speak again, she had taken flight down his staircase in the manner of one of her exits from the Bodleian.

As she stepped out onto the street, Kit took a great gasp of chilly air. *Farr*, *Christine Iris*, frolicsome and rollicksome, bloody fucking hell, she thought. All she had done was to say 'yes' a couple of times, instead of *no*; but it was as though everything was her fault. What *everything* itself added up to, she still couldn't say, except that her whole life felt like a meaningless screw-up.

She sobered as she trod along in the cold. There were,

she reflected, no rules. There was no one to ask. You made it up as you went. That was it. Precedent was bunk. Whose precedent? Everything was your own fault. So, she'd gone to a dance club, had danced with an unknown man, had, in the face of trenchant expectation, and to the seeming contempt of the other representatives of her sex, danced with him the wrong way round—after which, for no reason whatsoever, she had slept with him. Dressed up right, in another girl this could absolutely have sounded to Kit, well, sparky and adventurous.

But in herself, it felt like the pits. There had been moments, as when he'd asked her about *Oliver Twist*: he had actually been listening. So, fine, she thought woefully, so he paid by listening to me gab.

A few minutes of padding along and she was home. She whacked the hall light button with her thumb. After you did this, the bulb remained on for exactly four minutes.

'Where have you been?' Michaela stepped out of her room and pounced on Kit, successfully exuding an air of blame.

'Evening, Mum.'

'Come on.'

'I went, okay? I went. I *went*.'

'Seriously?'

'Yes.'

'Hey, brilliant. Don't tell me in those trousers. I don't believe it. You're the end. You look so pale. What happened?'

'If you must know, we ended up back at his place.'

'You're joking me. Kit! After all the grief you've put me through?'

'I've put *you* through? Bloody hell.'

'Kit you—hey, wait a minute. You naughty girl. You didn't just—?'

'Maybe.'

'Put that one away! What's he like? Why didn't you stay over? You're a close one. How was it?'

Kit smiled while trying to look arch, hoping by this means to convey sophisticated amusement—after which, feebly, she added, 'It was great.'

'Good for you,' cried Michaela.

And because Kit's mood was resistless, this made her grin.

'What's he like?'

'It was great,' said Kit wearily.

Michaela narrowed her eyes. 'Better than a slosh in the mush, I suppose.'

You are, Kit thought, a small and irritating person—infuriating, even. *Infuriating Michaela*, you know nothing. I dislike you, thought Kit.

'Fancy you!' said Michaela with a wink.

Kit grinned again, absurdly fortified by this second-hand enthusiasm; then, once again, she wilted. In bored tones, she said, 'I'll give you your dress back tomorrow.'

'Hey,' called Michaela, 'remind me in future not to tell you what to do. And, Kit, get some proper shut-eye, for God's sake, you look like you really need it.' As she retreated backwards into her room, Michaela slammed her door shut, thus cutting in half her sign-off, 'Sleep ti—'

CHAPTER 3

'Look what the cat dragged in,' said Michaela, swishing.

Kit got to her feet confused, exposed, her open notebook and a saucepan of custard in front of her on the kitchen table.

'He asked me if you lived here,' said Michaela.

Kit had assumed, without great regret, that she would never see Joe again, or at worst, that they would half acknowledge each other on the street some surprise day in the future. Michaela notwithstanding, she had hardly thought about him since the previous Friday, putting him to the back of her mind if for no other reason than to ward off shame.

She closed the notebook. She had stretched out to it instinctively, wanting something to do, to appear engaged. She wasn't ready for this situation.

'I knew it had to be one of these buildings,' said Joe, 'so long as you meant it last week about the other side of the Woodstock Road.'

'And you just happened to ask Michaela?' Kit delivered her rejoinder with considerable bite, hand arrested on the tabletop.

'She wasn't the first,' replied Joe evenly. 'And you left several glass slippers when you ran away.'

'I just *did* happen to be coming back to this shit hole,' said Michaela, 'bloody Friday and there he is wandering around like a lost dog, so we have a little parlez-vous and don't go glaring at me like that, Kit. He found me, I didn't find him. What do you think?'

Of course Michaela hadn't gone and found him. How could she have? As well as feeling confused, Kit now felt daft. Me, I'm the lost dog, she thought.

Almost before Joe had begun, Michaela spoke across him, 'She would'—as he said to Kit, 'I was wondering if you'd like to—as it's Friday, it's—'

Both of them stopped.

'Feel free not to answer on my behalf,' snapped Kit at Michaela, who was already removing herself from the scene. 'Later, darlings,' she crooned, as she backed merrily out of the kitchen.

'God,' said Kit. She and Joe, eyes askance, listened until they heard Michaela's door close. 'What exactly did she say to you?'

'It's all right,' said Joe.

Kit had been sitting there eating custard off a wooden spoon, reviewing her notes from the morning, which she'd spent in the library. Between the library and home she had gone to the supermarket, where she'd found herself mooching past the section with tins of Bird's custard powder—the shelf-stackers were discussing it, it didn't come in actual tins any more—and had remembered all about Bird's, eating it as a child. There she had stood, remembering how much she'd liked to eat custard off a wooden spoon when her mother made it, because, after her mother decanted the custard into a diamond-pattern

70

jug, Kit had always been allowed to scrape out the saucepan. All spoons should be made of wood, she thought. She had felt pained for herself as a child, thinking how solitary that character now seemed; which had caused her to buy a container of Bird's and extra milk, and to go home and at once make a pint of custard in a large, flat pan, letting it cool for a while because she also liked puncturing the skin. These days, her mother bought ready-made custard that tasted synthetic, had no skin, and poured over the carton lip in gouts.

'Did you know, in—' Kit blinked anxiously, unsure how long she'd been standing there failing to communicate, '—in the Co-op they put custard powder and Fray Bentos pies, yuk, and coffee sugar and I'm not sure, they put that kind of thing on the lower-down shelves, so that the old folks who like it can reach?'

She hadn't entirely allowed herself to take in that Joe was holding a bunch of freesias. When he handed them to her, she jumped. With a gruff, 'Thanks, thank you,' she pulled a slender knife from amongst the cutlery in the strainer and took it to the little elastic bands wound at intervals round the stems. Jerkily, as she severed them, they flicked off onto the floor.

'Flowers!' she said. She sounded almost mocking. Bother, she thought.

Her empty cherry jam jar from the week before was still in the recycling crate, glass and office paper. Kit didn't own a vase, so she retrieved the jar, filled it with water and cut the freesias short—too short, it turned out. She was making a mess of everything. She arranged the twelve stems in a crude fan shape, aware of being silent again as she did so.

When she had finished, she said, 'I guess I'll put these in my room.' She didn't want Michaela to enjoy them.

'Christ,' said Joe, 'it looks like you've been burgled.'

Kit stared at the scene. 'This isn't random,' she said, 'at least, not to me. I'm trying to work out some stuff. This is my mind spread out on the floor. And the laundry pile,' as luck would have it, embarrassingly heaped by the door, '—the house washing machine is broken. I was thinking I might just do it all myself in the bath. I was going to go to the laundrette in South Parade,' where she had had visions of meeting a handsome boy reading Kafka by the drying machines or, more obscurely, reading Donald Barthelme.

'This is all the space you have?'

She pulled a face.

'Right,' said Joe.

'Middle of the ballot. It's meant to be a married flat, but the college has hardly any married students this year. And then it was supposed to be being done up because it's in such bad nick, but they fell behind and—I don't know, they chronically lack accommodation, so the domestic bursar just decided to shove another bed into this room and—' Kit put the flowers in the corner on the tiny mantlepiece over the tiny, boarded-up fireplace. 'It's fine. It's nice being up high—high in the air. I like being on top of everything.'

'In this one respect, at least?'

'Thanks,' she said. Had she positively wished him to be there, his feeling free to tease her might have been pleasant. Instead, she felt criticised.

She didn't know what to do. Why had she gone and brought him into her room? She couldn't believe she was entertaining a stranger in her bedroom, and the business of having slept with him only made it worse.

Friday afternoon, time was sloping forwards. She didn't know what to do. By freakish chance he had succeeded in finding her; although it wasn't so much amazing that he'd succeeded as that he'd tried. She attempted to like him for it. It put him in a different light. It almost put *her* in a different light. He'd come and found her, with flowers. She gestured at her desk chair, seating herself stiffly on the bed.

Of course, she hadn't wholly forgotten, Friday, about the Intermediate class, had been passingly conscious that it would occur that evening, up out eastwards, St Christopher's church hall, on the night side of town. But her thoughts about it, all two of them, had been restricted to wondering whether or not Joe would go, and, if he went, who his partner would be.

'No TV?' he said as he sat down.

'No,' she said. 'I sometimes watch things on my computer.'

'If there's ever a programme you want to catch, come to my place,' he said, 'if you like.'

She clutched at this thought in a disconnected way; it was such a dull proposition. His washing machine, on the other hand? Perhaps not. Kit got up to move the jar of flowers again, which, because her arrangement was so inept, refused to appear symmetrical over the fireplace. Their smell was already clouding the room with sweetness. 'Michaela has a TV in her room,' Kit mumbled, 'I go and watch rubbish with her. She gets addicted to the most crazy things, I can't even tell you, like strongman races where they totter along carrying real cars, that sort of thing.'

She was feeling more and more claustrophobic. The flowers still looked wrong. She got up yet again, wanting to correct this one detail, if no other.

While she fretted, Joe began to read on the floor, and then picked up, an A3 photocopy she had made from microfilm of a page from an early Victorian copy of *The Times*. Kit turned suddenly around, alert to the rustle of paper and the subsequent depth of Joe's silence. She had highlighted sections of the minute newsprint in yellow, and could see that he was jumping between these lurid sentences, engrossed, until he broke his own spell by reading out loud: 'Coroner: "One of the wounds was inflicted by stabbing through the stays, and I imagine the murderer seized hold of the top of the stays on the opposite side with his left hand, and with the other hand then—" What is this?'

He held the photocopy away from him, then brought it back close, reading out more. '"I have altered my opinion since the first holding of the inquest as to the infliction of the wound at the back of the neck. I at first supposed that the injury was inflicted first, because I considered after the extensive wound in the front of the neck the murderer would have had no object in inflicting the second; but now I am of a different opinion, and I think that the wound in the back of the neck was perpetrated after that in the throat, for the purpose of severing the head from the body"—Kit,' said Joe, 'a beheading?'

'Are you actually asking me about it?' All week she had been struggling to make her thesis introduction sound lofty and judicious, but that morning, unpersuaded by her own efforts, and bored by this self-imposed task, she had fallen off the straight and narrow path, so beguiled by what she'd chosen to do instead that she had managed to miss the day's 'Best of British' at the Phoenix, *Performance*, not a film she knew.

'This is to do with your DPhil, is it?' Joe asked.

'Maybe slightly, a bit. It's a curious case, hugely famous at the time, an unsolved murder. It's pretty interesting, actually. I've just been working on it today.'

'Yes?'

She sat back down on the bed, freesias abandoned. 'Okay, well, that piece of paper in your hand gives the details of a second post mortem on the body of a prostitute, Eliza Grimwood, murdered in Waterloo, London, 1838, off the Waterloo Road. The actual terrace doesn't exist any more. It was a slum back then. Basically, she was killed a couple of minutes' walk from where you'd be sitting if you were at a concert in the Festival Hall.'

As Joe seemed perfectly attentive, Kit carried on, though she was mostly now rehearsing these facts for herself. 'She was found a little before dawn on the floor beside her bed, toppled over backwards from a kneeling position with a blanket half thrown over her. The medical witnesses hedged about a bit, as you were reading, but came to the conclusion that she'd been killed by having her throat slashed open. She was also stabbed in the breast and the womb area, but not until after she was dead, they thought, you'll see where it—' Kit jumped up and leant over to point at one of the sections she had highlighted, then read it out to confirm what she was saying: '"There was no effusion of blood from these wounds, and they were inflicted after death", equals, I guess, psychotic kind of stuff—I mean, they reckoned these further mutilations were severe enough that they themselves would have done her in if she hadn't been dead already.' As Kit sat down again, she realised that she wasn't feeling quite so awkward, and wondered whether Joe had asked her about her work with this in mind. 'Added to which,' she said, catching up with herself, 'as you were just reading, the murderer then attempted to cut her head off. *The Times* said—its first adjective, or rather, adverb, on the case—that she had been killed "inhumanly", which makes you wonder what "human" means, in a way.'

'Sounds a bit Jack-the-Ripperish,' said Joe.

'Absolutely. I quite agree. Although that was decades later. But I mean, yes. And her room was drenched in blood. There was blood all over the floor, and it was splashed across the walls four feet from the corpse, presumably because of how her throat was cut, or so they reckoned.' These were the gruesome details Dickens had judged too sordid for his family journal; and it was in poring over them that Kit had spent many absorbing hours of her day.

'Where does this fit in with your work?'

It was a fair question. 'I don't know,' Kit replied gaily, then felt stupid. 'No, it's just that—' She halted, retrenched, and said, 'Please tell me what it is you do.'

Joe put the piece of paper back down in its place amidst the chaos on the floor. 'I work for the university.'

'I know, you said that last time.'

She watched him as he weighed up whether or not to answer properly.

'I'm a lecturer,' he said.

'A lecturer?' She was astonished.

'Yes.'

'In?'

'Maths.'

They both paused now while she took this in. She clasped her hands together, then let go again. 'You're a *maths* fellow?'

'Yes.'

'A *don?*'

'Yes.

She shook her head, almost indignant at having been so completely misled—even if by her own imagination— admin?—though perhaps it was more accurate to say that she hadn't been led anywhere much at all. Whatever; she felt completely fooled. He was a lecturer? At the university?

'What did you think I did?'

She couldn't say, so she lifted up her shoulders in a shrug and then just held them like that.

'Well, now you know.'

Now she knew, yes. 'Is there any use my asking you what you work on?' she said, trying to control herself. He bore no relation to her image of a mathematician.

'You can ask,' he replied. 'My research isn't in good

shape right now. I've got what feels like an unmanageable teaching load this term, which is denting my will to live, frankly, compounded by the fact that I've just started giving a course of Part C lectures on algebraic geometry.'

'Oh,' said Kit. If only Michaela had still been there. Michaela, who was a physicist, might have understood. 'What—' Kit rued being so very ignorant, 'what—what subjects would that cover?'

'The lectures? Algebraic curves; affine and projective varieties; the Zariski topology; applications of the Riemann–Roch Theorem—' Joe broke off with a sardonic smile.

'I see.' *Affine and projective varieties*. So, *affine and projective varieties*, yes. Into the tense quiet that followed, Kit said, 'You'll have to forgive me.'

'Consider yourself forgiven.' He smiled at her again, more gently. 'I'm no great shakes at it,' he said. 'I'm nothing special. I'm about as good as ordinary gets, put it that way. I inhabit a dusty little corner of what the Americans call the "ivory basement".'

'I'm sure you're being modest,' said Kit. She thought about what she had done that day, and said, 'I don't think I'm up some ivory tower either, you know, although maybe I am, viewed from the outside. It feels more like I'm at an ivory horror show.' She was groping for a way to neuter this remark, when Joe took her aback by asking, 'Do you mind being tall?'

'No,' she replied doubtfully. 'The great thing is that it works as a disguise. People think, oh, that tall girl—and then they don't think anything more about it. So even though you stick out, or especially because you stick out—what I mean is, because you seem to stick out, you can hide away inside and people just don't think about you. And it's good when you travel. The sorts of countries where Western women are, are—'

Joe's mobile had begun to ring loudly in his pocket. He fumbled for it. 'Hi,' he said, then listened to the person the other end babble. 'What's—' He shot his watch out from under his sleeve and frowned at it. Kit glanced at her radio clock. If there was any thought, she shrivelled, whatsoever, thought of them catching the Intermediate class, they had dwindling leeway now, unless they were going to take a cab, or Joe had a car. He was a don, a maths lecturer, a grown-up. She was still astonished. It could be he had a car.

The person on the phone, a man, sounded keen, pressing. 'It'll have to be quick,' Joe said. He looked at his watch again, brow lowered. 'Yes, I did—I have. I'm with her right now. All right, all right,' he said irritably. 'Yes, no, I'm not— Humpty? Okay, bye.'

He lifted his annoyed gaze to meet Kit's concerned one. 'I have to drop in at The Forfeit,' he said.

'Oh?'

Joe stood up. 'What do you think of Lucille?' He looked at his mobile, then put it in his pocket.

'Lucille? Do you mean Michaela?'

'The dance instructor.'

'Oh, right, sorry. Yes. Well, she's great.' Kit felt acutely ill-at-ease. She didn't want to have to go to the dance club ever again. 'She's very shouty, though,' she said. 'I mean, she never stops. I find her teaching method a bit odd.'

'It's more than odd,' said Joe. 'I don't think she has any formal training. I'm not sure it's even real steps, but I do like her.' He stepped towards the door. 'You coming?'

As they went down the stairs, Kit asked, 'Who's Humpty?'

'My brother. What were you saying—if you're tall, when you travel?'

'If—? Oh, yes, countries where Western women are pestered in the streets. I guess—I mean the ones I've been to, they're also countries where the men are dreadfully short. I once said to a man in Egypt, "If you carry on like that, I'm going to *spit on your head*." And I could have done. And he went away.'

'Jesus.'

'I know, idiotic of me, but I'd had enough. Fucking hell. Lucky by sheer chance he wasn't a spit fetishist or something.'

'Carry on like what?'

'What?'

'You said you said, "If you carry on like that, I'll spit on your head."'

'Oh, you know, he wanted me to have a drink with him, and I'd learned a bit of swearing in Arabic, so I swore at him in Arabic and he said, "Not only are you beautiful, but you speak Arabic!" They always tell you you're beautiful. It's depressing.'

'Is it?'

'It makes you feel as though you don't exist.'

'You just told me the advantage of being tall was that it stopped people thinking about you.'

'Oh. Yes, I did.'

Kit walked along the street slightly behind Joe, kicking at the leaves that had started, that week, to fall. Though it had been Joe himself who'd been making her feel claustrophobic, this had left her with a compelling wish to get out of her room. Of course, by staying put she could have evaded whatever was to come; but she hadn't had the grit to do it, to say 'no', so now the dismal business of *no*, still remained, presumably.

At least she was outside, however, added to which, despite herself, she felt somewhat intrigued.

'We won't be long,' said Joe.

'That's okay.'

'You know The Forfeit? I usually meet him there on a Friday, that's why—' he sighed. 'It won't take any time.'

'That's fine. Whatever you like.'

As they strode along, they descended into talking about their colleges, how good the food was or wasn't in hall, how and where they worked, the exact nature of their workloads, Kit feeling more and more like driftwood.

She had been past The Forfeit often enough, and could summon to mind its front window, which was frosted and ornamentally etched; but the glass was all she had ever noticed about it. This was her first time inside. There was sawdust sprinkled on the rough plank floor, which she took to be an affectation, while the pictures on the walls

81

showed bombers and fighter planes from the Second World War.

'Humpty,' said Joe, and gestured palm upwards to a skinny but appealing-looking young man on a bench against the back wall. His clothing was trashed. He had black, curly hair. Joe rested a hand on Kit's shoulder. 'This is Kit,' he said.

'Sit down,' said Humpty.

Kit pulled out the stool in front of her, but then hesitated because Joe hadn't moved.

'Sit down,' said Humpty again. He smelled of cigarettes. When Kit had first arrived in Oxford, before the law changed, she had particularly liked tobacco in the air in pubs, late afternoon. She hadn't been a passive passive-smoker, but on purpose had sat close to people who were smoking.

Joe checked his watch again, then darted a look at her. 'You'd like something?'

She had no idea what was going on, but grasped that this was an unexpected opportunity to waste time. If there was any chance it would make dancing impossible, then—'Yes,' she replied.

To Humpty, Joe said, 'Be normal, all right?'

'Who's normal?' asked Humpty; or perhaps, 'Whose normal?' Kit wasn't sure.

Joe shook his head and went to the bar.

'What do you think of the war?' said Humpty.

Kit now sat down. 'The war?' she said. Humpty was staring off past her with great intensity. The war? Kit thought. The war? Which one? What kind?

'I think there ought to be a law passed that says, next time a prime minister takes this country to war, as soon as the first British soldier's killed, the prime minister's taken straight to hospital and has his legs surgically removed.'

He had a kind of twitch, Kit saw, and his mouth was never quite still.

'Make them think twice about sending other people to fight,' Humpty said. 'If you're the British prime minister and a British soldier's killed because you sent him to war, your legs get removed. Of course, don't get me wrong, there'd be a state funeral, for the legs.'

'Oh really?'

'Definitely. Come on, massive. If there was a state funeral for the prime minister's legs, wouldn't you go? *I'd* go. Massive state funeral, for the prime minister's legs?'

'What if an enemy soldier's killed?'

Humpty looked sage. 'For every single as-they-say "enemy" soldier killed by as-they-say "our forces", the prime minister has to go to the parade ground outside Buckingham Palace and execute a horse.'

'Himself? By hand?'

'Yes, himself. Execute a horse, in public, outside Buckingham Palace, for each guy on the other side who's killed.'

'Well well, that would cause a fuss,' said Kit.

Humpty's twitch got slightly worse. 'That's the point.'

'No, I get it. Make that cows, and you could help out with the TB problem. Or how about condemned attack dogs?'

'Human beings divide into two kinds,' said Humpty, 'those

who have certain knowledge they're going to die soon, and those who don't.'

'Whether, in fact, they're going to or not,' replied Kit.

This was simply a joining-in sort of a remark, but Humpty shook his head in jittery fashion so as to convey to her that she had inelegantly amplified a statement that had been clear enough already.

Kit wanted to shout, 'Stop twitching'—to see if it would work.

'How did you meet Joe?' Humpty asked, as Joe came back with a pint for himself and a half of something for Kit—shandy, she discovered, a drink she greatly disliked. She took a large mouthful anyway.

'At a dance club?' she said, not pleased to have the subject raised.

Joe sat down on the bench. 'You know what,' he said, 'someone once told me this thing, that you can't really dance until you can dance superbly on a brick.'

'What if the person who tells you things, who you can't remember who said it—if it's the same person,' said Humpty. 'I mean, what if it's the same person for everyone. There's this one person who goes round telling us all these things, who has this special quality that, you can't remember who they are. I'm talking like the Sandman, or Wee Willie Winkie, who, they have this thing that they can reach everybody, but with this person, the special thing is, you can't remember who they are. Wouldn't it be great to be that unrememberable person who says rememberable things? And it's your job that you have to go round saying things to people like, "You can't dance properly till you can dance

84

on a brick", or, "Everyone has a bird's eye view of the stars".'

Kit, assuming that not much was expected of her, found it in a way cosy to be sitting in a pub, Friday, late afternoon, with two brothers, having a drink and a chat; saw herself, in this way, as a person who had something to do and friends to do it with. 'It would be quite a responsibility,' she said, mentally answering her last thought with the observation that, far from them being her friends, frankly, to her they were nobodies. She tried out a smile that promised more than she knew how to deliver, a sort of a smile that she saw often in the movies. 'My mind is—'

'No—' speaking over the top of her, Humpty said, '—no, no—'

'—infested with all sorts of—'

'—no, this would have to be a life for someone completely *irresponsible*,' he said, talking her down.

Kit took another swallow of the shandy.

'The person no one can remember,' said Joe, 'who tells us memorable things, is the brother of the angel who dances on people's graves.'

Humpty looked entranced by this suggestion, unless it was that he looked as though he'd been caught out. 'Bet it was Evalina,' he said suddenly.

'It was Evalina,' said Joe.

'Evalina.' Humpty closed his eyes. 'Talk about *dancing*—'

Kit pictured the minutes ticking away. She didn't want to dance. The thought of being asked to dance again as the boy—even the thought demoralised her. If this was what Joe had in mind, she would absolutely refuse. 'You know what makes seraphim different from other kinds of angels?' she said.

Humpty's eyes flew open again. 'What?'

'They're the lightest.'

'Oh.'

'I learned that at school.'

'Humpty and I learned dancing,' said Joe. 'Our headmaster was about a hundred and considered it essential.'

'*Two* Rottweilers, he has,' said Humpty, jiggling his knee.

After a pause, Kit said, 'He who?'

'Guy who runs this place. Joe and me are convinced he keeps a woman locked away upstairs dressed in a WAAF uniform. Nothing new under the sun,' said Humpty, before topping this platitude with the conspiratorial observation, '—apart from all the new stuff, that is.'

Joe glanced at his watch—for the fourth time?

'If you don't sleep well,' said Humpty, 'you're—' Whatever he was after, it was evident from his expression that it was negative. 'Joe doesn't sleep well.'

'Sleep well—neither do I,' said Kit. 'You do?'

'Like the dead,' replied Humpty.

'That isn't well,' she said, for no particular reason.

'In your ill-informed opinion.'

'Humpty—' said Joe.

Kit laughed, but inside she was thinking, God, this was a big mistake. I should really have stayed at home. I could be at home, doing something worthwhile, like *working*.

'Have you eaten recently?' Joe asked.

Humpty did look starved. He dismissed the question, but

86

it struck Kit that if he had eaten anything much in the past month, it didn't show.

As he and Joe fell to discussing a person called Buddy, she allowed her mind to uncouple from their exchanges, and lifted her gaze until it snagged on a set of cracks that ran across the ceiling—a vision that occupied her fully until it came to her to ponder, again, the oddities of the Grimwood murder, as she had uncovered them earlier in the day.

She hadn't got as far as explaining this to Joe, but there were aspects of the case that didn't make sense. There had been two suspects. The first, never identified, had been a gentleman, Eliza's last-ever client, whom she had picked up across the Thames at the Strand Theatre, and had slept with hastily, or at any rate semi-clothed, in her back-parlour bedroom the night of her killing. The other had been her cousin, lover and pimp, William Hubbard, who ran the house and had spent that night up in the attics, as was his habit when she had a customer. It had been he who'd found her body when he'd come down before dawn the next morning.

The coroner had taken it that if it had been Eliza's final client who had killed her, it had to have been over a dispute about money—though why in that case the demented attack on her corpse? And how could this man have melted away again afterwards unnoticed, soaked, as her murderer must have been, in blood? This last question had struck people as so unanswerable that it had caused many to assume that the killer must have been Hubbard, in a jealous rage, not that he was known for them—a reading that appeared to explain why Eliza, who had defence wounds across her hands, hadn't screamed for her life. There were other people in the house who would have heard her if she had, a maid asleep in the basement kitchen, and a second girl and her client in the room above Eliza's.

Yet there were reasons against its being Hubbard—Kit took a long draught of her shandy, now nearly finished. The inquest had determined that Eliza's injuries had been inflicted with a weapon something like a single-bladed Spanish switch knife. There was no blade even remotely similar in the household inventory, these being poor people whose possessions could be entirely listed. Charles Field, investigating, had had the privies, drains and sewers dug out, had pulled up floorboards, ripped out fireplaces and so on. No matching weapon could be found anywhere. If Hubbard had disposed of such a knife secretly, how had he done it? Okay, perhaps he had crept out through the house's cellars into Belvedere Road, had run down to the Thames and flung the weapon in. But even if so, there were only three water bowls in the house, and none of this water had the least sign of blood in it, and no set of Hubbard's clothes was missing, so how had he got himself clean again? He had had not a single sign of a struggle on him. How, as her murderer, could he have come out of such a splatterfest unmarked? And *one*, and *two*, and *three*, and *four*. The case didn't add up.

Kit toyed with the half-inch that still remained of her sickly drink. She had the embarrassed feeling she'd missed something, though Joe right then looked as though he, too, was having to recall himself to the moment. 'Humpty certainly shouldn't be able to sleep well,' he said. 'He recently fell in love.'

'Oh?' Kit cleared her throat, obscurely upset by this remark. 'And how did that happen?'

'For her own reasons,' Humpty gripped his hands between his thighs, 'she was changing out of her trousers in the kitchen—it's open plan, don't get me wrong; it's a dive, but it's open plan, and I walked in just right then and I saw her unzipping her trousers, the low kind so you can see her belly, so that—the moment she did the zip they fell, voomp, but—identically the same moment she was wanting whatever out of the wall cupboard above her head. So she undoes the zip but, identically the same moment she lifts her right leg up behind her bent at the knee and goes up on tip toe on her left foot and reaches up and the trousers catch at the crook of her knees so her legs are stopped in place just exactly like that, stopped completely still, so that she looks like—like a Renaissance painting of a nymph running away. And there's something, the shape of her, her knickers and the light on her skin and the way her trousers have fallen and are—and the sun, she has this pale hair on her legs so that the sun, when she's cold and they're pricking up, she glows. You'd think a skinny girl wouldn't have much hair like that, but it could be it keeps them warm, like a vole or something, just a light brushing—'

'Humpty—' said Joe.

'—a light *brushing* of hair.' Humpty laughed, a big laugh for a small funniness. 'The thing is,' he laughed more, for no obvious reason now, wound into himself on the bench, 'the thing is, she'd had two thoughts at once.'

'That's impressive,' said Kit. His choice of analogy, a Renaissance nymph, had piqued her.

'Her knickers,' said Humpty, 'were *ruched*.'

'Humpty—'

He turned jerkily to face his brother. 'She fucking asked,' he said.

'She was being civil.'

'That's impressive.'

'Enough,' said Joe.

Kit had the dreary feeling that she had misrepresented herself. 'Please, don't mind me. I don't—' What was she trying to say? What was she *saying*? '—I don't mind myself.'

Humpty turned back to look at her. In a voice of dangerous friendliness, he said, 'Everyone has a bird's-eye view of the stars.'

'I've got to take a leak, then—' Joe caught Kit's eye to ask her if she'd be okay. Would she be okay if he left her for a couple of minutes?

She nodded. No problem.

Still, she didn't much wish to be alone with Humpty, now. Joe was right.

When he had gone, Humpty said, 'You know who he was meant to dance with at the club—not last week, the first week?'

I see, thought Kit. Despite asking, you already knew how I met him.

And what was the answer to his question? Yes, as Joe had mentioned to her in Pams Cafe—a point she had lost a while ago, that now came back to her—yes, someone had stood him up that first Friday. Someone—Kit felt the elements in her mind mesh and looked cloudlessly at her interlocutor. 'You,' she said.

'Clever girl.'

So, after all, Joe had meant to dance with another boy, his own brother.

'Why didn't you show up?' she asked. 'Lose your nerve?'

Humpty spoke as though he found this suggestion derisory. 'I didn't show up,' he said, 'because I'm a *bad character*.' He leant forwards. 'You know why he was after doing it reversed?'

'He wanted to be carried away—sent,' she replied. Here, at least, she knew what she was talking about.

'Wrong,' said Humpty. 'What he wanted was—' but he couldn't put it into words. He scraped wearily at his temples with the heels of both hands. 'The thing is, I'm a burden,' he said. 'He wants me to go and live in a field. He told me that, before he died, he wanted to try dancing the following part, so I offered him it, which would have been good, except I didn't make it over there in time. *I* was meant to do it. But you—you said yes. Because, what wouldn't you say *yes* to? You don't mind yourself, right? You're not bothered if people respect you or anything.'

'You think he doesn't *respect* me?' she asked, audible but barely, upset at being spoken to like this by someone she didn't know.

'How it is,' said Humpty, 'he'd have respected you more if you'd've said no, but he wanted you to say yes.'

Sarcastically inside her head she thought, oh, so Joe had to make do with getting what he wanted? It felt like a riposte worth delivering out loud, but—she clutched her hands together—she was sure it probably wasn't.

'Hey, Kit,' said Humpty, as Joe came back and hovered, before sitting down again in a provisional-seeming way, 'can birds sing out of tune, do you think? Meaning, do birds ever think to themselves, I wish the fuck that starling would shut up, it's tone deaf? And if the answer to that is, "No, a bird can't sing out of tune", then is the human ga—' he'd got the word mangled, '—ga-pa—' he said, 'ca-*pacity*, for singing out of tune, a by-product of—' he paused, '*su-per-i-or* intelligence?'

'I think we're off,' said Joe.

Humpty slewed round to his brother and began to speak urgently. 'Don't, okay. I've been talking to her. She's one of those type—she sees a person down—she's one of that type of girls, she's just curious, she's—'

'Humpty,' said Joe, 'she's sitting right there.'

'—she—' Humpty looked back. 'Oh yes.' This came out in an easy way: 'Oh yes,' he said. Then he shivered. He shivered and rose to his feet. 'That's me.'

Joe reached a hand into his pocket.

'I'm fine,' said Humpty.

'You mean it?'

'I'm fine. Hey, Joe,' Humpty took a step backwards, 'guess what? Who just became a fully paid-up member of the Royal Elastic Society?' He winked at Kit, who didn't respond.

Joe, too, sat rigid, three twenties in his hand.

As Humpty stared at the money, he changed his mind. 'Well, okay,' he said, 'thanks.' He came back, reached for the notes, shoved them in his jacket pocket and left.

Joe looked towards Kit, his face unreadable. 'Right,' he said.

'In at the deep end,' she said.

'That was nowhere near the deep end,' said Joe. His shoulders sagged. 'I'm sorry, all the same. He's a pest. I shouldn't have let us stay.'

The word 'pest' felt hardly adequate for the situation. 'Is he, as it were, all right?' Kit asked.

Joe became markedly edgy. 'What do you want me to do about it?' he said.

'No, I was just—'

He shook his head to dismiss the matter. 'Look,' he said, 'if we scram, we can still just about make it.'

'That's okay.' Kit smiled wanly at him. 'I'm really tired.'

It was both true, and at the same time an excuse. To fortify her resolve, Kit summoned to mind the battered church hall, the twinned bodies, the insidious stench of the place, the hostility she had encountered there, the fraught closeness of it all. I was pissed on, she thought suddenly, and couldn't bear the idea of more.

'Are you sure?'

'Completely,' she said, though because she was equally sure she had disappointed him, she did then add, 'We could have another drink if you like'—perpetuating the evening, oh God.

'What do you fancy?' he asked. 'Actually, can we get out of here?'

'Fine, yes.' Kit stood up, clasped her coat around her, pushed her hair back.

Joe followed her through to the front of the pub. As they threaded past various tables, he said, 'So, what are we going to do about this dance I owe you?'

'This what?'

'I owe you a dance, right? You made that pretty clear last week. The right way round?'

Kit's ability to talk temporarily failed her. 'Did I?' she stuttered.

'In the café, afterwards, you said—'

He opened the door of the pub for her and out they went into the bland, early evening. On the pavement she stared at him, mollified and dismayed in equal measure. He had sought her out in order to discharge a debt?

On the other side of town, Intermediate would shortly be beginning. They could have been half way there by now had she played her hand differently. She could have been half way to being held, led, danced to oblivion, the very thing she had wished for. Yet instead, here she was stuck on a pavement feeling complicated. Well, how stupid.

Kit feared that the tenor of her reflections might show, and said, 'I didn't think he'd be so—'

'Humpty?'

'Yes.'

'What did you think?'

'I don't know how to say this. It sounds so prejudiced. I guess I was kind of expecting he'd be an egg.'

Joe wasn't amused. 'Can I take you for a meal somewhere, or cook you something?'

She affected to be unable to decide. The truth was, she didn't want to do either.

'What do you like to eat?'

Kit couldn't think of an answer. 'Anything,' she said. 'Pigeons, dandelions.'

'All right,' said Joe, 'how about I make you a pigeon and dandelion risotto?'

As though it was all decided, he began to walk; and so, once again like driftwood, Kit did too. She had had the chance to suggest where they ate, or to bail out of the whole, futile exercise. Now they were going to his place again. She had completely blown it.

The trip to The Forfeit had been a senseless and peculiar experience, but senseless, peculiar and different, so she didn't really care. Now, though, she had absolutely had enough— more than enough. She was tired. She hadn't slept well for days. And she had work she needed to catch up on, after all her fooling around with the Eliza Grimwood stuff.

She and Joe wandered along together exchanging the odd remark, twilight glimmering in the air, the pair of them looking, Kit imagined, extraordinarily content. And *no*, and *no*, and *no*, and *no*—

Up Joe's shabby staircase, they were just coming level with the door to the middle flat when an elderly gent stepped out onto the landing. He seemed surprised by them, appeared haggard.

'Are you all right?' Joe asked.

'Frank died.'

'No—Buddy, no.' Joe lifted a hand in tender salute.

'Funeral was this morning. St Michael's.' Buddy nodded to confirm each of his points. 'Vicar's a real stuffed shirt. References to sin, to my mind, not the right thing, Joe. Anyway, coronary. Quick exit. There's worse ways. Only time I smarten up these days is for a funeral.'

The two of them stood huddled on the landing while Kit remained a step below on the stairs.

'I'm so sorry,' said Joe, 'that's—I know you were close.'

'There were only about fifteen people,' said Buddy, 'and I think someone rather went out into the hedgerows to get *them*.'

'Are you all right?'

'Don't you worry about me,' said Buddy. 'I've seen it all. You've your lady friend here.'

'We'll talk tomorrow. You're okay for supper, right? You have—'

'Bits and bobs, Joe. I've a wodge of Stilton. Don't you worry. Bit of a shock to the system, that's all. I've known him—' silently he mouthed the sum he now undertook in his head, '—forty-two years. You go on up,' he said. 'I'm just taking out my rubbish. Nice to meet you,' he said to Kit.

'Yes, I'm so sorry,' she said.

'Never you mind.' Buddy bent behind him to pick up a meagrely filled bin liner, waiting for her to pass so he could carry it down the stairs.

This time, Joe let Kit chop up the vegetables.

'His flat's unbelievably worn. He hasn't done a thing to it in years. The pictures are slipped in their frames, you know?—which is symptomatic of what the whole place is like. Everything's threadbare and chipped. Humpty and I have offered to help him often enough, but he always refuses. He has a niece in New Zealand. He does have friends. He's a hotshot at the bowls club on the Marston Ferry Road.'

'Where does the name "Buddy" come from?' Kit asked.

'Brian, but I've never heard anyone call him that.'

'Brian. Right. So how come this flat's so slick then?' she said. 'I mean, I guess I hear dons grumbling about—they get paid so little, and how it's such a doss in the States, compared.'

'The answer is that it isn't my flat. It's an investment property of my father's.'

'Oh, God, I see.' While Kit mulled over his reply, Joe melted butter in a pan, which caused her stomach to turn hungrily. So far that day she'd had breakfast, a pint of custard and a few mouthfuls of shandy. At the prospect of a square meal, a meal made by somebody else, she felt almost ill.

'You're right. I would never live like this on my own account, even if I could afford to.' Joe glanced round at Kit, then said, 'Michaela's a bit of a one, yes?'

'She has this boyfriend,' Kit replied. 'Everyone in our house pretends he's imaginary. He's not, but everyone pretends he is because basically for the past year and a half he's been in the Amazon rainforest doing analysis of soil samples, and when she shows you a photo you pretend it looks nothing like the last photo of him and so on. It's just a joke, but the truth is she's lonely without him. She's a bit of a good-time girl, and I think she finds it hard that he's away. She's very sociable, but she pines, and—'

'And you're good friends?' said Joe.

Kit tried to think. 'Yes, maybe. Not exactly. When I first met her, before we started sharing, I quite disliked her. But I came to see that this was very much a snap judgement on my part. I mean, I saw that there was more to her, naturally enough. But it turns out—' she stared at the vivid colours of the vegetables, a red pepper bleeding under her knife, '—it turns out that, you know, like constellations of stars holding steady, my snap judgements have definitely lingered. They may only come out when it's dark, but they're always there. I mean, I do realise there's still a lot about her that I don't—' Kit broke off to wonder why she was being needlessly ungenerous in this way, and finished her line of thought inside her head: there was still a lot about Michaela she didn't know. Of course, Kit reflected, there were only so many people you could take on properly in a life, whatever that meant. And as she starkly thought this through, she found she suspected—more than suspected, really—that so far as people she cared about went, she was some way from having reached a human limit.

She was so hungry that the meal seemed to come and go without her sensibly appreciating it, until they arrived at a point where Joe, pushing a coffee in front of her, said, 'Shall we shift through?'

The enormity of saying, 'Oh the kitchen's all right, let's stay here'—she couldn't make herself do it.

Drink this in sips, Kit thought. She stood up, picked up the coffee and followed him, glancing, as she had done on her previous visit, into his impressive, antique mirror. *Drink it in sips*, she told her reflection, *string it out*. In the speckled, silvery glass, she looked distinctly flushed.

'Oh—this picture,' she said, and stopped to take in properly a large pencil study that hung to the side of the mirror, next to the archway through which they were about to pass.

'Ah, you've noticed,' said Joe. 'What do you think?'

'Well, I mean, at the risk of sounding completely silly, am I—doesn't she look like me?'

'I know.'

'You think so?'

'Very much I do. I was startled when I first saw you for that exact reason.'

'Yes?'

'Yes. I thought, here's my picture, she's jumped off the wall and gone out for a dance.'

'Was that why you followed me to the bus stop?'

'No,' he said. A look flitted across his face. 'No, I followed you because—you know it was such a crush and everyone had to divide into boys and girls? The way you managed the steps on your own; it was unlike anyone else there. For an hour I watched you, and wanted to be the person you were imagining dancing with.'

This answer made Kit feel so shy that she simply blanked it out. 'Who is she?' she said, pointing at the girl.

'Just a model, I think. It was done by a friend of Rodin's. My father picked it up for a song in a junk shop, and he can't sing.'

'You mean, extremely cheap?'

'Yes, considering. The artist's called Rothenstein. I think he was an early director of the Tate. I should find out. I'm not quite sure.'

'You know there's this whole schtick about the image of the female reader in Victorian art?'

'No, I don't know.'

'I mean, boring, boring,' Kit paused, '—well, actually, it isn't *completely* boring—in art and in literature, I mean. I wonder if he drew her because she was reading, or, because he was drawing her, he let her read to get through the time.' She leant in closer. 'She's very peaceful, isn't she, despite looking like she's effectively unwrapped for display. It really is disconcerting how much she looks like me. I just have to say that. It makes me feel odd.'

'It's even odder for me, now I'm seeing you both at once.'

'Your father gave her to you?'

'No.' Joe laughed a little, and not happily. 'No, this whole place is his and most of what's in it. She isn't mine. I shouldn't have said that. That's mine.' He gestured through the archway to the sitting room, and an impressive black piece of furniture with shell inlay on the doors. 'It's a replica of a desk by Charles Rennie Mackintosh; original was one of the most—I think—one of the most expensive pieces of twentieth-century furniture ever at sale.'

'Blimey. I quite like it.'

'Yes. This is supposed to be the ideal double bachelor pad. Chrome and antiques; probably passé, who knows.'

'With mildly suggestive sketches of late nineteenth-century women readers?'

'One.'

'One.'

He took her out onto his balcony. Kit, on her previous visit, hadn't noticed the picture, had barely considered the sitting room and hadn't realised the balcony even existed. Here it was, though. Joe shifted a Japanese screen to one side. To get out, you had to climb through a window.

'It's Buddy's bathroom underneath,' he explained, 'and

the ground-floor kitchen under that. The extension isn't original to the house. They put this balcony on top without ever
making proper access, hence the need to clamber.'

'Buddy's flat has to be enormous,' said Kit, climbing out
after him. Inside the flat it had grown quite dark, but outside,
the sky to the west was holding its light—an empty, fading
brilliance.

'It is. Must be worth a lot these days, but he lives like a
mouse.'

'With his wodges of Stilton.'

Kit peered briefly down into the garden below, which was
dotted with plastic toys, a lidded ladybird sandpit, a trike on
its side.

'Ground floor is married graduates with two little kids,'
said Joe, 'French. They've only been here a couple of months.
It's a rent—change and change about.'

But Kit wasn't looking down any more, or even really
listening. The balcony formed a striking contrast with the
flat. On either side it was walled, and these walls were
covered with wooden lattice, while at the front there was an
iron parapet. In and out, in a jumble, wove a passion vine
and a clematis, a jasmine, a rose; a white rambler rose in
bloom. The brickwork, too, was strewn with plants that had
been slipped into holes in the mortar.

Kit put down her half-empty coffee cup on a flaking and
rusty, painted metal table. 'Amazing,' she said, as she peered
at the blooms and the clinging clumps of foliage.

Joe waved from one to another, 'Snapdragons, thrift, val-
erian, daisies, pimpernel, wall lettuce, moss.'

'Amazing,' said Kit again. There were baby snails on the

walls, no more than a couple of millimetres across, perfectly formed miniature knock-offs.

'You see this red honeysuckle tucked away here?' he said.

'It's pretty.'

'I don't know, I've been thinking about whether to keep it. I keep thinking it looks like the trailing parts on some pimped-up tropical fish. Early October, most of these plants shouldn't still be in flower, but they are.'

'I like the way it's almost entirely on the vertical plane, this garden, apart from these three pots,' said Kit.

'Yes. They're actually a bigger challenge than the walls,' he replied. 'I wouldn't mind having bare terracotta; but there are tricks to container planting, if you want them to look good all year round, that is, without endlessly adding new plants. This is a Japanese maple,' he added. 'It should turn soon and go practically magenta. Exotics tend to turn before the native trees, although, these days—'

'Isn't there something about prime numbers and fir cones?' said Kit, dredging up the question without thinking about it very hard.

'You're perhaps looking for the word "fractals" as it relates to ferns?' he said. His lesser eyebrow twitched. 'Or was it the connection between Fibonacci numbers and, for example, the ordering of seeds in the head of a sunflower?'

Kit grinned. 'Just so you know, it was a miracle I scraped a "B" for maths in my GCSEs.' She nodded at one of the containers. 'I guess people must occasionally *give* you new plants, though?'

'It's not my custom to let anyone see this,' he replied.

Not for the first time that evening, Kit felt outmanoeuvred.

What a funny situation, she thought, when escaping it required you to climb through a window.

She reached for her coffee cup, searching, once again, for something inconsequential to say, and settled on, 'I don't usually like wallpaper, but this is a bit like wallpaper that's alive.' She glanced at him hopefully. 'I like *this*, I mean; and it must change all the time.'

'I know. I think of this, the balcony, as being my real room,' he said. 'Even though it's open, I don't feel over-looked. I could be, if one of the neighbours bent right out of their skylights, or if a person in one of that block of flats beyond the trees had a pair of binoculars on me; but why? And when I lie down on my back and stare upwards, I really am invisible. I can get to feeling sometimes as though I own the bit of sky above me here—not own it—as if, as if that's the right bit of the sky for me to be staring at. I like it. Humpty says he'll put it on my gravestone: "He liked looking up at the sky."'

'When you said "invisible", I thought for a second you meant "see-through", "transparent"; that when you lay down and couldn't be seen, it was because you became trans-parent.' Kit put a hand to the window frame. She wanted to go back inside—to leave, in fact. Life was confusing. She'd had enough of it for one day.

'About Humpty,' said Joe, 'you know you asked if he was all right? I just want to mention; you know how if you're crammed into a seat at the cinema and your legs don't fit, you feel too big, but if you are on the side of an enormous mountain you feel quite small, right?'

Kit let her hand drop again. 'Believe me, I know all about

my legs not fitting into seats at the cinema, or on buses, or aeroplanes, sleeves not reaching my wrists, trousers floating above my ankles. I could go on,' she said.

'Yes. The thing about Humpty is that I think he feels exactly the same size whatever he's doing, wherever he is. He always feels as though he's exactly the same size,' said Joe, 'except at the weekends.'

'You mean he's a bit mad?' she said.

Joe replied to this question merely by dipping his head. 'What's your full name?' he asked.

'My full name? Farr, Christine Iris.'

'Really?'

'Yes.'

'Christine Iris Farr?'

'Yes. Christine was my mother's choice, and my father's mother was called Iris. I chose to be Kit when I was about nine, because I didn't like being called "Chris", or "Chrissy". And by the way, I also have a brother—a half-brother— called,' she sighed, then said quickly, 'Graham. He's miles older than me. We have the same father. My father's seventy-four. Graham's mother ran away with a man from Dundee, but left him behind, Graham, I mean. So we grew up in the same house and everything, but not at the same time, essentially. I mean I'm fond of him, but he's more like he's my uncle, kind of thing. There's twenty years between my mother and father, working out that Graham is considerably closer in age to my mother than my father is.'

'Right,' said Joe, not apparently that interested.

Kit downed the remains of her coffee, realised what she had done and felt a pang of concern. 'So?' she said.

'So?'

'What's your name?'

'Leppard, Joseph.'

'Leopard?'

'Leppard.'

'Leppard, sorry. Beg your pardon.'

'That's all right.'

'No middle name?'

'No.'

Her coffee was all gone. Kit decided to announce that she was leaving. She began to gear herself up for it. 'You know what I think's strange?' she said.

'What?'

'There's the sky up above, and we're down here surrounded by plants, but this is not the earth. It seems funny, you know? Do you know that Paul Muldoon poem about, one blue eye and one brown?'

'Why do I get the feeling it would be better to admit to syphilis or something, than to not having read Paul Muldoon?'

'No, no.'

'What about it?'

'The poem?' she said fretfully.

'Look,' said Joe, 'you might want to factor it in that the answer to any question you ask me that begins, "You know that poem where"—the answer will almost certainly be, *no*.'

'That's okay. I apologise. I mean, I'd quote it to you,' said Kit, 'but I can't remember it. And it only has four lines. To me, that's me having—that's, I've got syphilis as well, that I can't even quote it, four lines. I often find myself wishing I'd been brought up to memorise, as a matter of course, the things that I really like; not that I—' What was she on about? Never mind. I'm leaving now, she thought: the window. 'But in the poem, you know,' she said, trying to wrap up her remarks, 'it's that, there's this girl with eyes different colours, and it's the brown eye for the earth, and the blue eye—' she threw a hand skywards.

About as lightly as it's possible to ask such a thing, Joe said, 'Would you like to sleep with me again?'

'Oh I just *couldn't*,' she exclaimed.

A woman's voice burst out from a window down below. '*J'en peux plus de ce bordel!*'

Joe looked away, over across the gardens, taking in Kit's reply. With a touch of amusement, he said, 'I didn't mean out here.'

After this, they stood, for what felt like a long time, just as they were, mute and still, in the city-whacked dusk, undecided.

CHAPTER 4

Kit lay in bed looking at her clock radio, 8:37—8:38—8:39—
8:40—whereupon she put out a hand to turn it off; except,
as she confusedly then understood, she hadn't been listening
to the radio, she'd been watching the time. And the time you
don't turn off.

Another Friday, not enough sleep.

Michaela came thumping into the kitchen with the post.
'Yours,' she mumbled, and tossed Kit an envelope.

'Thanks.'

'For nowt.'

Spoon, bowl and cup, knife, a box of parched health stuffs,
fruit, soya milk: noisily, Michaela made herself a collection
on the table.

The envelope was stamped with the information that it
came from Shropshire, was an appeal for funds for the reha-
bilitation of careworn donkeys, and was 'IMPORTANT'. Kit
slung it unopened into the paper recycling box under the
counter by the oven.

'For fuck's sake,' said Michaela, leaning back out of
her chair, 'office paper here, *window* envelopes and cardboard in with cans and plastic bottles.' She retrieved the
letter and threw it into the correct crate. Out flew a wasp.

'Sorry,' said Kit, who found herself wondering whether it was because Michaela's father owned a bottle factory that she was so militant about recycling.

'I've labelled the bloody crates. I've done all the work.'

'Believe me.'

'You haven't put vanilla in your coffee? Why do you do that? Vile. You're so free and easy.' Michaela fished around in her bowl, trying to get just the pineapple bits on her spoon. 'Well, in some ways,' she added, 'nudge, nudge.'

'Betsy Trotwood, yes,' Kit wasn't paying attention, 'yes, Betsy Trotwood, *David Copperfield*, hates donkeys. I suppose they still have them, do they, on beaches? They haven't been banned yet?'

Michaela looked up. 'Planning another little adventure this evening?' she asked. 'And don't say, "With who?"'

'With whom?'

'Piss off, okay? What's he called? Jack, Bob? It's a Friday night thing, right? Friday nights? Right? What does he do other nights?' Michaela sat back and pushed her bowl away from her. 'More's to the point, did you sleep with him again last week? I've been very good. I haven't asked.'

Kit endeavoured, as a performance, to look wry— although, how was she supposed to tell what face she was pulling? No one practised, did they? Or was a wry face the exception? She felt she had seen it in the movies, young men, timid, faintly smiling at themselves in the mirror. She *had* seen it, more than once; though was this in English-language movies only? She took in her fair share of Korean, French, Japanese films, naturally, the odd Iranian one,

German ones, heaven knows; but she couldn't instantly place the scene she had in mind in a setting with subtitles, which perhaps meant—

'Not very talkative, are we?' said Michaela. 'Too early for you, ten past nine in the morning?'

—which perhaps meant that the business of using a mirror to be certain you were pulling off *wry* was a defining experience common only to the writers of English-language film scripts.

This was the sort of line Kit could imagine being delivered by someone funny, who would say it funnily, so it sounded funny. But was it true? Did—'What?' she said. Oh. Yes. Yes, she was meeting him again, Bob?—*Joe*, up the hill, dancing, yes. He owed her, apparently, wished to discharge his debt. The rest of the week, goodness knows what he did. Yes, she thought, it's a Friday night thing, and today is Friday and—why was it that she and Michaela always seemed to want breakfast at the same time?

'Kit,' boomed Michaela unpleasantly, 'you're off in la-la land, you twit. You slept with him again, I'm asking? I take it you did, right? Was it better than before?' She stared narrowly across the table. 'I see. Yes. Good. Sweet. I knew it. I *knew* it. Maths lecturer sounds a bit crap, frankly, but, I don't know, he's got presence, hasn't he? Don't look at me like that, the wind might change. I mean, seriously, for you, Kit, twice is practically married.'

Kit flicked a scattering of toast crumbs onto the floor. She doubted it was humanly possible for a person to feel less married than she did.

*

She knocked off a reading list for Orson—she was getting increasingly efficient about them, and he was as ready as he was ever going to be to tackle *Bleak House*—then spent most of the day between two libraries, with a break in the middle to watch *Get Carter,* a film that buoyed her with the illusion that she was more alive coming out of the cinema than she had been going in.

She had started out that morning trying to make progress with her regular work, but had swiftly abandoned it. Friday had become the day she allowed herself to pursue other courses, and besides, while hunting for traces of Eliza in the catalogue of all Oxford's libraries, she had come upon an irresistible title, the very thing she had been hoping might exist. *Eliza Grimwood, a Domestic Legend of the Waterloo Road* was a supposedly true, contemporary account of the murder, initially printed in instalments, and designed to capitalise on the public's fascination with the crime. The author had been catalogued as, 'Grimwood, Eliza, fict.'—wrong all ways round. Eliza was by no means a fiction, but at the same time, could hardly have written up her own death. Kit had ordered the book in a whir of excitement. The film had then put her in the perfect mood, so that she felt a terrible, happy jump within herself as she danced back up the Bodleian staircase. She was even happier as she collected the book from the issue desk. It smelled great. Her hands felt suddenly heavy as she tucked herself in at a table, seat 109, and began to read.

At first she scrabbled to try to understand the material. Then she slowed down. The narrative was formulaically circuitous, to pad it out, and formulaically titillating. It was, after all, about a prostitute. What was unusual, though, as Kit soon began to understand, what was bizarre, was the book's explanation—Kit pulled out her notebook—of Eliza's murder.

From the start of the 1830s, the author wrote, the big newspapers had all had their 'tame incendiaries', and 'special and general criminals', subdivisions of their more aboveboard labour force. If there was no news, news would be created. These illicit employees were 'consummate concocters of London crimes'. Thus the destruction by fire of the Houses of Parliament in 1834, so the author asserted; and thus also, during an 'insipid' down patch in 1838, when the public was stuck waiting for all the excitements of Queen Victoria's coronation, the merciless killing of a prostitute in Waterloo. The city's heaving populace—the newspaper readership—had been notably restless, and so, 'the initiated gentlemen of the press', drawled the narrative, had 'expected that something would happen to horror-strike the nation'.

Eliza had been executed to boost the sale of newspapers? Kit patted her cheek compulsively. But then, as she tried to think this nonsense through from various angles, she was led to a question she couldn't confidently answer. Might Dickens have been accused, with much more justice, of something not dissimilar, when earlier killing off *his* prostitute, Nancy?—of having tried to boost his entertainment value by crassly horror-striking the nation?

When Kit had put *Oliver Twist* on Orson's reading list a few weeks before, she had done nothing more than skim it herself, to remember its general feel; so she pulled a copy off the shelves now and dipped into a few of the appendices, trying to gain purchase on how it had been received when it first came out. She hadn't much time left, though, and only just scraped getting to the dance session as it began. This wasn't polite of her, but she naturally wished to arrive after Joe, not before him, if one of them was going to have to wait around. Let him wait, she thought.

It was a pleasantly blowy evening, an evening to be on the streets. She looked along the pavement to see if he was folded into the railings, but he wasn't.

He was, however, inside. Kit picked him out, through a shifting crowd of bodies, leaning against the battle-worn plaster at the back of the hall, self-contained, but also perceptibly tensed; at which, entirely out of concert with her spirits, she was afflicted by a thrill of desire—at which she *then* thought to herself, oh shit.

All she wanted to do was to dance.

She made her way over to him. 'So it's definitely on,' nervous, 'the right way round kind of thing? I'm the girl this time?'—dropping her bag down, stripping off her jacket.

'Hi, hello,' said Joe. 'You're here, good. Yes, sure. As agreed.'

'Thank you, thanks,' she replied, speaking much more sincerely than she would have known to had she never attempted what she was now expecting of him.

Joe straightened up. Kit was wearing her flattest shoes. There wasn't much between them like this. I didn't need to ask, she thought, I made myself look—'*Okay*, people,' the instructor yelled, 'over here. Come on. That's right. Great. So, yes, this week I'm going to really make you suffer, okay?' She switched on the elderly music system. 'Let's step it up now,' *Lucille*. 'Eyes this way. You, yes, excuse me, yes, can I borrow you, love? Yes, yes, you.' A young man with scabbed elbows came forward reluctantly to partner the instructor. 'Right, listen to the music,' she yelled—they were all embroiled now—'counting in slowly here and—*Quick-quick* one; and *quick-quick* two; and *quick-quick* three; and *quick-quick* four—again? *Quick-quick* one; and *quick-quick* two; and *quick-quick* three; and *quick-quick* four—Let's—spread yourselves out, okay? Cooee? Let's all have a pop at this. Find yourselves a partner. Boys and girls, in a minute you're going to take it in turns dancing with your eyes closed, so please pay attention. Okay, ready, here's the music—whap, three, *four*: QUICK-*quick* one; and QUICK-*quick* two; and QUICK-QUICK THREE; help!, QUICK-*quick* four; good—*quick-quick* one; and *quick-quick* two; and *quick-quick* three; and *quick-quick* four; and—' Kit? And Kit was lost already, whirling amongst the phantom bullets, gone.

'Bloody fucking hell, you really did it,' she said, jumping off the hall steps onto the street, other people flooding out around her.

Joe, though thin, was so much the stronger of the two of them that even when she'd made errors, he had guided her through them by force. He was a beautiful dancer. Only a very few times in all two hours had either of them distinctly stumbled.

He had tried to help Kit back on with her jacket, but it was cut tight, and she was so unused to this gesture that it had made things more difficult for her, not less. She had flailed with her free arm trying to find the sleeve, pleased, nevertheless—on a bit of a high.

'Did *it?*' Joe repeated, catching up with her, entertained.

'I didn't have to think at all. It was so lovely, and—' Kit shrugged her jacket up, 'I just really enjoyed it. Thank you. Thank you. *That* was what I—'

'I know,' he said.

On the bus heading back into town, warmly squashed together, he asked how she was, 'And how's the work going?'

'You know, Dickens is fucking interesting,' she replied. She was in an exceptionally good mood.

'I don't think he'd approve of that as a compliment,' said Joe.

Kit looked round at him. 'Dickens? How do—? Oh no,' she said, mortified by the expression on his face, unable to keep the pleasure out of her voice, 'you went and read a Dickens?'

'I've started one,' he said.

'*Bleak House?*'

'No, *Oliver Twist.*'

'Good God. Because of me?'

'Of course because of you. You said it was interesting, and violent, if I recall correctly. I saw the movie as a kid, the musical, didn't particularly remember it as violent— psychologically perhaps. I thought I might as well read it, start at the beginning.'

'I don't think any screen adaptations have come that close to the real thing,' said Kit, 'as far as I'm aware, although there have been a lot of them, I mean in the order of forty, I think; because, they make them for kids to be able to see, whereas if they were accurate to the book, you'd be talking X-rated, certificate 18. It's a funny point, but if Oliver Twist could read the book he appears in, he'd faint away in horror.'

'He's a fainter too, isn't he? You're right. You must mean the ending, though. I haven't got there yet.'

Kit hardly noticed the scene outside the bus as they made their stop-start way in heavy traffic. 'I can't believe it,' she repeated delightedly. 'I made you read a book.'

'True,' said Joe. 'And how's your maths coming along?'

She covered her eyes with her hands and made a small, agonised peeping noise.

'Forget I mentioned it,' he said. 'It's all right, I was joking. Tell me again what it is about *Oliver Twist* that interests you so much?'

Kit took a deep breath, held it tight, smiled at him, and then spoke in a whoosh: 'For example, the death of Nancy, which you haven't read yet but Bill Sikes bashes her to death, is objected to by modern critics as being absurdly melodramatic. But at the time Dickens wrote it—well, a few years later, 1840—Thackeray offended him deeply by describing Nancy as, "the most unreal fantastical personage possible". Thackeray thought that if you took account of the actual prostitution element, which Dickens was forced to gloss over, then any goodness Nancy manifested would be rendered void by her immorality. And anyway, Thackeray didn't believe in her good side. He thought it was senti-mental rubbish.'

'Her self-sacrifice, you mean? When she betrays Sikes for Oliver, if I remember correctly? I haven't got there yet, although she's already afraid of getting herself killed.'

'Yes, she recognises the danger from the start, which makes her doubly martyrish, I guess. And yes, she puts her life in jeopardy to save Oliver. But her self-sacrifice is even more extreme when she gets caught, because she begs Sikes not to kill her *for his own sake*, to spare him the consequences of becoming a murderer. She's not indifferent to her own fate, but she pretty much dies trying to save Bill Sikes from himself.'

'You don't consider that melodramatic?'

'Sure, fine. But consider, Dickens was criticised for this being unbelievable, and yet—just imagine what he can have thought when, a little while later, Eliza Grimwood's slaughter hit the press? Remember the photocopy you looked at in my room? As it happens, one of the main arguments that swirled around when people tried to interpret the details of that murder scene was exactly the following: that Eliza must have been done for by someone she knew, and wished to protect, because she had defence wounds on her hands, and yet hadn't screamed out and ensured that her attacker got caught.'

'One–nil, Dickens.'

'Absolutely. And I mean, in very similar circumstances, too. You have a pimp-suspect, bedroom death scene, prostitute, poverty. I guess once Eliza's killing had happened, then whatever else you wanted to say, if you were prepared to think hard about the details of the true-life case, you couldn't so easily dismiss Nancy as the most unreal personage possible. And you know, Dickens was so cross about Thackeray's comments that he wrote a retrospective preface to the novel where he answered back, and said that examples like Nancy's, of goodness in desperate and wicked circumstances, weren't so hard to find in real life, and that she was, in effect, "TRUE", was "God's truth", and on and on like that.'

'You're sure Dickens would have known about Eliza's killing?'

'Yes, yes,' said Kit, 'that's as sure as can be. I mean, the case was huge. You know you said it reminded you of Jack the Ripper? Okay, Jack the Ripper happened fifty years later. But guess what I found out? When the Ripper murders got going, how did the *Telegraph* try to communicate the insanity of the thing to its readers? It said, here we go again, this is just like Eliza Grimwood.'

'Oh really?'

'Yes. The exact quote—'

'Which you've memorised?'

Kit hesitated a fraction. 'I read it today. It just sticks in my mind,' she said. 'The *Telegraph* noted that how the women were being butchered in Whitechapel, and the manner of Eliza's death, were of "closely analogous horror". In other words, for the *Telegraph*, whoever Eliza's killer had been half a century before, a full fifty years later that unidentified murderer remained the best available benchmark for the person known as Jack the Ripper.'

Kit did now gaze out of the window. They would soon reach the High Street.

'All right,' said Joe. 'All right then, I accept your judgement that Dickens probably heard about it.'

She looked back at him. 'It's not just that. Dickens himself wrote about Eliza later on. And I mean, leaving aside his moral argument with Thackeray, he loved this kind of thing, shocking crime cases. He's known for it.

And—you know what else? Until two years previous to Eliza's murder, the Strand Theatre, where she picked up her last client the night she died, was managed by someone Dickens actually knew, called Douglas Jerrold; and it was still being managed by Jerrold's brother-in-law the night of the killing. Guess what else? On stage, the night of her death, while she was hunting amongst the audience for business—' Kit grinned at Joe and threw her arms out sideways—so far as she was able to—in a gesture of satisfaction, 'on stage,' said Kit, 'unbelievably enough, they were performing a version of *Pickwick*—a work *by Dickens himself*, ta-da! I mean, of all the possibilities, it was an adaptation of a work *by Dickens* that Eliza walked out on to be slaughtered. She and her gentleman got a cab outside the Spotted Dog pub on the Strand, then trundled through the tolls on Waterloo Bridge. Can you possibly think that all these threads were in place, with Dickens not aware of any of it? Hundreds of people milled in the streets waiting for news updates from her inquest. Everybody knew.'

'How's the thesis going?' said Joe.

Kit laughed. 'I have to admit, I did spend most of today on this stuff, again, which was very bad of me, but I really feel as though, if I keep following these details, I'm going to stumble on I-don't-know-what.'

'I can see that looking at you,' said Joe. He smiled, then glanced away, his whole demeanour altering in the process. 'Is it all right if we drop in at The Forfeit?—just check Humpty's doing okay?'

'No, no. That's fine.'

'He's not in great shape at the moment.'

118

'That's fine,' said Kit. 'Whatever you want.'

Humpty in poor shape wasn't at all what she felt like; but she was in a carefree mood, the dancing had exceeded her hopes and she was pleased to be able to oblige. 'Lectures going okay,' she asked apologetically, 'algebraic geometry? Affine and projective varieties?'

'They're going okay, yes, thank you.'

'Good,' she said, 'no, yes, sure.'

Humpty was slouched at the table where they'd found him the week before, at the back of the pub, slightly removed from the rest, jiggling his knee. 'How's Baddie?' he said. Along with its bench, stools and chairs, this particular table was boxed in on one side by a decorative glass partition, designed, so it seemed, to shield any drinkers from a door to the patio at the back.

'*Buddy*,' said Joe.

Kit felt a twinge of regret that she hadn't asked about him herself.

'Did you take him out?' Humpty looked so pale, he could have been carved from a bar of soap. He looked, thought Kit, like Shelley in a Byron wig.

'Yes, I did,' said Joe. 'But you know what he's like. He's all right. Remember when the secretary died at the bowls club?'

'Yes, but how long had he known Frank?'

'About forty years—I think he said? Decades, certainly. But he mostly talked about other things, you know? He told me there was a lady who lived in our flat years ago, "She wasn't really a lady, Joe, and one day she started seeing a fancy man, upped and had her hair bleached, and after she'd washed it a few times back at home", this was—'

'"—it turned green",' said Humpty, 'when they still had the old copper water pipes: "Blue rinse is fetching. Green rinse, that's another story." You reckon she was secretly after Buddy, or what?'

'All right,' said Joe. 'I hadn't heard it before.'

'Let me tell you,' Humpty sounded vacantly aggressive, 'I've heard it all before. Fifty-five, thank you. Sixty anyone? On my right at fifty-five. Maiden bid at fifty-five. Sixty, sir? Thank you. Sixty at the back. Sixty-five? No? Anyone at sixty-five? Going at sixty. Hammer's up—'

'All right,' said Joe flatly.

'Haven't I got—you don't think? Me on the rostrum, sell anything.'

'Now there's an idea.'

Joe, Kit felt, was speaking with the absolute minimum of enthusiasm his words would allow.

'He wants me to go and live in a field,' said Humpty.

'Really?' said Kit. 'Who, Joe?'

'Ah,' said Humpty, as though changing the subject. He tipped his head back and for a moment closed his eyes.

Round the partition, three young men came to their table. Kit could imagine her father muttering, 'As if they owned the place'.

'Oh, yes,' said Humpty, with the gesture of a person who's forgotten to explain something. He wasn't twitching any more.

'As you were,' said the first of them.

Kit looked to Joe.

'Kit, this is Dean Purcell,' he said, 'and this is Donald,' he pointed to the second of them. Donald's eyes were strikingly colourless. His eye whites looked grey. He was the only person amongst them who might have been described as fat. 'And this is Pauly,' said Joe.

Baldy Drinkwater, thought Kit, *Ebenezer Ward*.

The third young man was much littler than the other two. Kit was pleased that it was he who sat on the stool to her right; less pleased that Donald slid in beside her to her left along the bench. Dean sat between Donald and Joe. The three of them all bore half-empty pints. They had evidently come in from smoking outside. They had very short hair, as Joe did, and Dean and Donald each wore an earring. Who they were—who could say?

'Hey, Professor,' said Donald, 'I've got a question for you. Is the earth the moon's moon?' He sipped his drink. 'Like, is earth the moon to the moon? Would you know a thing like that?'

Pauly said, 'I know. Why don't you ask me?'

Joe said, 'What you—'

—but Dean cut him off: '*Think* about it. We'd be talking a *blue moon*,' he said, 'if the earth's the moon's moon. Wouldn't it, it'd be *blue*.'

'Green cheese,' said Donald, with a gleam in his ugly eyes. 'Dean's little sister,' he said, 'I mean, she's so thick, she thought the moon and the sun was the same thing until the other day she noticed them both in the sky the same time. Got her well freaked.'

'Sixty-five,' mumbled Humpty, 'thank you, sir. Sixty-five on the bench. Seventy, anywhere? Seventy, am I bid?'

Dean gave Humpty a sidelong glance. 'She's just a kid, she's only eleven,' he said. He turned to Kit. 'You should have seen her when I told her, not only the sun isn't the moon, but it's a star. That screwed her head up even worse. You know what she said, mate?' addressing himself now to Joe. '"If the sun's a fucking star, how come it don't shine at night?"'

Everybody liked this question. It gave rise to a feeling of communal merriment. Joe leant forwards, poised to speak, but Dean hadn't finished. 'And you know how small she is,' he said, 'she stands there, like—I mean upright, right? You know pelican crossings? She stands there and she bloody presses the bloody crossing button with her *nose*.'

'The moons don't go with the months,' said Joe, 'so some years there are thirteen instead of twelve. And on old calendars, if there was a thirteenth full moon it would be shown coloured blue, so they—'

'Right. Cool,' said Dean.

'—so they say, hence—'

'Hey,' said Pauly, 'you heard NASA's planning to put a colony on the moon by 2020?'

'Leave it out,' said Donald.

Humpty's mumbled commentary slid once more into the snatch of quiet that followed. 'Eighty on my left, yes. Fresh money at eighty. Eighty-five, anywhere?'

'It's true,' said Pauly.

'What for?' said Donald. 'Fucking cocky-knockers. The moon? The *moon*. They should bloody leave it alone.'

'A functioning colony?' Kit was strongly conscious that

this was the first thing she'd added to the discussion. Because, here she was sitting on her own at a table with five blokes, implausibly enough. Taken together, apart from Humpty but including Joe, they looked like what Bulwer Lytton would have dismissed as the 'vulgar-ruffian' class, the low-end criminal element it was probably demeaning to read about. 'That sort of leaves you feeling really helpless,' she said, 'like a serf hearing about the crusades,' noticing, as she spoke, that Pauly's left ear didn't, the way a normal ear would, curl over at the top, but was straight-edged and virtually yellow, as though the top had long since been pared off with a knife.

'Hark at her,' said Donald, '*serfs*.' He gulped his drink. 'Hey,' he said, 'I mean, hey, we should, you know—we should set up a quiz team.' The others scoffed. 'No,' he cried, 'no, I mean, I mean, we've got the moon covered, right? The professor here can do the maths. Dean knows the canals. And AX7s. Pauly knows about French polishing.' Pauly raised two fingers at Donald. 'Fuck off yourself,' said Donald. 'Humpty's on cricket and everything. Me and Dean, we're both geniuses on Oxford United and Mini engines. I know all *Doctor Who* stuff. And if I say so myself—' he paused to nod sagaciously at them, 'yes, my friends, if I *do say so myself*, I know everything about everything about how to make a bitch happy between the—' His incipient boast was whirled away in a blizzard of catcalls and jeers.

Kit tried to summon to mind the huge tables in the Bodleian, the hush, the light and the high ceilings; the vast space the reading rooms seemed to provide a person for thought.

She wasn't uninterested. She felt like a trespasser trespassing. When she caught Joe's eye by accident, they exchanged a look, but to what effect, she didn't know. Behind him, a tidy young man paused uncertainly. He seemed to Kit, from her vantage point at the table, as though he might be hesitating over whether or not to join them. Maybe he was one of Joe's students. Or maybe he—

'Like our dance club, then?'

Kit did the mental equivalent of blanching. The young man walked away.

'Go tonight?' Dean asked.

'Ladies and gentleman,' said Humpty, speaking with effort, 'this, surely, is worth ninety-five of anybody's money.'

Dean twirled an imaginary moustache.

'Have I seen you there?' Kit asked.

'I've seen you, love. You had my water bottle off me, what, two weeks ago?—when your circuits fried? I gave you, like, the hospitality of my water bottle? You drunk my water, babe,' he said, darkly satisfied. 'You know how priests carry knives into jails?' he said.

Kit could feel her cheeks warming.

'Priests,' said Dean, 'when they go in the nick, you know how they carry knives?'

'Really?'

'In case they have to cut a man down. Hopefully, in case they catch him in time, unless it's Adrian Marcett, in which case, let the fucker dangle.'

'Look—don't,' said Pauly. 'Just don't.'

Dean's whole body went rigid. In a menacing voice, he said, 'I'm having a *conversation* here.'

'Leave her alone,' said Humpty.

Kit's heart began to thump. Involuntarily, she caught her breath. *Senator Voorhees*, she said to herself, *Meta Cherry, Hunker Chisholm, Young Billy Nay—*

Pauly stared downwards.

Joe raised a hand in warning.

—Nettie Slack, Polly Ripple, Baldy Drinkwater, Ebenezer Ward—

'Yo.' Donald made an idiotic quacking noise, then lapsed back into silence.

The others remained as they were: static, arrested.

Dean looked round the table at his leisure, pitched a loud quack back again, like someone saying '*boo!*', then mockingly laughed at them all.

Kit breathed again in a secret gasp.

'You cunt,' said Dean to Humpty. He rearranged himself in his chair with exaggerated ease. 'If your brother wasn't here, I'd clip you one. Tell you what, you know what Adrian Marcett's mother says to him when he gets out? She says, "You don't belong in this family. You're the *shit on our shoes*."'

'That's not nice,' said Donald. He snorted at the idea of it. 'Man, that's fucking horrible.'

'No it's fucking not,' said Dean. 'He misbehaved himself. What d'you expect?'

'Gobshite,' said Donald. 'She's his mum.'

Dean's mobile rang. He pulled faces for everyone's amusement as he said to the person the other end, 'Look, fair play, I told you I'd get the tickets but it was like *four* quid on my phone because I had to ring from work.

They keep on bloody give you all these options, round the bloody houses. Like, *four* quid. I mean, I said I'd do it, but, like, if you want to buy me a pint or whatever, it's up to you.'

'What's your line of work, then?' said Pauly. 'Student, right?'

'Fat Steve,' said Dean, putting his phone back in his pocket. 'Cunt.'

Kit, who had been transfixed, changed register with difficulty. 'My work?' she murmured. She turned to Pauly and tightly shook her head, as though she was, by this means, reordering the glittery bits in a kaleidoscope. 'I kind of study Charles Dickens,' she said.

'Kind of?'

'Amongst other things,' she said.

Heart-sinkingly, Dean called across to them, 'Wasn't Maria in a Dickens film?'

'Thomas Hardy,' said Pauly, adding, for Kit's benefit, 'she used to be an extra, from she was—' he held a hand out to indicate the height of a child. 'Her mum was into it. She did *Jude*, *The Saint*, all sorts of shit.'

'Maria?'

'Pauly's wife,' said Donald.

'My ex-wife.'

'Oh, I'm sorry,' said Kit.

'Ran off with this bloke, then she finds out she's bloody got throat cancer,' said Pauly. 'You have to laugh,' he said.

'No you don't,' said Donald.

'You know what's the first thing she does when she finds out?'

'No,' said Kit.

'She lights up.'

'If you can't have a fag when you've just heard you're going to die—'

'All right, Donald,' said Dean, swatting him.

'I'm sorry,' said Kit again.

'Well I'm not,' said Pauly. 'I'm glad. She pops her clogs, it gives me less to think about.'

Kit was worried by the fact that she hadn't quite understood whether Maria was already dead or not. 'And the man she went off with?' she said. They seemed to be talking about it, so she asked.

'Used to be a fucking postie,' said Pauly. 'Two years he got his mates to nick all my letters, like everything's *my* fault. Had to have stuff sent to my nan's, my sister's, if I even knew. Bollocks. I was an extra once, kids' thing, BBC. Took us out to Great Tew in a monster fucking bus. Remember Billy Walsome?' he said to Dean. 'His dad was driving that bus. We had to be Victorian firemen, but there was no fire and no water. Put it on afterwards, CGI. All they had was smoke bombs, and these little kids jumping out the windows.'

'Really?'

'Put it all on afterwards. Except, like, these little kids. I was surprised they was allowed to, like, little kids—' he whistled a downward slide, '—out the windows. Got fucking tedious running around with these empty buckets and everyone screaming and it's only a couple of smoke bombs. I left my hat on that bus. I thought I would've got it back, but I never did.'

Kit stood up, murmuring, 'I need the ladies.' Which wasn't true, or not very. Had she wished to, she could easily have held on.

The toilet, at the back end of the building, left Kit feeling sullied, with its drip-spattered seat, barely functional door bolt and its banked rolls of loo paper on the floor, all with swollen, ruffled patches on them where they'd been wetted and allowed to dry out again. The sink was so dirty, she decided it would be more insanitary to wash her hands than to leave them.

As she sloped back again, past the rear side-exit, and into the closeness and warmth of the pub, level with the partition next to their table, clear as anything she overheard Dean say, 'So, Joe, about that blonde you was out with the other night. Quality goods, my son.'

Kit stopped dead and focused her thoughts narrowly on the elegant sheaves of barley and hops etched into the partition's opaque glass; though as she stared, it came to her that through a spray of hop cones she was seeing a distorted image of Joe's face, he himself, she now made out, looking intently across the pub towards the bar. Kit was so unpleasantly affected by Dean's remark that her immediate thought was to go back and hide in the loo. What a pitiful thing to do, though. She turned her head to follow the line of Joe's gaze, not to the bar itself, it transpired, but to the mirror behind it; to Joe's reflection as he looked at her reflection in the mirror behind the bar. For a split second their eyes met in the glass.

She had overheard Dean asking him about a blonde. Joe

had seen her overhear this, which meant that—he knew that she knew that he knew that she knew.

So much for mirrors. With a dull sense of her own worthlessness, Kit stepped round the partition.

She squeezed herself back down onto the bench. The mood at the table seemed drunker. She had intended, as she went past him, to compare Pauly's right ear with his left ear, but forgot to do this. Humpty looked almost asleep.

'Give it a year,' said Donald, 'one of us probably will be capping it on St Giles.'

Kit, who no longer cared about something indefinable that she *had* been caring about before, asked, 'How so?' She wasn't sure she'd heard correctly, and if she had she didn't understand.

Donald swept a phantom hat off his head and held it out as a beggar—held it out to her, and as a beggar waited, and waited, until she began to feel uncomfortable, not handing over any coins.

She tried and failed to stare Donald down, before quoting disdainfully at him: '"They haunt the shadows of your ways, In masks of perishable mould: Their souls a changing flesh arrays, But they are changeless from of old".'

Donald retracted his arm. 'Come again?' he said.

'What is that, Kit?' asked Pauly.

'"The Statues"?' she said. 'Poem, 1899, Laurence Binyon. He thought London's real statues were its beggars, considering that they were always there, out in the open, and motionless, I guess; *capping* it.'

'You do my head in,' said Donald.

It suddenly struck Kit—how had she missed this before?—that Binyon's use of 'changeless' could be read as a pun; presumably not deliberate though.

I am a very stupid person, she said to herself, because, up until Dean Purcell asked Joe about this blonde he asked about, I wasn't especially minding what happened next, and now I slightly feel quite upset, even though Joe doesn't owe me anything, even though—

Kit's thoughts scattered as a pinched if not-blonde girl put a wine glass down beside her, filled with a blush-coloured, gas-rich drink, indicating with her thumb a wish to sit down on the bench. Kit was forced to shunt up close to Donald, who nodded his approval.

No one acknowledged the meagre girl's arrival. The talk had moved to football. She glanced at Kit several times, unimpressed. Kit was unimpressed back. After a while, the girl murmured confidentially, 'How does it feel then, to be sat here with us lot, a rose amongst the thorns?'

'What?' Kit inclined closer, not because she hadn't heard, but because she wanted to feel as though she hadn't heard.

Before the girl could repeat herself, Kit jerked back again. She turned round to catch Joe's eye, who questioningly tilted his head towards the door at the front of the pub.

Kit was filled with relief. To the girl she said, 'Could I ask you to—'

'Joe, Joe,' said Pauly anxiously. He had a hand on Humpty's shoulder—Humpty, who was now slumped over, legs knotted, eyelids barely open. 'Back to yours tonight, or what?'

Joe looked at his watch. 'Are you here till last orders? I

could walk Kit home and be back in time to get him?'

'Go ahead. It's okay,' said Dean. 'We'll keep an eye.'

Donald snickered. 'Unless Alison Stannard walks in.'

'I'd rather fuck an exhaust pipe,' said Dean passionlessly.

The skinny girl snickered too. If she had moved her legs, it wasn't detectable. Kit was forced to edge out round the table with her body kept bent in sitting position.

Joe, as he observed this, appeared displeased.

'I can go home on my own,' Kit said, but he quelled the suggestion at once with his eyes.

'I'll be back in a bit,' he said to Pauly. 'He hasn't been doing this during the week?'

'No, mate.'

'I'll just—' Joe fished some money out of his pocket and gave it to Pauly. 'In case,' he said.

'No need,' said Pauly, though he took it.

'Don't worry, mate,' said Dean.

'I won't be long.'

Humpty struggled towards speech. 'Hundred,' he slurred, and raised a limp fist.

Kit stumbled over a plastic bag the girl had left on the floor.

'Have a nice trip,' called Donald, before adding more quietly, 'Fuck me, she's tall.'

'Don't think she'd have you, mate,' said Dean.

'I'm crying already,' said Donald.

Kit heard the girl laugh hysterically.

'I mean, what—Joe uses a fucking step ladder or what, when—!' There was a plosive cry.

Kit looked back. She couldn't help herself. Dean was gazing ceilingwards. Donald was clutching his stomach.

'Come on,' said Joe.

At the door of the pub, their way was barred by a strikingly pretty girl—as Kit observed, instinctively on her mettle—in an outfit of white denim fringed with silver. 'Dean back there?' she said.

'He is,' said Joe.

'Wanker. I knew it. I'm coming out the toilets in The Bunch of Grapes, because, God forbid I should ever drink lager because I just, like, *piss*, and Dean comes up to me and—'

'Look—' said Joe.

'—he goes—'

'—look, I'm sorry,' said Joe, 'but I don't have time to—'

The girl stepped backwards out onto the pavement to stop him passing her. 'Is Ailie in there?' she asked.

Again, Kit remembered too late that she had meant to check Pauly's other ear.

They left the girl standing amongst the cigarette ends that lay in a spattered arc outside the pub. When they were a little way off, she screamed after them, '*I'm not a fucking nobody, you know.*'

Joe shifted the line of his walk closer to Kit's, and gently touched her elbow. 'Hey there, woman,' he said, 'I thought you told me you didn't have any poetry memorised?'

'Me?' she said. 'Oh. Yes—no. No, no, I have some lovely things stored inside my head.'

As they turned into the Woodstock Road, Joe said, 'Thank you.'

'For?'

But there was no answer.

After a few minutes of silence, Kit pulled herself together. 'Joe, what's going on? What are you thinking?' she said.

'Sorry.'

'No, don't apologise.'

He sighed. 'I was wondering—most wars, to date; Humpty's always talking about—I suppose they're still usually only going to be possible if a large number of people can be persuaded to kill whoever's immediately in front of them, right? Even now, this is still true, right? But with Dean, I can't figure out whether he's the sort of person—whether you can sense he's someone who'd be almost happy to do this, at least at first, or whether—whether he'd be impressively more ready than most to resist.'

'You're toying with the idea of him being perfect trench fodder, as it were? Can one still say that?'

'No, not that,' said Joe slowly. 'I'm toying with the idea of him being immediately willing, in a way I wouldn't, to take up arms to defend my mother and father. I don't know. When Humpty loses Dean's protection, then I think we're really in the shit, and I'm—'

Joe was jumping about too fast for Kit to follow. 'Protection?'

'Sorry,' he said. 'It's complicated.'

'Why does Humpty say you want him to go and live in a field?'

'It's complicated,' said Joe again. 'I don't want him to live in a field. Kit, my parents have never really known how to handle either of us, so it falls to me to—' He sighed exasperatedly.

'My parents don't understand me either,' she said. 'I had a dream the other night that my father jumped out from behind a tree wearing, you know, a Homburg hat.'

Joe looked bemused. Kit smiled at him.

'That's *it?*' he said.

'What, you want more?'

Joe laughed, which caused Kit to laugh. She counted it as their second joke.

Their first, which this exchange now brought back to her, had felt propitious. When Joe had helped her back in off his balcony the previous week, in through his sitting-room window, he had kept hold of her hand and had kissed her.

Out on the balcony he had said, in his humorous way, 'I didn't mean out here', and she had omitted to reply, and things had grown awkward.

But upon being kissed, for want of anything much better to do—and for want, it felt like in her whole life, of being truly wanted—there it was. Like that, once again, Kit gave way.

As he'd taken her in his arms, however, she had found herself still bothered wondering what it was to kiss someone you knew so little. And no doubt because of this, as they'd tended towards his bedroom, he had said to her, 'Perhaps this time you'd consider a little less of the old—of the, lie-back-and-think-of-England approach? How about it?'

And she had said, 'England? But—but I find the thought of England so tremendously *sexy*.'

Which had made him laugh, which had made her laugh: propitiously, their first joke.

They went across the Woodstock Road at one of the pedestrian-operated light crossings, too lazy to dodge through the traffic; not either of them, though Kit thought of it, stooping to press the button with their nose.

'You know, you have a curvy voice,' said Joe.

'Curvy?'

'I can't think how else to put it. There's a curviness to your voice.'

Kit shook her head. 'A girl I knew at school once said she wished she sounded like me.'

'I can believe it.'

'Well, thanks.'

'Pleasure.'

'Now I'll feel self-conscious talking.'

'Please don't,' he said. 'I like it when you talk.'

Out in the night air, with the trees shushing in the wind, the scene they'd left behind them at The Forfeit already felt to Kit as though it had taken place hours before. 'What branch of maths are you in?' she asked. 'I may not have heard of it, but please tell me anyway, the general area.'

'Number theory.'

'Oh, yes. That, I have heard of.'

'Yes?'

'I liked Pauly,' she said.

'Pauly? He's a French polisher,' said Joe. 'It's skilled, but tedious. I suppose it gives him the freedom to think a bit. I think he's wanting to shift out of furniture and into guitars, but I don't know if he has what it takes or not. He's a good bloke. Makes the heart bleed a little sometimes.'

'I can see that.'

'Frankly, I think any of them might—if you knew them better. What's more,' Joe said, 'don't assume that if they knew a bit more about you, you wouldn't have the same effect on them.'

Kit struggled. 'You mean, I'd make *their* hearts bleed?'

'It's not impossible.'

'Maybe I would,' she said. After all, it wasn't such an outlandish idea. 'There seems to be a lot of talk about birds, one way and another,' she said, rather changing tack, though not on purpose.

Joe glanced upwards in the semi-darkness. 'Starlings. Medium-size passerines,' he said.

'What?'

'Passerines. Basic sparrow-shaped perchers; though for whatever reason, a sparrow's *size* isn't a benchmark of the term.'

'Good for them?' Kit ventured.

'It's disorderly, I think.'

'How come Dean was at the dance class?' she asked. 'I didn't see him. He told me he was there the last time; I mean the time I sort of fainted.'

'Yes. Well, that's—I mean, it's because of Dean that Humpty ever heard about it. And it was Humpty who proposed it to me.'

'He mentioned.'

'He did?' Joe, without slowing down, kicked a small stone

sideways into the road. 'Did he tell you it was my birthday present?'

'What was?'

'I happened to say that I'd like to know, just once in my life, what it was like to be led on the dance floor—just to know what that felt like. So Humpty offered it as my birthday present, which was inspired in a way, or would have been if he'd actually gone through with it. He owes me so much money, if he'd bought me something there would have been the annoying sense that I'd effectively paid for it myself. I don't know how you avoid that, really. And although the greatest thing he could do for me would be to leave me alone, you can't just give that to someone as a present.'

'Happy birthday, by the way,' said Kit.

'Not at all.'

'I mean—well. I mean, of course I didn't realise any of this when it was me instead, dancing you around.'

'No, you didn't.'

'It's okay,' she said. 'Can that be my birthday present from me then?'

Joe said, 'Kit, you know, I—you were late, and I'd waited for you the day before as well, in case; and I was still angry, pointlessly enough, with Humpty, for failing to show up the week before. I didn't plan to ask you instead, I just—asked you.'

'It's okay,' she said again, 'seriously.' To her, it *was* okay somehow—now. 'What do you do other evenings?' she said.

'I don't know, Thursday nights I play a regular poker game.'

'Really? You mean it? Who'd play poker with a mathematician?'

'Other mathematicians.'

'Of course. Silly me.'

'Mondays, Tuesdays and Wednesdays, I suppose things tend to come up, or they don't. I try to have dinner in hall at least once a week. But otherwise, well, I tend to try and get on with my research. Often I lie on my balcony when I'm working on a maths problem, pad of paper, pencil, so long as the weather's bearable.'

'You have a mattress kind of thing?'

'I do, yes. And a brain.'

'Indeed.'

'There's a camping mattress rolled up behind my sofa,' he said. They had reached Kit's house. They wandered through the gate posts and half way across the gravel drive. 'Why?' he asked.

'Here we are,' she replied, and came listlessly to a halt. He had put a question to her, but she'd lost hold of it. She was remembering how much she had desired him at the start of the evening, when she'd caught sight of him leaning against the back wall at St Christopher's, tensed, waiting alone, she wouldn't have—

Joe gathered her up and held her, speechlessly, just long enough for her to start to wonder quite when he planned on letting her go again.

She stood there and told herself that, wonderful as the dancing had been—or perhaps because of it—on balance, anyway, she was glad there didn't have to be any question now of, *yes* or *no*—not this time. She was glad they could part simply as friends, so she told herself. 'I have to go and do Orson's reading list,' she said apologetically, only to remember that she'd done it already. She took a step back towards the house.

Joe said, 'Meet you here in a week?'

'Here?' she asked, pointing at the ground. 'Sure,' she said. 'Absolutely.' Next week; she hadn't got that far yet.

'Kit,' said Joe quietly, 'would I be right in thinking that your romantic history is one to which the word "romantic" doesn't really apply?'

In a mumble, she replied, 'Pretty much.'

He pulled one of the faces she couldn't interpret.

She wanted to say something further, but didn't know what, and any sense of it slid rapidly away.

Still Joe hesitated.

'I know you've got to go,' she said, 'but just tell me, what happened to your eyebrow? I've been meaning to ask.'

'This?' He touched it. 'I was hit by a firework as a kid, at a friend's house, one of those occasions where everyone says how lucky you were not to lose an eye, but you yourself are thinking, how unlucky to be hit in the face by a firework. The dad who set it off was disturbingly upset, I remember, but I healed up fine except for this slight scar,' he rubbed it with his thumb, 'and the end of my eyebrow not growing back.'

'Do you still like fireworks?' Kit asked, thinking that it wasn't long till Guy Fawkes Night.

'Yes, I like them.' He took a sudden deep breath and looked at his feet. 'Next Friday, then.'

'Great,' said Kit.

'Right.'

And he left her like that, so that she felt a little sad.

Kit baulked at the idea of being back indoors again so soon. The night breezes had revived her. Only when Joe was out of earshot did she murmur, forlornly, 'Goodbye.'

She went up the stairs to her room praying that she wouldn't have to talk to Michaela, and was relieved when she reached her own door unaccosted.

She closed it behind her, dropped her bag down and did a somersault along the length of her bed, and as this felt good, stepped round and did another one. This time, however, coming out of it, Kit deliberately punched the plywood headboard, which, being poorly attached, gave a little so that her knuckles were grazed. She hunched up at the pain and licked her hand like a dog. *Oliver Twist* lay on the floor next to her bed. She bent down to retrieve it and began to read:

The housebreaker freed one arm, and grasped his pistol. The certainty of immediate detection if he fired flashed across his mind even in the midst of his fury, and he beat it twice with all the force he could summon, upon the upturned face that almost touched his own.

She staggered and fell, nearly blinded with the blood that rained down from a deep gash in her forehead, but raising herself with difficulty on her knees drew from her bosom a white handkerchief—Rose Maylie's own—and holding it up in her folded hands as high towards Heaven as her feeble

strength would let her, breathed one prayer for mercy to her
Maker.

It was a ghastly figure to look upon. The murderer staggering backward—

'You in there?' shouted Michaela's voice through the door.
Fuck, thought Kit.

—murderer staggering backward to the wall, and shutting out
the sight with his hand, seized a heavy club and struck her
down.

Still reading, Kit quickly got herself into her desk chair,
placed the book open in front of her and in meek tones sang
out, 'Yes?'

'I've been thinking,' said Michaela as she walked in; she
threw herself onto Kit's vacated bed, 'he's a bloody lecturer.
He's taking advantage. You should get out of it, girl. I've
been thinking about it. I should've never encouraged you. I
don't know what I was on about. You should chuck him.
You should chuck him. It's all wrong.'

'Please.'

'You don't ever stay over at his place. Why not? I don't
reckon you even *like* him all that much.'

'God, a lecturer doesn't matter. We're not the same subject,
college or anything. What do you know about how I feel?'

'So where is he now?'

'What do you mean? He had to go and look after his
brother.'

'You believe that?'

'*Yes*, I believe it.'

'Has to look after his brother? Seriously? Did he tell you that? What, he's his dad or something? Come on, Kit. What's wrong with his brother?'

'I'm not completely sure.'

'He's pissing you about. Don't be a fool about this. He's making you do everything his way. Stand up for yourself. What do *you* want? You have to make things happen in your life.'

Kit thought about the dancing, how extraordinary it had felt, blissful, until she had almost ceased to be herself—and about how for her sake Joe had read half of *Oliver Twist*. He had been reading a book because of her. What did she *want?* What did anybody want?

'If you asked nicely,' said Kit, 'do you think you could persuade your father to give someone a job in his bottle factory, I mean a non-skilled job?'

'Sure, probably, but don't change the subject.'

'Okay,' said Kit. 'Okay. Not changing the subject, I really don't think you know what you're talking about.'

'I'll tell you what I'm talking about,' replied Michaela, her eyes now shut, 'I'm talking, he's probably just been dumped or something, and he wants to make this girl jealous, so he thinks, I'll get a quick one in, and make her want me back. I'll bet you anything he's using you, Kit. You don't believe me, but I totally bet you there's something else going on. He'll keep coming back until he finds some other girl he wants to sleep with, or his girlfriend takes him back. He's got some girl, right, he's just using you, and—'

As Michaela started going round in circles, Kit allowed herself to look down once again at the page in front of her:

He had not moved: he had been afraid to stir. There had been a moan and motion of the hand; with terror added to hate he had struck and struck again. Once he threw a rug over it; but it was worse to fancy the eyes, and imagine them moving towards him, than to see them glaring upwards as if watching the reflection of the pool of gore that quivered and danced in the sunlight on the ceiling. He had plucked it off again. And there was the body—mere flesh and blood, no more— but *such* flesh, and *such* blood!

He struck a light, kindled the fire, and thrust the club into it. There was human hair upon the end which blazed and shrunk into a light cinder, and, caught by the air, whirled up the chimney. Even that frightened him, sturdy as he was, but he held the weapon till it broke, and then piled it on the coals to burn away, and smoulder into ashes. He washed himself and rubbed his clothes; there were spots that would not be removed, but he cut the pieces out, and burnt them. How those stains were dispersed about the room! The very feet of the dog were bloody.

'—don't you?'

Kit jolted to attention. 'Say again?'

'*Don't* you?' said Michaela peevishly, opening her eyes.

'You just don't get what it feels like,' replied Kit, hoping this answer would do.

'What it *feels* like is all in your head,' said Michaela. 'I'm telling you, you're too free and easy. Just think about it for a minute, please? You've made mistakes before. You don't tell me stuff, but I'm on your case and I see. I don't care whether you like me or not—'

'Michaela!'

'—it doesn't mean my advice is wrong.'

Kit couldn't come up with any sort of reply to this. Advice? She sat there, dumb.

'Well, I'm all done in. I've had a shocking day, thanks for asking. I am *so* looking forward to the end of term, already.' Michaela swung herself up into a sitting position, then got back up onto her feet. 'I'm going to hit the hay. Won't be a minute in the bathroom.'

Kit nodded to acknowledge what she considered the one practical remark.

Not so much later, in a tepid and functional bath of her own, worrying about her worthless existence, Kit was assailed from nowhere by the thought that it was odd, wasn't it?— was it not odd?—that Dickens had opted to kill Nancy by having her pimp, Bill Sikes, savagely bludgeon her to death in their sparse bedroom in Spitalfields, only for Eliza Grimwood, a few months later, to be no less savagely butchered for real, also a prostitute, also in her sparse bedroom, not so far away in Waterloo, very possibly also done in by her pimp, both women struck down to the floor from a kneeling position, both omitting to cry out for help, blood absolutely everywhere: were the two cases not curiously similar? It was a crazy idea, as well as a terrible one, but for a flickering instant, Kit wondered whether Eliza's killer hadn't been inspired by reading Dickens—hadn't been unhinged even, by Sikes killing Nancy the revolting way he did in *Oliver Twist*.

Kit stood poised and freezing in the middle of her room in her pyjamas. She had started to shiver violently in the bath, had got out in a panic and had done a kind of war dance, while drying herself, to try to warm up.

Now she assumed ghost position, as it was apparently called, her arms in jointed arcs, one foot part way through a slide, whap, *whap*, whap, *whap*. Not that Kit did dance. She just stood there, thinking nothing.

Then she went to bed.

So who was Evalina, the girl who could dance on a brick? And who was the quality-goods blonde? Kit replayed, in her mind, the incident in the pub with the bar mirror—fuck Michaela. Her mind returned to Dean Purcell's encouraging question. What had happened to the blonde? *Quality goods, mate*.

Kit, on her uncomfortable mattress, lay uselessly discomposed; in *bed* ghost position: lonely.

CHAPTER 5

The following Thursday, Orson was ill; a hangover, Kit decided. He emailed at the last minute asking whether it would be possible to move his tutorial back twenty-four hours. As Kit had set Friday aside for the Bodleian, she arranged to meet him at 8:30 in a café on the High Street—absurdly early, to punish him for messing her around. But he took it on the chin. Perhaps it hadn't been a hangover after all.

She set out at 8:10 in a light mist, which lingered, so that she and Orson, tucked in at the counter along the café's front window, seemed the more enclosed in their retreat, and also warmer. He looked depressed, despite caffeine and two chocolate croissants. What about a sugar rush? Kit took a rapid decision not to push him, or even tease him, much. Why should it matter to her whether he was paying attention or not? Everyone had warned her—first teaching job—not to put too much work in. Typical beginner's error was to attempt to do so much of a student's work for them that they would find it more of an effort to fail than to succeed; but besides this being a waste of your own time, she'd been told kindly, if you did their thinking for them, they didn't learn how to learn—a line Kit had come to think of as the teacher's sink-or-swim get-out clause.

After a meagre discussion of Orson's essay, forty minutes

maximum, Kit opened her eyes wide at him, as a sort of exclamation mark, and said, 'Okay, well, I took the liberty of bringing a new reading list for you—' Orson plainly relieved it was all over, '—since we were meeting today anyway.' He slumped down an inch or two on the counter top. 'I've pointed you towards as much material as you could possibly need to get cracking on next week's essay. We can discuss it if you like, but I thought you'd probably be happy just to plunge in. You look to be getting on well with this stuff. You can always email me any queries if you have them.' Kit searched through her bag for the piece of paper.

'Can I get you another coffee?' said Orson.

Kit bit back a response along the lines of, 'no'. She was desperate to get out of there, couldn't find the list, not tucked into her notebook; where was it? She had a heap of reading on order, and precious hours set aside for hunting needles.

But this, here, this is *real life*, she told herself sternly, perceiving that Orson was propelled by a strong desire to detain her. Why, she had no idea. Shape up, she said to herself, and to him, 'Very kind, thank you.'

'Same again?'

'I'll take the small, "minimo" thingy.'

Orson bent into his backpack, extracted an appallingly vast print-out manuscript, and, with what struck Kit as inauthentic confidence, thumped it down on the counter beside her. She was tempted to say, then and there, 'Can we just agree that whatever this is, I think you're brilliant and fantastic?', and she would have been quite happy to say it, too.

Orson turned away without a word.

The title was *Score*. Kit peered at it at an angle, unwilling to turn her head. Discreetly, she started in the middle of the second paragraph:

He grunted, eyeing the sunlight as it drizzled down dazed through the tattered afternoon. He wanted to kiss her even though it wouldn't work out, he knew. Something snapped in him. He stepped into the light like some avenging angel. He left the guys without a word and walked over to her. She was leaning against the wall the other side of the alley. Heels. It made his eyes sting how high her heels were. She smiled at him and he flicked his cigarette casually into an oil stained puddle where it hissed and spit like a snake. The guys' eyes bored into his back as he leaned over her. Bad move. Her smile was seriously fake. He felt an icy shiver slide down his spine. Some angel, he mused.

Let alone some opener, Kit thought in reply. She stopped reading, or even really thinking, until Orson came back with their coffees.

'Oh, great,' she said. 'Thanks. Thank you. Okay. Well, so I should have a look at this?' She put her hand on the monument beside her. 'Not that my opinion is—I mean, I'm not exactly a, what's-it-called, a *now-literature* person, you know?'

'It's *now*, but it's also deliberately retro, right?' said Orson, getting back on his stool. 'But that's okay.' He was in command of himself. Kit felt a twinge of irritation. 'What I was wondering,' he said, 'was, like, if this could, like, count towards my grade? Like, informally? My mom and dad—' He was staring out of the window. 'I need the grades, you know? Like, it cost a lot to send me here? And—'

Kit tried to wave this effort away, as though it was understood between them that he didn't really mean it. She hadn't ever considered what the value might be to Orson of his grades. On reflection, though, sitting there, it came to her that his particular ration of intelligence and luck was surely ample to win him a life of material comfort, if that was what he wanted, or to reject it with splendid arguments if it wasn't. Yes, she thought, that was the grade she would like to give him: congratulations, you win, there's no good reason why your time on earth shouldn't pan out just fine compared with the overwhelming majority of people on the planet. And by the way, before you say anything, this qualifies as an 'A'.

Kit looked down again at the top page of his novel. 'It seems very—American, punchy. I'll look forward—' she glanced round at Orson, 'to reading it. Of course, I can't say till I've had a go at it properly.'

'I want to get an agent? When I get home?' said Orson.

'Great,' replied Kit, foreseeing several years' worth of rejection letters, with a sideline in Internet self-justification. She wedged the manuscript into her bag. 'What's the basic subject, may I ask?'

'Street gambling,' he said, 'is the primary axis. I mean, it's about so much more, chicken trials, you know? But kind of street things, mostly, dog fights. But, like, retro?' Only now did he appear suddenly anxious. 'I don't really know what I'm *doing* in Oxford?' he said. 'Like, this isn't where I want to be, in my existence, like, *at all*. Like, you're great and everything? But—I don't know, you know, Oxford's just one big fucking lunch-out and I want to be wired into something that's *happening*. I want things to *mean* something. I didn't ask to come here. They never even thought I might not *want* to. Like, it's supposed to be this great *opportunity* and everything; but, like, Classical Civilisation and shit? The History of Philosophy—?'

Whatever exactly it was that was bugging Orson, Kit felt neither qualified nor inclined to help. Was it really her job to give succour to a person hardly much younger than herself as he struggled through thickets he couldn't be bothered to describe?

'Listen, Orson,' she said, 'you're bright. I shouldn't tell you this, but your essays are considerably better than I was expecting. I don't think you need to give me other stuff to help you out, even if it is allowed, which I'm pretty sure it isn't. I'm no more clued up about things than you are—'

He interrupted her to agree, 'I know.'

Kit, who had been planning to continue with the word 'except', now smiled, and instead threw out cheerfully, 'Thanks.'

She put a hand in her coat pocket. And there was the reading list. Who was she to counsel Orson? She hoped it would be enough just to cart away his daunting manuscript. What did she know about the meaning of life? Nothing, nothing, she thought glibly. 'Let's finish off our business,' she said. 'Here's this. I take it you're still going to do some work for me?'

'Oh sure. You don't understand, I *have* to get the grades, they'll kill me.'

'Because there's lots of interesting stuff on here,' she said. She took the mashed piece of paper and smoothed it out on the counter top, then, holding it down with her index finger, used her thumb to rotate the sheet until the writing faced her student.

'I mean, I like that you're so enthused?' said Orson, ignoring the list. 'I totally get it. Fully. I was just—I've had my mind in a different place this week, you know? I've been, like, knees down in this really fucked-up brain space. But,' he struggled with himself, 'I want to complete your course, for sure. It's quite good. And, hey,' he said, 'who knows? I might write a detective novel one day.'

'What does "knees down" mean—kneeling?' Kit asked. Half of what he said she couldn't understand.

He was tickled by the question and shook his head, before bending his whole body to one side as he gripped the handlebars of a notionally impressive motorbike. 'Knees down,' he said, and demonstrated a bend the other way. 'I'll take you for a ride if you ever come visit—like you will, huh?' His tone now tilted also, towards the ironical, before he righted himself again. 'Where I come from,' he said, 'we have, like, these great roads? That just favoom way to the horizon, brrrr, forever?' He made a sound in his throat to suggest massive forward propulsion.

How wonderful, Kit thought, as she slid off her stool, to ride with Orson, of all people, through vast American nowhere-land, for a thousand thousand miles, at a million miles an hour, with nothing to look at and the—before she, too, corrected herself. 'Orson,' she said, doing up her coat buttons, and remembering the genial Midwestern course director who had interviewed her, the pleasantries, the euphemisms, 'Orson, please tell me it's not the case that I'm being, as it were, paid to give you a good grade?' She realised her little coffee cup still had dregs in it, and finished the rest standing.

Orson seized his head histrionically. 'That is seriously the most fucked-up thing I ever got asked by a professor,' he said. He held this posture, then smiled at her.

'Fine,' she said. She placed her cup back down in its saucer. 'Fine. No problem. Bye, Orson,' she said. But he hadn't quite finished with her, even now.

Once, finally, the tutorial was done and dusted, or was partially done and not really dusted, but was at least over, Kit slipped back out of the café—the mist gone, burnt off by pale sunshine—and crossed the High Street and hurried to the Bodleian, temporarily losing a century or two, or three, as she hit cobble stones, and slowed to admire the gleaming light on the ancient walls around her. She had noticed this before: that the pleasure she took in Orson became painful whenever she held it in mind that her pupil would soon be lost to her, out in the wide, wide world.

Kit laboured in the library for many hours, possessed by her subject, and didn't leave again until the early evening, punch-drunk, unpleasantly unfed, her right eye splitting the images it received so that everything was a touch blurry—an unusual exit for her in that she walked down the stairs.

As she hit the outside air, though, she felt a wash of pleasure. It was windless, cooling and exceptionally clear.

If only she could call Joe, she thought, the sole person who knew something of what she was up to—whose number she, however, didn't have, though he was supposed to be coming round anyway, God, what time was it? She stumbled along, bought a flapjack from a sandwich joint and consumed it as fuel, wondering whether she should catch a bus for two stops to get herself home the faster. A yogurt-topped flapjack, what did that mean? Bleached corn fat beaten up with sugar?

Many witnesses, Kit noticed, had testified to Eliza being beautiful. She had been known around Waterloo as 'The Countess', twenty-eight when she was killed, a grown-up in Kit's way of looking at things. Perhaps Eliza, too, had been a quality-goods blonde; one of those—Kit flung the flapjack wrapper into a bin—*quality-goods-blonde* style blondes. The yogurt stuff left a chemical taste in the mouth. Kit's insides hurt.

When, a couple of times that week, she had passed by the end of Joe's street, she had been unable to resist casting a look at the bend in the road beyond which his house lay, fearful that she might see some glamorous, platinum-haired girl shimmying forth; not that that would have told Kit anything. All she had really learned from doing this was that Joe had infiltrated disorder into her already unruly mind. He had provoked tedious thoughts, like, who was this blonde Dean Purcell had spoken about, and when was she; not to mention, *was* she, somehow, still?

Kit hurried along, willing herself to stop it. Think about your work, she said to herself, think about that. But, released from bondage in the Bodleian, her research seemed to have left her bursting with a sense of her own insignificance. There were herons on the wing these days, late butterflies, still-ripe blackberries in domestic parcels of wasteland. The goodly folk of North Oxford were beginning to leave buckets of spare apples out on the pavements, with damp help-yourself notes sticking to the fruit. What mattered so much to Kit was of no importance to the world. Who cared? Nobody cared. Why should they?

She turned through the gateposts of her house, hoping against hope that Michaela wouldn't be in. The one morning Kit had got up before 8:00, in fact at 7:15—the only morning in weeks that she'd got up at 7:15—Michaela had got up then too. And once again Kit had succeeded in pissing her off, by failing to recycle a yogurt-pot lid correctly.

'If everyone did their bit—' Michaela had said angrily. 'It's the same principle as taxation, without which, n.b., you wouldn't even have a university place to pursue your crappy little studies.'

'Please,' Kit had said, 'isn't it a bit early for you to do this to me?'

'It's a bit late in the history of human civilisation for me not to,' was the wilting reply. 'You know,' said Michaela, 'I reckon one of the things about what's happening now is that people are getting a more peasanty mindset about manufactured goods, you know? In the past, people who were close to the land, which was most of them, would know how to butcher and use every last morsel of a pig, for example, entrails, bladder, liver—'

'Teeth?' said Kit, looking glumly at her toast.

'Plus the manure, and then crop rotation. And now, in a similar way, in a way, people are beginning to get plugged in to exactly what elements make up a product, and its packaging, where it all comes from, and what's the consequence of disposing of the constituent parts in one way or another: plastics, batteries, polystyrene, foil. What I mean is, like peasants in the past, we're beginning to pay heed to how we can dispose of every component of what we buy as scrupulously as possible, how we can use it for other things. And why?' she asked triumphantly. 'To stop the sky falling in on our heads.'

'Yes,' Kit mumbled, 'that's an interesting way of approaching it.'

'You're so lame,' said Michaela.

Once in her room, not long back home, and the whole house inspiringly quiet, the top-floor bell rang. Kit rushed back down the stairs and trembled as she opened the front door, yes!—took a deep breath, felt winded. She quite wanted to hug Joe, but also quite felt like ending it, *ending* it, so that he didn't any longer cloud her mind with—what had Orson said?—didn't fuck up her precious brain space, her quality-goods mental processes, not that—whatever.

'So,' he said. 'Hi. How's it going?'

She shrugged, and felt inexplicably deflated as he leant against the porch wall. Even though, on the occasions when they kissed, she would impulsively observe to herself that this implied an intimacy she certainly didn't feel, she would still have liked to be kissed.

Joe frowned. Kit's mind leapt ahead: Friday night. 'How's Humpty?' she asked.

He put his hands in his pockets. 'Please don't feel you always have to ask me that,' he said, though he then added, with effort, 'Actually, Humpty's in Milan. Sorry. Not an unreasonable question.'

Milan? Had she heard right? What, a football game or something?

'No, no,' she said, catching up with herself, 'sorry. It's me. I'm a bit out of it. Sorry. I had to teach Orson incredibly early this morning because he had a cold yesterday, or anyway he felt rubbish, and I've been working non-stop all day ever since and I'm—I haven't had a chance to eat lunch yet, and it's getting to be more like supper now and—oh, that's amazing, look, it's beginning to get misty again. That was quick. It was clear just now. Did you see the mist this morning?'

'Yes,' he replied. There was a withdrawn sense about Joe that bore no relation to what he was saying. 'Yes, I cycled down the canal path this morning, and it wasn't only that mist was hanging over the trees, but the whole canal itself was steaming. It was beautiful—trees bulking out of nowhere, and these forlorn-looking ducks coming in and out of view.'

'Clocks go back next week,' said Kit.

'Yes, so they do.'

There was a pause, during which she couldn't think of anything further to say.

In the end it was Joe who filled the gap. 'How was the tutorial? All right?'

'Oh, fine. Step in,' she said, 'it's chilly. Yes, I love Orson.

I often have no idea what he's on about, but every time we meet, he makes me laugh.' She shut the front door, but they then stayed in the hall. 'Today he actually asked me to a party. I was saying, you know, "Goodbye", when, out of the blue, he asked me to this party.'

'Tonight?'

'Yes.'

'Don't let me stop you if you want to go,' said Joe.

'He's, I mean, five foot four,' she said. '*Five foot four*, Joe. To me, the world is made up of men, women and men-who-are-too-short. And, five foot four, Orson's—I mean, let alone any other consideration in the world, of which there happen to be numerous—'

'You could spit on his head,' said Joe.

'Yes.'

'All right.'

'Bloody hell,' said Kit, aware she had just answered a question she hadn't really been asked. She felt silly. She *was* silly, foolish.

Joe looked perhaps mildly entertained for a moment, then said, 'Right.'

Right?

'You're as pale as anything,' he said. 'If you try and dance in your present state, I should think you'll probably faint within five minutes, so I'm going to take you out to dinner instead.'

Now Kit did hug him. 'Thank you, thank you,' she said.

Before he could get his hands adequately out of his pockets, she had let go again. 'Not at all,' he replied. 'Let's wander into town, try and find somewhere decent, yes?'

'I'll just zip upstairs a minute and get my bag. You can come, but I'm just going to zip up and zip right down again.'

'You zip,' he said. 'I'll wait here.'

'Thank you,' she shouted as she ran up the stairs.

Dinner out—could he even remotely guess what this meant to her, old-fashioned, no nonsense, take-you-out-to-dinner? As she went into her room she hopped two steps, thinking, this can't be me.

But it was.

'Can we just agree right now that we'll meet at the dance hall next week, so we know what we're doing?' said Joe, as they strode along. 'That is, if you want to. Make it a definite plan? I mention it because I'd have to go straight there if we do, because I've got a department thing beforehand. Is that okay?'

'Yes, fine,' said Kit. 'Which way round are you going to want to do it?—so I know what I'm in for.'

'Don't worry, that was a one-off,' he said. 'I don't want to make you black out again. I was curious once, that's all.'

'But didn't you like it?'

'Don't tempt me.'

At this, she thought maybe she should; but she didn't.

'Do you want to give me your mobile number, in case?' she said.

'Ah, mobiles,' said Joe, 'I hate them. But, yes. Remind me when we're sitting down. We can exchange numbers then.'

Apart from her pressing need to eat, Kit felt that she could easily have spent the rest of her life pacing along like this with Joe. Even as they walked, the mist grew denser around them. They began to speak inconsequentially about poker, dancing, Virginia creepers, the news; until Kit broke the spell by saying, 'You know that thing where your brain is quietly fizzing away on its own and it makes a connection you completely hadn't thought of, and it's so exciting it makes you want to laugh, or you find that you *do* laugh, or at least exclaim something or something?'

'You realise how bad a person would feel if you said that to them, and they couldn't say "yes"?' Joe replied. 'But, I'm happy to say—*yes*. That's what my balcony's for, in good weather.'

'Well it often seems to happen to me when I'm in libraries, so I'm forced to keep quiet,' said Kit, 'for some irritating reason; because if you do laugh in the Bodleian, they make you feel like a criminal, speaking from experience. I'd like library notices to say, "No talking, eating or mobile phones, but don't worry, laughing is allowed". What is number theory, by the way?' she asked. 'Bear in mind I know nothing. I've decided to ask you for information in small increments.'

'I see.' Joe glanced briefly upwards. 'Well,' he said, 'it's the study of solutions of equations where the answers have to be whole numbers. For example, it's easy to find a solution for x squared plus y squared equals z squared, but once you use integers, it becomes much, much more interesting.'

In her nervousness, Kit was wholly unable to concentrate on this answer; was instead busy thinking, oh God, I'm such a goof, am I *absolutely* sure what an integer is? She passed smoothly on to the next thing. 'I know you're going to hate

me asking this,' she said, 'but is there any practical appli-
cation for what you do?'

'Hard to predict,' he replied. 'And it would be disingen-
uous to pretend that that's why anyone does my kind of
maths. It is true that a solution within number theory can
have knock-on effects in other areas of maths. I'm playing
with the idea—' but whatever he had been about to say, it
was lost as they got caught up in town, lights, traffic, people,
shops, commerce.

After a couple of attempts, he secured them a table in an
Italian place. It was hot in there, or seemed so after the
streets. They idled through the menu and made similar
orders.

'I want to explain something,' said Joe, while they waited
for their starters. 'You realise, I think, that Humpty and I
have an arrangement to meet at The Forfeit on Friday nights,
yes? That's the reason I keep being sort of semi-double-
booked. Because, it was because Humpty was supposed to
be meeting me at the dance club the evening I first met you,
that he picked a place that happened on a Friday, so it would
be when we were supposed to connect up anyway. That was
the point. And then he didn't make it. And now it's you and
me trying to dance on Fridays, when we get over there, and
it's a bit of a muddle.'

'I understand. It's okay. Semi-double isn't what you mean,
for a mathematician, by the way,' she said. 'But yes, I get
it.'

It came to her that she should say something about meeting
some other night, but she was paralysed by the attendant

thought that perhaps he had a specific night for the quality-goods blonde. Perhaps she was Saturdays, for example. This hadn't occurred to Kit before, but it occurred to her now. Perhaps Kit was Fridays, and the blonde was Saturdays and Tuesdays. How awful.

As the waiter brought them their soup, Joe flicked his napkin out of its folds one-handed. 'So, you've been doing a shitload of work?' he said.

'Yes.' Kit immediately began to eat. 'Oh great,' she said, shoving her unwelcome thoughts aside. 'Delicious.'

'I imagine it's pretty simple to make,' said Joe as he tasted it.

'You think?' Kit felt so restored by a little nourishment, that she began to devour her broth in a manner to rival Oliver Twist himself.

'Do I take it you had a brainwave in the Bodleian?'

'No, no,' she said, 'not this week, sadly; although, I have had a funny thought. Probably daft, but I—Joe, what do you think? There are so many details in common between Nancy's case and Eliza Grimwood's, coincidence, I'm sure, but I can't get rid of this mad idea that whoever killed Eliza was partly inspired by reading Dickens.'

'That's a bold leap,' said Joe, his expression more scep-tical even than he sounded.

'I know.'

'What coincidences are you talking about, specifically? I've finished it, by the way.'

'*Oliver Twist*? You have? Brilliant. Did you enjoy it?'

'I did, yes. I see what you say about the plot not being well planned out, but it carries you along anyway. There's things about it that—' He broke off and looked at Kit appraisingly, then said, 'Tell you what, let's go through it. So you don't bias the argument, I'll list what strike me as the key details of Nancy's murder, and you persuade me that Eliza's killer used them as a primer.'

'Okay.'

'Okay?' he said, with a grin. 'You think you can do it?'

'I don't know,' she said.

Joe pulled a funny face, then began. 'Well, obviously they're both prostitutes, killed in their bedrooms by, or possibly by, their pimps, and they are both found dead on the floor in a sea of blood, right? Agreed? Beyond that, Sikes first bashes Nancy in the face with a pistol, then clubs her to death on her knees, and then, if I remember right, gratuitously clubs her some more.'

'Yes,' said Kit, still hungrily downing her soup. 'Well, Eliza, I grant you, was, by contrast, killed with a long-bladed knife, probably a switch knife. But she was evidently also killed on her knees, and also fell over backwards, and also continued to be attacked after death—I think worse than Nancy, as it happens. By the way, I say *also* backwards, because Nancy's corpse lands so that she's staring up at the ceiling, right? So she must be on her back? And Eliza was on her back, so it's the identical position.'

'Different weapon, though.'

'I know. I said.'

'And Sikes burns the club to ashes in the fire.'

'Yes, but this is what I'm thinking. Eliza's killer successfully made his weapon disappear, clearly realising it was necessary and important.'

'Any murderer would figure that out, surely? No sensible killer is going to walk around with a bloody knife in his pocket.'

'Okay,' said Kit, 'fine, but how about the fact that Sikes throws a rug over Nancy's body, then plucks it off again? Remember that? Eliza's body was also semi-covered in bedclothes that had been taken from the bed; and then Hubbard, at the inquest, described how he pulled back the quilt when he discovered the body, hardly knowing what it was, he said, and saw underneath Eliza's blood-drenched face and drastically cut throat.'

'Really?' Joe appeared to add this detail to a list in his head.

'Yes.'

'You're cheating. I'm meant to decide which features are important.'

'Oh, yes. Okay, go on then.'

'What do you say about Sikes cutting the blood stains out of his garments and then burning the scraps in the fire?'

'Yes, but again, one of the troubling points about Eliza's killer was the question of, how did he get away with the fact that in the aftermath of the crime he must have been covered in blood?' Kit clattered the spoon down into her bowl. In her haste, she had already entirely emptied it. Rich pasta would follow; a good thought, a satisfying thought.

'That, too, though,' said Joe, 'in the circumstances, any killer would have to deal with, no?'

'Oh fine,' said Kit, 'fine. What about the dog?'

'The dog? Sikes's dog? Bull's-eye?'

'Yes.'

'That was a nice touch, I thought. You can have that. Okay, so Bull's-eye walks round the room and gets blood all over his feet. What of it?'

'Hear me out, okay?' Kit bent down into her bag and extracted her notebook. 'Witnesses testified that a dog barked in Eliza's house the night she died, I think about three in the morning, can't remember, but it came up at the inquest as hinting at time of death. Listen to this letter to *The Times* a few days later. This codger wrote in that, sure, okay, the dog may have barked, but all the same, it must have known the killer. Because,' Kit put her finger under the lines she wanted, 'quote, "Was the dog bloody? No. How come such a faithful animal was remiss in its duty? Ought we not to have expected to see the animal likewise murdered?"'

'Forgive me, but what conclusion are you drawing from all this?' said Joe. 'Even if your old codger thought up his question having read about Bull's-eye's scarlet footprints, that doesn't tell you anything about any influence on Eliza's murderer.'

'I'm not convincing you this is at all strange?'

He shook his head, then said, 'I'll tell you the main reason why I'm not convinced. Forget all the discrepancies. Really, it's what the two stories have in common that I think rules out any influence.' Joe had been eating much more slowly than Kit, and only now finished his soup. 'The main thing that makes Eliza's case sound similar to Nancy's, if you ask me, is that both murders are savage to the point of total derangement. But for that very reason, I can't believe Eliza's killer was half-following a pattern out of a book. I don't know, but to me that just doesn't ring true.'

'Sorry to have wasted your time,' said Kit, scowling.

'No need to apologise.'

'All right, I won't.' She knew she was being childish but felt too cross to contain herself.

'Look at this another way,' said Joe, trying to appease her, 'at least it leaves Dickens in the clear, if he didn't spark off a gruesome, real-life murder.'

'Yes, but you see, that's another thing,' said Kit. 'He was still interested in Eliza years afterwards, including he asked Charles Field about the case in 1850, over a decade later. I was wondering if that mightn't have been because he felt guilty about it, kind of deal.'

The waiter brought them their pasta. 'Oh, superb, brilliant,' said Kit. 'God, I'm going to be stuffed at the end of this.'

'I notice you're always very polite about food,' said Joe.

'Polite? You're being polite calling it polite,' she said with a laugh. 'Appreciative, yes.' A small alarm in her mind was telling her that the evening was about to go wrong; yet, not knowing how or why, she carried right on, eating and talking by turns. 'I can't be bothered to do things for myself in the kitchen, so I'm always impressed by anyone who likes to cook. My mother's all prefab meals these days. I think it's a big relief to her to have given up. If she cooks an actual cooked dish it leaves this thick smell in our house like fried soap. I find I have bordering on this sentimental thing about it, when I smell that smell after being away.'

'Kit, I didn't mean to destroy your theory,' said Joe.

'You'll think I'm crazy,' she replied, 'but even if you have, for now, I can't promise you I've given up on it.

Orson says—' she regretted mentioning him again, but too late, 'he says, "I like that you get so enthused".'

'Yes, well, I agree with him,' said Joe.

'Orson is having trouble with the nature of his being or something,' said Kit.

'I'm with him on that, too.'

'What do you mean?'

'I, too,' said Joe, 'am having trouble with the nature of my being or something.'

'Really?' said Kit. 'Is it infectious? I ran away when he tried to talk to me about it this morning. I felt bad afterwards, but I was just so bored. I don't mean I'm bored about you,' she added awkwardly.

Joe, who had seemed disenchanted with his food from the start, put his fork down now and held his hand up in surrender.

'But I mean, that was why he asked me to this party thingamabob,' said Kit, wanting to explain, 'so he could pour out his woes over a glass. Though why he thinks I can say anything useful, I have no idea. He doesn't think he truly exists here in Oxford. Joe, I still feel, the Eliza case, I can't explain, but there's—I feel there's something I'm not getting that it would be interesting to understand.'

'Well, I'd be very sorry if you gave up because of anything I said. You know, your eyes shine when you talk about all the details. I don't know any other way to describe it.'

This observation caused Kit to start glowering at him again. 'This isn't some version of, I don't know, "you're beautiful when you're angry"?' she said.

'It what?'

'You're so sweet when you twitter on about your work?'

'Hardly.' Joe laughed. 'Kit, what?—you're so sweet when you twitter on about women being clubbed to death, mutilated and having their heads chopped off?'

As she wasn't wholly mollified by this reply, Joe changed tack and asked, 'Have you tried talking it through with your tutor?'

'No. No, I ran into him on Wednesday, but he splurted out—splurted?—blurged?—anyway, *poured* out, that he's getting divorced; so luckily he forgot to ask how my work was going. I mean, I don't mean to be callous, but I'm getting quite behind. He said his marriage has gone totally phut. He once characterised his wife to me as being—he said, "She's the sort of woman who stays in touch with all our daughter's ex-boyfriends".'

'Ho-hum.'

'I know, it does sound a bit ho-hum. I can't believe he's been a super-brilliant husband either. Anyway, none of my business; but he was upset, so I just did the being-sympathetic bit, and that was all we talked about. But what am I—? Yes, sorry. You know, I have *definitely* done a shitload of work this week. That's what you asked me, wasn't it, a large amount of food ago. How are you? Aren't you hungry? You've hardly touched that. I feel so much better now I've eaten. Yes, shitloads of work, basically, and not just on Eliza, I don't mean, far from it. Although I have flipped through a lot of incredibly unhelpful *Oliver Twist* articles, believe me.'

'Is there anything else you want to say about it all? I'm still open to argument.'

Kit put her elbows on the table. 'Okay, one tiny thing, okay, and then that's it.'

'So long as you don't tell me you think Dickens himself killed Eliza Grimwood.'

'Give me a break,' said Kit, 'I'm not a complete nutter. No, there was this pirate publisher, Edward Lloyd, who plagiarised *Oliver Twist*, instalment by instalment, and sold his version to the public in seventy-nine penny parts renamed *Oliver Twiss*—called it a "literary bantling", but added changes, improvements to the text can you believe, which doubled its length. So I had a look at it this afternoon, out of curiosity. I don't know what I was after, really. But one of the most peculiar things about it, to me, was that, where Nancy, in *Twist*, more or less signs her own death warrant on London Bridge, right—remember?—when she betrays Fagin's gang to try and save Oliver? Well in *Twiss* this is altered so that her fate is sealed, not on London Bridge, but on Waterloo Bridge. *Waterloo Bridge?* I mean, don't you think that's weird? I double-checked on a map, and Waterloo Bridge, logistically, is in completely the wrong place for the plot. Nancy needs to get from her room in East London to whichever bridge and back again as fast as possible before Sikes wakes up. Waterloo Bridge is much further away. So why did they make that change in the pirate version?'

'And what's your answer to this question?'

'Apart from Waterloo being London's number-one suicide bridge at the time, because it was a toll bridge with little recesses, and was therefore the most private, so it had this reputation as kind of a bridge of ill omen—well, that's the rational theory why. But isn't it like a weird little prophecy?'

Joe shook his head. 'I'm sure you don't want to hear this,' he said, 'but sometimes a coincidence is just a coincidence.'

Kit sighed heavily, finding his rigour oppressive. 'I have this feeling I can't put into words that if I try hard enough, I'm going to see something else here.'

'Brute force.'

'What?'

'Sorry: a brute-force search,' said Joe. 'It's a maths term; means working out an answer by going through every possible option, rather than by devising a short cut that will eliminate a proportion of the trial runs.'

'Oh. Thanks. Well then, I suppose. Although it's not the same, because I'm pretty much compelled to look for evidence anywhere it might be. Although, in a brute-force-search way, perhaps. I have to say, I think I'm scraping the barrel now— or at least, the barrel I know about. Not that I haven't got a thousand other more important things to do. I mean, apart from my thesis intro, and knocking my Conrad chapter on the head, which I've virtually not done any of this week, I've been slaving over a paper I've got to give at the Victorian graduate seminar next Thursday, and my plan was that, even if it's rubbish, I'd at least try to win them over by amusing them all to pieces—but that's a scary option in itself, and I'm finding what I'm saying less and less funny the more I work on it.'

The restaurant was packed, the service slow. Kit assumed that their waiter had decided he could neglect them. They were a couple, after all, and though they weren't any longer eating, they still had wine. He might soon need their table, but he must have calculated that he didn't need their approval for being efficient.

'I'm sure it won't be rubbish,' said Joe. 'You're planning to do a comic turn?'

'I thought it would be good if I could make them laugh.'

'How do you aim to do that, as a matter of interest? Amputations? Cannibalism?'

'You know what? *Yes*,' said Kit. 'You think I'm a maniac? Wrong in the head?'

'I don't know,' said Joe. 'What's the paper about?'

She swallowed hard. 'It's, "A Short History of Sudden Death in the Reign of Queen Victoria". Because—really, Joe, you've got to admit—in the Victorian era, the opportunities for dying by accident increased beyond belief, which from a literary point of view equals authors having much more choice over how to kill off their characters. If you read Victorian newspapers, the number of whole houses that got blown to smithereens while gas was being installed, or the number of workmen frizzled to death when they were trying to get the country electrified, or the number of people, you wouldn't believe it, killed on the railways, hundreds, thousands, seriously, crushed, or with bits fatally severed, let alone pigs and cows—and then there was sleep-walkers falling out of high windows once the masses were crowded into city tenements; honestly, you could do a whole book on this subject, factories, construction projects. But, yes, for the purposes of surviving my talk, my idea was that the press notices of these disasters can be quite hilarious, and of course, every one of them has a guaranteed superb ending. You didn't answer my question, by the way.'

Joe shook his head uncomprehendingly.

'How are you?'

There was a long pause, then, rather than answer, he said, 'What is it with you and violence, Kit?'

She herself paused, before replying lightly, 'Oh, God, violence—well, what I think about violence, crime, I don't know. My feeling is, that people who have the imagination to do crimes properly should have the imagination not to do them at all. Mostly people do them rather badly. No, that's a stupid thing to say—depending, as ever, on what's meant by "properly"—and, of course, by "crime".'

A wave of terrible fatigue assailed her; the warmth of the restaurant, her overfull stomach, the wine she had drunk, and the knowledge that her answer had been garbled because she hadn't known what to say.

'But violence in particular interests you?' Joe asked.

Of course it was hopeless of her not to be able to understand the least particle of what he did, but he seemed so unwilling to talk about himself, unless she had missed something. 'I wouldn't say that it was a notable feature of my daily life,' she said.

'It is a feature of mine,' said Joe, and he lifted his right hand up, and showed her the knuckles.

'What happened?' she asked, a little shocked.

'I didn't think I could cook for you,' he said, staring at the scabs and bruises. 'I've been eating with this one,' and he indicated his left.

So he had. She had noticed without thinking about it. 'What happened?' she said again.

'Humpty got in a fight last weekend.'

'You're kidding.'

He wasn't.

'And you?' she said. The thought that she was having dinner with someone who hit people unsettled her.

'Let's say I helped extract him.' At the look on her face, he added, 'I did boxing at school.'

'Oh. Goodness. Isn't it banned in schools?'

'Not formally, no.'

'Oh,' she said. 'You mean it, though? You actually punched someone?' She peeped at her own knuckles, which she'd scraped doing the somersault, but they were healed again.

Joe put his hand back in his pocket. 'What I was wondering was, you get something out of it at a distance, yes?—on the page, or the screen, or in old newspapers? You like *clean*-dirty, right?'

'Have I done something wrong?' she whispered.

'I'm just asking. I didn't mean to—whatever. I'm just trying to understand you,' said Joe.

'Well, thanks.' On reflection, Kit added, 'Maybe I should mention that I find you quite hard to understand, myself.' As he didn't reply to this, she continued, 'I get caught by what I'm reading, you know, and all the world looks bad to me for a while, even if it's just wasps and starlings and apples and fog and blackberries. I don't know what to do with the bad bits inside my head. It doesn't feel clean in there, definitely not. Did you really, fully slow down and picture to yourself, when you read about Nancy, what it would be like to beat a woman to death with a club while she knelt in front of you; or what it would be like to be the person killed that way? Don't you ever think sometimes that the things inside your head are too violent?— and that smacking something solid would be easy, in a way?'

Joe looked down into his lap and said quietly, almost to himself, 'Although I wanted to hit him, the *reason* I wanted to is that I'm so sick of being in a position where doing something like that, where hitting someone, is even remotely imaginable.'

Kit found herself at a loss for how to reply, so she merely gave Joe back his line a little altered, as if this were a psalm: 'You wanted to hit him because you didn't want to have to.'

'Kit,' Joe flicked a look at her for a second, 'I should tell you, I want to tell you—Humpty, even for him, Humpty's in a bad way. I have a bad feeling about it. Christ knows, we've been through enough with him already in my family, but, right now—this isn't a great time, and,' Joe was looking all around the restaurant now, 'he got sent away to Milan to get him out of the way, I deduce, which may be the last favour any of them ever does him—' he shook his head. 'I wish I'd met you when things were simpler, but they just aren't.'

Kit paled. His finishing remark sounded oddly rehearsed, and it arose in her mind that perhaps this was it, that Joe was preparing to terminate their friendship, Michaela had been right: *The End*. Michaela—'I know someone who could get him a job,' Kit said, 'in a bottle factory, near Rochester, Humpty. You—' Joe was visibly flinching, Kit began to get in a snarl again—'last week, you said—I found out for you in case it was a help.'

'You spoke to someone about my brother?' he asked, his tone caustic.

'I didn't say who it was about.'

'I'm glad to hear that,' still icy.

'I just asked about it,' she said, adding without conviction, 'for his own sake.'

'A *bottle factory?*'

She quailed. 'Isn't that—the kind of thing he might do?'

'He's a furniture restorer,' said Joe crushingly, 'a craftsman. A fucking bottle factory, I'm not so sure. You know the Mackintosh desk in the flat?' His voice began to rise. 'You don't just decide to send my brother away and stick him in a fucking factory, Kit. Where did you get that idea? What—have you found him somewhere to live?'

She felt sick. Joe was swearing at her. 'I'm sorry,' she said. 'I'm sorry. I didn't realise—I didn't know what he did. He keeps saying about living in a field. I didn't decide anything. It was just—' She remembered now, the first time she'd met Humpty, saying to Joe afterwards, 'In at the deep end,' and Joe saying, 'This is nothing like the deep end.'

The waiter came, crashed their plates together, and said, 'Can I bring you the menu?'

Joe cleared his throat. 'Kit?'

'No, no, I'm good,' she said.

'Coffee?'

'No thanks.'

She tried to split the bill with him, but he wouldn't let her.

Outside, the temperature had dropped so far that their clothing was no longer adequate to keep them warm. Kit hugged her coat around her tighter than the job done by the buttons. A thick fog was making everything damp now, not just the air.

'This way?' said Joe, pointing up towards the Woodstock Road.

Kit nodded.

'Do you want to take a bus?'

'Walking's fine,' she said, and thought that, this way she could pace herself into readiness for a fumbled goodbye. Perhaps he really was going to finish it, was just waiting for a suitable turn in the conversation: *The End*. 'Unless you want to, I mean,' she said. She looked round at Joe, startled by a misapprehension that he was choking. He had merely cleared his throat. He seemed so much more definite to her than she felt she was herself, with his low voice, scarred fist, and his eyes, that her tallness didn't compensate for how slight he made her feel.

They proceeded to walk, and spoke about this and that, woodenly at first, before a sham ease came over their conversation. They strolled along together through the stage-set fog, chatting like friends, until, all too soon, they drew near to Kit's home.

'Where are we going?' she said, birdlike in the tilt of her head, and was almost fearful when Joe suggested coffee at his flat.

As they turned down his street, Kit recognised the elderly gent who emerged from the mist into a pool of street-light ahead of them. 'There's Buddy,' she said. It was intrinsically quaint to her to be able to call an old man, 'Buddy'.

'Yes, right, you met,' said Joe.

'Joe,' said Buddy, with a well-worn nod; and then, staring around, he said, 'How about this, my word. And you can just smell winter, the sniff of it.'

'Kit,' said Joe, introducing her.

'Evening,' said Buddy. 'I won't keep you. This feeling keeps—reminds me of when I was a boy. My father died when I was twelve: didn't really know him. Bit of a reprobate, like Humpty.' Again the gruff nod to Joe. 'I went to the Public Record Office at Kew the other day. Very interesting. Read all his dispatches from the Second World War.'

'The Public Record Office,' breathed Kit, thinking, of *course*.

'Gave an account every month, two figures at the end of each: so many wounded, so many dead. He filled them all in till he got his fingers shot off and became one of them. Never took a bullet again.' At this, Buddy sounded almost regretful. 'He died of a fever in the end. To be honest,' he said, 'not many young take an intelligent interest in the war these days.' And then, returning to where he'd started, 'This fog reminds me of when I was a boy.'

'Absolutely,' said Kit, touched with excitement: she hadn't really been listening. The Public Record Office, how could she not have thought of it? Imperatively, yes, she must check their catalogue—because, what if they had holdings on Eliza? 'Brilliant,' she said.

Buddy took stock of her, surprised. 'Well, in that case,' he said, 'I've a little something you might like to look at.'

'I—yes?' Kit glanced round at Joe for help, whence no help came, only a smile.

'He wasn't much of a correspondent,' said Buddy, 'but

177

I've my grandfather's letters from the Great War, and they're a gold mine, a treasure trove, mostly the Macedonian front. He was a padre, but he insisted on sticking with his battalion when most of the chaplains flunked it. Spent months in front of the guns, took services in the trenches, constantly under fire. Had to organise the burial of the dead, a massive job in this case, out on the mountain slopes.'

'Thank you *so* much,' said Kit. She had begun to concentrate now. 'I'll look forward to that. It sounds excellent. But you mustn't trust me with anything too precious.' This funny old man had supplied her with an opportunity to be kind, to appear kind; and yet, a first-hand account of the horrors of trench warfare, let alone Orson's 600-page novel—where was she going to get the time? Oh God, what a messed-up day.

'Don't you worry about that,' Buddy was saying. He gave Joe a wink—of approbation, it seemed, a not-bad sort of a wink, evidently with reference to Kit. 'Won't keep you. Cheerio for now, then,' he said.

As Buddy ambled off, Joe murmured, 'That made him happy.'

'No, well,' said Kit, 'I'm extremely grateful he made me think of the Public Record Office.'

'You think you'll go? Keep hunting?'

'If they have anything, yes.'

Joe nodded at this information. He let them into the house, the front hall of which wasn't much warmer than outside.

'Where do you imagine Buddy was off to?' said Kit, as she hung up her coat. Her heart began to race at what she was doing.

'Buddy?' said Joe. 'You mean, will he be back soon, and will he come straight up here with his war notes?'

'Exactly. A hundred per cent spot on, because I—' a nervous carelessness overtook her, she didn't want the day to end badly—didn't really want it to end at all, 'because— I quite feel like taking all your clothes off; but, if Buddy's going to show up, yes. I mean, he was going away from the house, right, wasn't he?'

'If Frank hadn't just died—' said Joe.

Ah, he was turning her down. That was a *no*. Kit's heart thumped yet harder inside her. A 'no', then. Ah. Well, never mind. So what? Did it matter?

She yelped as Joe slid his icy left hand under her tee shirt, and pulled sharply away from him—a reflex. 'Sorry,' she cried, clutching the cold imprint of his hand on her belly. 'Sorry. I'm sorry. Sorry.'

He looked at her. 'Finished?' he said.

'Yes.' All of a sudden they were joking together with their eyes. Kit listened, in pantomime, for footsteps on the stairs, then said, 'Well, this is a silly situation.'

'Only quite,' Joe replied. 'Anyway, Buddy's no fool.'

'Let's go out on the balcony,' she said. 'Let's jump out of the window.'

'Why? It's freezing.'

'Please.'

'Kit—'

'Please.'

Outside, aloft, up above the great array of back gardens, visibility was so poor that it hardly extended over the balcony's rim, apart from the weak glow of lit windows trailing away to either side. Across Joe's vertical flower beds, innumerable spiders' webs gleamed with water droplets. The sodden air was heavy also with the scent of wood smoke, and there was a light splashing sound as drips fell from gutters and soaking trees. The scene was strange, yet earthly; quiet, but also fantastical.

Kit communicated her next thought with one eyebrow and a gesture of the hand.

'Out here?' said Joe. 'You mean it?'—his voice subdued by the deadened air. 'I'm at your mercy, I'm just asking.'

'Out here,' she replied, with artless determination.

'This puts a whole new slant on the concept of a blanket of mist.'

'Blankets would definitely be good,' she said, 'and,' stooping back in through the window, 'we could—' she began to attempt what she was describing, 'get your mattress thing—' She hefted it towards her. After all, she understood now how he organised himself, when he lay out on the balcony and thought about maths.

Joe laughed, climbed back inside, disappeared, then returned with a heap of bedding. 'Pillows, two blankets, a quilt,' he said. 'This is going to be uncomfortable.'

'I'm not fussed.' Kit took a deep breath. 'We could be on the moon out here.'

Joe looked up into the invisible distance. 'Not that you get mists on the moon.'

'No.' Not that you did.

'Also cold, though,' he said.

And these were the last words either of them spoke, 'also

cold though'. Whatever else they might have said, understood or not understood, they put it aside for now. Nobody wanted them, nobody cared, as the fog lent a kindly, obliterating halo to their wishful human forms.

CHAPTER 6

Kit crawled out of bed, her hands shaking. The past few days she had suffered a series of debilitating headaches, though she felt mysteriously sure now that she was clear of them; only her hands, and the dullness of fatigue, slowing her down. Friday: it should have been a high point of the week. But maybe not this time.

She had parted from Joe seven days earlier unsure she hadn't offended him, and had become increasingly stricken since at the thought that her generous attempt to get rid of Humpty had been really a big mistake. She had become convinced that Joe must still be planning to drop her—he could make do with the quality-goods blonde, right?—that in the unfortunate minute that she had spoken of the bottle factory, he could only have relegated her to the position of false friend. After all, real life wasn't like some pulp Victorian novel where you sent your unwanted relatives away; and even if it were, nine times out of ten, she thought wryly, in a book of that kind, the dreadful relative came back at the end and made things worse.

Kit brushed her teeth, her hands still unsteady. Joe had made a date with her the previous week to meet at the club this evening, it had been almost the first thing they'd discussed. But whether the date still stood, she didn't know. She had felt confused when she'd climbed back in off the balcony; euphoric, wrung out, and so suddenly angry that she hadn't wanted to speak—hadn't asked about it, hadn't been told.

She would go to the dance hall in the hopes he might be there, but wouldn't expect it.

First, though, right now, Friday morning, she was going to make a lightning trip to London. It wasn't a sensible plan but she was doing it anyway. She hadn't gone on Wednesday as she'd intended, had slept through her alarm and woken in a haze at around eleven. But today, here she was awake in time, and, if shaking, still determined.

She got herself out of the house and stumbled along the cold and quiet streets to the railway station, picturing for no good reason how it might have been had she been murdered on Joe's balcony, killed like Eliza or Nancy, but out on a balcony, a great amount of blood spurting scarlet over the rail and falling down, down, down through the fog, to the untended garden below.

On the train Kit slept again, densely. She awoke at Paddington feeling sick, dozed on the Underground to Kew, drank a large amount of coffee in the Public Record Office cafeteria, then made her way up to the main reading room to work.

She had ordered in advance two murder confessions, the sum total of relevant material she could find listed under 'Grimwood, Eliza'. As these had to be *false* confessions, Kit was very aware that she didn't really have much excuse for bothering with them, interesting though they might prove, in their own way.

Buried amongst the correspondence in the first of two boxes was a letter that implicated a girl who had supposedly admitted to killing Eliza out of jealous affection for Eliza's last client. The tenor of the note was frankly unconvincing. The second box yielded up a confession made directly by a pathetic individual, 'of extreme bad character', who had hoped by this means to get himself discharged from the army, preferring prison. As he turned out to have been unavailable at the time of the murder, this wasn't convincing either. What the documents did both show, however, was that raising the Grimwood case at this time was a sure-fire way to get yourself noticed. In the 1840s, if you claimed to know who had killed Eliza Grimwood, even where the chances of your being right were unbelievably slender, the police would still be summoned. The government had continued to be anxious to see the thing solved.

It took Kit all of twenty minutes to decipher the two relevant bundles of papers. And that was that. She had come a long way for nothing.

She was still deeply tired, and didn't at all feel like setting off back to Oxford again at once, so, with half-hearted curiosity, she began to look through the other miscellaneous documents in the boxes before her. Most appeared to have been stored together on the sole ground that they had been sent in the same general period to the reigning Under Secretary of State: a letter agitating for road improvements around Bolton in the Moors; a copy of a pamphlet aimed at the rate payers of Newbury, traducing 'the American, whom you have the misfortune to call your Rector'; and, as Kit read with particular sympathy, a furious epistle from a Mr

Cox, who believed he had been unfairly refused permission to read in the British Museum Library.

As Kit drew close to emptying the second box, and was on the point of pulling herself together and leaving, she turned over a loose file that made her heart jump. Uncatalogued but unquestionably real: she caught her breath and bent down closer to the near-impenetrable, nineteenth-century script— here, no, *yes*, God Almighty, was the official police record, Charles Field's handwritten, signed police notes, every last detail, logged by him day after day as the investigation unfolded, of every step he had taken, every false step, all the evidence he had gathered, everything, in his painfully unsuccessful attempt to track down Eliza's killer.

*

Kit stood with her arm around the bus stop, her knees sagging, trying to relive the moment of her discovery. Hard to believe she had been in Kew only a few short hours before. She and Joe hadn't had time to speak before the dancing began. They had simply smiled their greetings, and she had then more or less collapsed into his embrace, so wiped out had she felt, weakly elated and unhappy—thrilled that he was there, but worried, even though he *was*, that he didn't much trust her any more.

And then, well into the first hour of steps, Joe, without warning, had broken ranks and begun to turn her round and round in their corner at the back, ignoring everyone and— he had concentrated them, blindly but on purpose, within their own primitive dance: one *two*, one *two*; one *two*, one *two*; Lucille yelling 'Hello?' at them, 'Hello? *Hello?*'—they ignored her as well—the pair of them dancing seamlessly as one, lost in rhythmic oblivion, tranquil.

They had continued like this, just as they pleased, until the music next stopped, when, still without speaking, they had left.

'So, hello there.' Joe also grasped the bus stop, with his good hand. The other, Kit noticed, he was still protecting. He sounded okay though, cheerful.

'Hello, yes, hello. How are you?' Kit replied.

'This is where I first spoke to you,' he said.

'Yes. Yes, and I thought you were some kind of—what? I don't know. Because of the way your hair is cut so short, and you look like—tough, you know.'

'Perhaps you'd better not explain,' he said humorously.

Nearly November, the frost in the air was making her nose prickle. There had been heavy rains earlier in the week, but the sky, now, was clear, clean, black, star-strewn, icy.

'Come to my place. I'll give you a feast,' said Joe.

Kit let out a small cry of dismay.

'What?' he said. 'I got artichokes. What is it?'

'What about The Forfeit?' she said.

'We don't have to. Humpty's in Milan. I'm completely free. Come to my place. I need to talk to you.'

Kit didn't know how to proceed. 'He's still in Milan?' she said.

'Oh, yes,' said Joe, 'last week, when I told you he'd gone, I thought he had, but he turned up the next morning about six a.m. Christ knows, if you'd stayed the night instead of scarpering, you'd have seen him. But anyway, there he was, six in the morning, in a terrible state, fuck it. Turns out he and Pauly didn't manage to leave until Tuesday; something about the car they were using.'

'Bloody hell, I've totally messed up,' said Kit, feeling fraught.

'What do you mean?'

'You know I told you I have a brother, much older than me, Graham?' she said. 'Do you remember? I only usually see him a couple of times a year? Well, he phoned me up today at lunchtime, when I was in London, and said could I have a drink with him this evening because he was coming to Oxford for a meeting tomorrow, and where did I suggest, and—it's just, he called me out of the blue, so I thought the best plan was The Forfeit because—I was going to say the pub around the corner, but I couldn't remember what it's called and, and listen, you don't have to come. I can have a quick drink with him then meet you at your place, if that's good. A really quick drink, fifteen minutes, is that all right? He'll understand. He's probably there already because he said he'd arrive before we finished at the club, because I didn't know we'd leave early. I wasn't even sure you'd come. I thought you might not,' she said falteringly.

'Why?'

'Let's not talk about it.'

'We forgot to exchange numbers last week.'

'True.'

After a pause, Joe said, 'See that pied wagtail?' and pointed at one that was bobbing along the pavement.

'I like them,' she said.

Joe looked back up at her. 'You thought I might not come, but you came anyway? You're a funny combination of being happy and scared. At least, I thought it was funny at first,' he said. 'I've come to wonder whether the two don't go hand in hand.'

'Well, my impression,' replied Kit slowly, 'is that you are a bit too weary at life to be scared much of anything.'

The traffic roared past them as each considered what the other had just said. 'I think I've become more scared since I met you,' remarked Joe, after a while.

'Oh,' she said, 'sorry.'

And he said, 'If you ever had anything to apologise for, it isn't that.'

Kit shivered as her body warmth began to dwindle. 'Did you see the sun setting before class?' she asked, 'how red it was? It was blue-black that way,' she gestured vaguely east, 'and then, that way,' westwards, 'the horizon was ablaze, but with a couple of low-lying clouds in long streaks above, in this lovely, threatening, purplish colour? And above that, the aeroplane vapour trails were lit right up making brilliant orange squiggles over the sky, like the after-image on your retina when you stare at a lightbulb filament, except, I mean, all up in the sky.'

'It was beautiful this morning too,' said Joe.

'Yes,' she replied eagerly. 'But like they said before—Humpty's friends, remember?—this evening it was the sun and the moon both there at the same time, and the sun was rich and scarlet and blurry, and the moon—' she waved a hand at it, rising, three-quarters full, 'well, it's incredibly distinct right now, incredibly precise. It was really possible to understand, looking at them both at once, that they're these orbs out in space, and we are too. You know the clocks go back this weekend? I hate it. Look, here comes a bus. What am I saying? Sorry. Yes, I—'

They got on and settled in side by side.

'How was your sudden-death talk?' Joe asked. 'And you said you went to London today?'

'Yes,' she replied, exhaling bleakly. 'Oh. This week's been very up and down. The seminar, I survived—I think. I hope. People did at least laugh here and there. I don't know. It was okay. I should have done it better. My stomach was in complete knots while I was speaking, but I think my voice sounded normal. I hope so. Michaela's been being incredibly narky, still. I mean she's been being unpleasant for ages, for no reason I can make out. She seems to have this permanent bug up her butt: so critical.'

'About what?'

'Oh, stupid things, anything, small things. My clothes, for example.'

'What about them?'

'Exactly. Anyway, I don't care. I'm completely out of it at the moment,' said Kit. 'God, last Saturday I had to go to a lunch thing at the Master's Lodgings, and I was talking to this bloke about what I did, just blabbing on in a superficial way, and for the life of me I couldn't remember whether I'd already asked him what he did or not, you know—in, you know, our opening exchanges. I was talking to him pretty much on automatic pilot, thinking, if I ask him what he does and he's just told me, I'll give the impression I'm completely uninterested by him—which I was, by the way. But if I haven't already asked, and I *don't* ask, he'll think I'm rude.'

Joe laughed. 'So what did you do?'

'I decided to ask, possibly *again*, and then be ludicrously interested whatever he replied. But just at the point of me getting the words out, he got taken to talk to this virus expert person, so I was effectively rude anyway, and may well have seemed uninterested as well, I don't know. I mean we're talking last Saturday lunch. It still qualified to me as basically the morning after the night before—so far as I was concerned. And you know about the night before.' She glanced at Joe under her lashes.

'I'd say the sacrifice in civility was worth it,' he replied, with a little smile of his own. 'And tell me about London quickly, before we tackle your brother?'

'He's a sweetheart.'

'I'm sure.'

'No, well, I got a train to Paddington this morning, got the Tube miles across London to the PRO—I mean, why exactly is the Underground so hot, when it *is* underground?'

Kit had intended this question to be rhetorical, but to her surprise, Joe replied, 'In large part because the friction caused by the movement of the trains through the tunnels heats up the surrounding air.'

'Oh,' she said, 'what a wonderful thing to know.'

'I have a friend who worked as an engineer on the Jubilee Line extension.'

'Very good. Brilliant. Have you been there?'

'Where? The Jubilee Line extension? Oh, the Public Record Office. Me? No.'

'I kind of liked it. They have this mosaic globe sculpture outside, called something like, "The World as Seen by Representative Lunatics".'

'Any good?'

'Very disappointing, because it looks just like the world as seen by everyone else. Come on, lunatics! Try a bit harder! Anyway, strangely enough, I had an exceptional one of those laugh-out-loud-in-a-library experiences that I mentioned to you before. In fact, yes, prepare to be staggered.'

'By you,' said Joe, 'I'm prepared to be staggered.'

'Sort of by mistake,' said Kit, 'guess what I found? Only Charles Field's actual daily log of his investigation into the Eliza Grimwood murder: Charles Field—Bucket—the actual police inspector in charge. Can you believe it? When I tell you it was handwritten, of course it was, because this was before typewriters. But it's just such a thrill to hold these things for real, God; the real, real thing, the paper he breathed on; his own hand. The Home Office evidently called in his notes when they started receiving false confessions to the murder, then omitted to return them again. But they weren't listed in the PRO catalogue, so I found them there entirely by surprise. I almost *didn't* find them because I was just muddling through the rest of these boxes for fun. I mean, *Charles Field*: I can't tell you how brilliant this is. This, I can really make use of in my thesis.'

'A bit of a coup, then.'

'Actually,' said Kit, trying to look modest, 'it is. I wasn't there long enough to decode all the handwriting, but from what I was able to glean in the time, it indicates that the police had absolutely no extra, secret evidence against anybody.'

'Right.'

'They were utterly foiled. Which isn't all that helpful regarding the murder, but does prove Field to have been an out-and-out liar when he talked about it to Dickens. I'll have to go again and work through the thing properly, but I had to get back here for dancing, as you know. Anyway, I've been conked out ill in bed half the week,' she said.

'I'm sorry to hear it.'

'Headaches.'

Their bus was crawling down the Cowley Road, past Chinese stores, Russian stores, tattoo parlours, wig shops, sex shops, Bangladeshi restaurants, bead stores, all muddled up with government and other outlets seeking to service variously bungled lives.

'Yes?' said Joe.

'And I've stopped going to the cinema,' said Kit.

'Is that a good thing?'

'I don't know.'

'I've had a stupid week,' said Joe. 'One of my students pissed all over this girl's door: quite a good mathematician. I've had to have endless meetings about it. Her parents want him sent down. I thought I'd already had my quota of this kind of idiocy for one term; but no.'

When they reached the bottom of the Cowley Road, Kit suggested they get off the bus again and walk. They waited for the rear doors to open, then stepped out into the frosty darkness. Cold as it was, they dawdled their way towards The Forfeit, by no means overly keen to arrive.

'Can I run a thought by you?' said Kit, as they paused to look from Magdalen Bridge down into the chilly river waters.

'Not by any remote chance to do with Eliza?' Joe asked,

entertained when her body language confirmed that his suspicion was correct.

'You know your comment, "Sometimes a coincidence is just a coincidence"?' she said. 'Can I tell you some more?'

'Sure, go ahead.' They started walking again.

'Because, you know, I still feel,' she said, 'if nothing else, that there's just too many of them.' She sighed. 'Anyway, Bill Sikes, remember after he clubs Nancy to death he's plunged into a terrible state of "dread and awe", goes off for a couple of days, is completely unhinged, comes back still mental, and is desperate to know whether or not her body has been buried yet? And when he's told it hasn't been, because the inquest isn't yet complete, he bursts out, *why* do they keep such "ugly things" above ground? Yes? Well, how ugly? one might ask. Or, putting it another way, what sort of shape do we think he left Nancy's corpse in by the time he'd finished? Because, note that when her friend Bet has to go and identify it, what she sees drives her stark, raving mad. She begins banging her head on the floorboards, and is hauled off to be straitjacketed in a lunatic asylum. You remember that?'

'I do—remember.'

'So, you have to imagine that the corpse is in a truly horrendous and horrific state, yes?—if Bet goes mad at the sight of it? Okay, so bear with me. Sikes then tries to escape a mob that forms, "hurling execrations" at him, by climbing out onto the roof of the building he's in. And, to wrap up, he then by convenient accident slips off the tiles with a rope around his neck and hangs himself. We're agreed about all this?'

'Yes. You've reminded me I wanted to point out to you that he falls thirty-five feet, as specified by Dickens, which without question in reality would cause your head to be torn off. But hey, never mind. Let the fucker dangle, as Dean would say.'

'Yuk, I didn't think of that,' said Kit. 'Thanks. *Yuk*. So anyway, now we come to Eliza's murder. I'm not saying anyone made this fit a pattern, I'm not saying that, because I don't see how they could have. But consider that when she was killed it was very hot weather, so her corpse rotted. We know this because, when the inquest jury was reconvened after five days of Charles Field gathering useless evidence, the jurors were unable to examine the new wounds that had been found on Eliza's torso, after her underclothes were removed, because, after five days of heat, these stab wounds had become undetectable due to having putrefied, *deliquesced*—I mean, obviously this was before scene-of-crime photographs, it was before photographs, so you just left the corpse where it was until you'd finished the inquest. So anyway, yes, for rising a week she was left to decompose in her bedroom, while Hubbard, the main suspect, her cousin-lover-pimp, was under house arrest in the same house, and on suicide watch because *he* was going mad. Think of the smell, by the way. And he was eventually implicated as the murderer by an anonymous letter that looked like it had inside information in it, but which the press speculated the police had sent to themselves. Anyway, whatever, it enabled them to *get* him, as it were. But the accusations couldn't be made to stick in court. The magistrates said Hubbard must be allowed to go free. And the governor of the prison where they were holding him, Horsemonger Lane Gaol, let him escape out of a back window, apparently, because a mob had gathered at the front, and was "hurling execrations" again, according to *The Times*, and there was this fear he'd be pulled to pieces. I mean, I'm not saying anything, except, doesn't this sound, in its main points, strangely similar to—'

She broke off as Joe took her arm to guide her safely through the traffic and over the street.

'Drat, blast and bother,' she said, when they got to the other side, smiling round at him blithely. 'You still don't find this all a bit close?'

'Kit?' said Joe.

'Yes?'

'This isn't exactly a change of subject, but I'm curious, do you want to be an academic?'

She took a deep breath. They were nearly at the pub. 'Not especially,' she said. 'I'm not thinking ahead about it, really. I don't really know. I don't want to *be* anything, particularly. I just like thinking about things, except when I don't want to think at all; which is why dancing is so brilliant, for example. Thank you for this evening. Why did we leave? We just—*did*?'

Joe shook his head as though he didn't have an answer.

'I don't know what else kind of thing I could do to earn my keep, though,' she said.

'You could join the police force.'

She laughed a lot at this suggestion. 'I could compose their anonymous letters for them, right? I'd enjoy that,' she said, adding, as an afterthought, 'You're lucky you have a good job.'

'Ah,' said Joe, 'what does that mean?'

As they walked in through the door, into the stale air of

The Forfeit, Kit squeezed Joe's arm, acknowledging an intimacy now to be suspended.

'Hello, beautiful.'

'Graham.'

Up stood a tall, middle-aged man who looked as though he'd been forced to grow used to being portly. He kissed Kit and stroked her cheek. 'Okay then? You doing all right?'

'Great, yes, I am. This is Joe, Graham. Graham, Joe.'

Graham stretched out a manly hand. 'Mate. Good to meet you. Been dancing, I hear. What's anyone having?'

'Have you eaten?' Kit asked him.

'Had a bite in town. A tasty baguette,' he said. 'All right, actually. Nice. I liked it. Grilled brie with, what d'you call 'em? Can't remember. Tasty, though. Nice place too. *Cranberries*, yes. I liked it. What about you two? Order you something? Take you out? What does anyone prefer?'

'We'll wait,' said Joe. 'We'll eat later.'

'Sure?'

'We're fine. We'll eat later,' he said.

'Well, so, what's anyone having?'

Joe asked for a pint; Kit for a glass of wine. She realised it felt funny to her not to be sitting at the table at the back.

While Graham stood jovially chatting to the barman, Kit said, 'I'm so sorry you have to do this.'

'Not at all,' said Joe. 'How could I possibly object?'

She shrugged her acceptance of this reply. 'You know I told you Michaela had been getting at me a lot recently?' she said.

'Yes.'

Why had she embarked on this? Kit folded her hands together, then continued, 'It wasn't really about my clothes.'

'Oh?'

'It's about you.' *No, no, no.*

'Me?'

'Yes.'

'What about me?'

'Don't get cross.'

'Do I appear cross?'

'You know when we were in here with Dean and Donald and Pauly?'

'Yes. They're here now, Dean and Donald are, out the back at one of the tables under a burner.'

'They're here?'

'Yes. When you come up the street, you can see the edge of the back patio through the railings down the side of the pub.'

'Oh. Right.'

'What about them?'

'No, yes. No. You know I went to the loo? You probably don't remember, but when I came back—' And *two*, and *three*, and *four*—Graham put their drinks down on the table. 'Murruh!' he said, spitting out several crisp packets that he'd had dangling by their corners from his teeth, before replacing himself solidly in his chair.

'Thanks,' said Joe. 'Excellent.' They opened the crisps. Joe looked at Kit, who had gone silent, then turned to Graham. 'What brings you to Oxford?' he asked. 'Kit said you had something on.'

'Did she tell you what?'

'I don't think so.'

'Dozy girl,' said Graham affectionately. 'I'm attending a session *adjunct* to a preliminary Euro-region meeting ahead of a breakaway congress next year of seed crushers and waste grease and oil processors.'

'Of—sorry?'

'Seed crushers? Waste oil processors? You know, sunflower, soya bean, linseed?'

Joe glanced at Kit for confirmation that he wasn't having his leg pulled, which he wasn't.

'I decided last minute I'd get here ahead of time in favour of having to drive down crack of dawn tomorrow,' said Graham. 'Thought I'd see Birdy here and take my leisure for once. Can't take getting up early any more. Going to kip at a mate's house off the Botley Road. Came by train. Handy for the station. Old friend, lives off the Botley Road. Handy all ways round. And there's always ye olde Cotswolds to fill up the view out your carriage window. What a lovely part of the world that must have been before cars.'

'Can I just mention that that's rubbish,' said Kit. 'You have to think of the past as having been excessive hard work and extremely dirty. Think of dreadful infant mortality rates, goitres, bad harvests, deaths in childbirth, stinking rotten teeth—'

'She's off on one,' said Graham.

'Birdy?' said Joe.

'Birdy? Christine. Skinny legs when she was a kid,' said Graham. 'Radio aerials. Bean stakes. A right little miss, too, sometimes. But yes, seed crushing, all in turmoil right now. Thing is, when I was young, obviously people older than me had authority as far as I was concerned, only natural.

Then I hit my thirties, began to notice that—boy did I notice—certain people were starting to have authority over me despite the fact that they were younger—patronising, you know? Arrogant little twerps in their twenties telling me what to do, in the context of, that things move on and they knew more about it than I did, now. Fat lot of good, all those years of experience; and don't talk to me about palm oil; and anyway, but *now*—' whatever he was thinking about, it was borderline too much, '*now*,' said Graham, taking a deep breath, 'now that I'm firmly into my *forties*—'

'More like firmly on the way out of them again,' said Kit, with a little sister's grin.

'Now I'm *this* age, I'm finding people have authority over me *because* they're younger than I am. Not despite—*because*. Which is like, I'm past my shelf life, is the general idea. *Adjunct* session. I tell you, this meeting's not unimportant in respect of keeping my end up, between these four walls, in the revered world of international seed crushing. It's not just going bald,' he waved at his head, 'it's my private-parts hair's going thin. I cough when I don't need to. Hear myself do it. I drip after I think I've finished peeing. Day I hit forty-five, I said to myself, well done, mate, now you're a has-been. You're a *has-been*. I'm a great believer in carpeying the bloody diem but I thought, this is it. Past your shelf life, a has-been. I knew it. But was I right? I was *not* right. Was that it? That *wasn't* it. By no manner of means, no. And how long did it take me to realise? Till just the other day, when I said to myself, shite, what am I on about? I'm not a has-been. I'm a *hasn't-been*. I'm a hasn't-been, never-was: a nothing, a resource hog. Willa's doing it at school, resource hogs. The things they teach them, I'm telling you, steady on! Problem with my wife, Joe—I mean, don't tell the *resource hogs*, will you.'

'Graham,' said Kit, caught between laughter and distress, 'what on earth are you on about?'

'Don't ask me, Birdy,' he said. 'Not exactly roses right now. Feeling a touch rough, to tell you the truth. Drinking on my own,' he said to Joe, pointing apologetically at his glass. 'Don't know what I'm talking about. I've got my pubes going white, the ones I have left. Birdy here,' he slapped her shoulder, 'when she was a tiddler, cried the whole bloody time. Wouldn't stop. Only way to get her to stop was to blow in her face.'

'In her face?'

'It surprised her, then it calmed her down.'

'I don't really know anything about babies,' said Joe.

'Well,' said Graham, standing up, 'they change everything.' And he stumbled away to the toilets.

Kit and Joe sat in joint, surprised silence. It was Joe who ventured to speak first. 'You were saying about Michaela?'

'I, what—?' said Kit, and then, 'Oh, yes. No, never mind.'

'Tell me.'

Kit, who was tired, hungry, over-warm and over-weary, and assailed by cares that she felt were beyond her, found that a moment for which she had been dangerously preparing herself had arrived. 'Who was Dean Purcell referring to,' she looked, just for a second, straight at Joe, 'when he said to you about a quality-goods blonde? She was "quality goods", was his phrase. He wanted to know what had happened to her. Michaela made me ask you,' said Kit, 'I mean, she thinks—'

'Ask what you like,' said Joe, 'but ask me because it's you who wants the answer.'

'Yes.'

'The "quality-goods blonde"?' He pondered the phrase. 'Clare, was she called? Clare. Yes. I had a date with her—must have been about a week before I met you. Dean cycled past us on Broad Street, saw us together and winked. She was—you know—blonde. I don't think she noticed. Why would she notice?—a person like Dean? She was very uptight. Humpty and I couldn't decide whether she meant a word she said. She taught art history somewhere or other. I don't think she liked me all that much. But I doubt she'd have let it show if she was upset, I have to say.'

'She what?'

'Like you do.'

'Oh. Thanks.'

'You give away more of yourself than you realise.'

'Not usually, I don't think.'

'I'll take that as a compliment, then.'

'Maybe it just means you're incredibly annoying?' said Kit.

'Listen,' he said, 'if you're going down this road, the person you should be asking about is Evalina.'

'Who could dance superbly on a brick?'

He was amused by the speed with which she made this rejoinder. 'I nearly married her,' he said. 'Or rather, I refused, in the end. We broke up because she wanted to have children. She was—is, older than me. She's the most selfish person I've ever held on a dance floor. She's from Chicago. She isn't here any more.'

He stopped talking as Graham swayed back into their

orbit. 'Who's up for another one?' he asked, leaning breathily over the table.

Joe began to fish for his wallet.

'No, no, no,' said Graham exhibiting the heaviness of a person who's determined not to be resisted.

'Why don't I at least go up and get them?' said Kit. She accepted without demur the note that Graham pressed into her hand.

'Same again all round?' she said.

Kit stood, confused, at the bar. She felt as though she'd just lost her grip on something. But what? Here she was, up at the bar, the quality-goods blonde, that bugbear, cast aside in a couple of sentences—and Evalina: *phut*. Nervously, Kit thought to herself, it's just me and Joe now. That's what it is. It's between him and me, now. It's all on me.

'You still with us?' said the barman. 'There you are, love.'

'Oh. Thanks.' Kit, thinking that it was she who was dancing on a brick, gathered up the drinks and revolved slowly on one foot.

'I was just telling Joe, here,' said Graham, 'thanks, wonderful, mmm—yes, thinking of investing in the double-handle toilet tank. Man of the moment, me.' Kit sat back down, exchanging glances with Joe.

'Thank you,' said Joe to Graham.

'It's *no more* complicated,' said Graham, 'than the concept of a *hot* tap and a *cold* tap. Complex? I don't think so. One handle's a semi-flush—peeing, in other words—other one gives you the full cistern, say no more. Water savings, meters, of course, more and more prevalent. Make a tidy packet off it, I'm thinking. Neglection of green investments is bloody foolish—you just can't deny it. Look at the weather we've been having. And there's corners of this market the lightliest regulated you can imagine, given the bandwagon effect.'

'I went to London today to do a research thing,' said Kit, 'the Public Record Office, Graham. Honestly, you know what? The girls' loos, they have these circular mirrors over each sink, and they're put on the walls so low down that if you're standing normally, me, I could just about see the bottom edge of my chin. Perhaps they were installed by little Polish people, I don't know. I mean, I may not be Rapunzel or Cinderella, but it comes off a bit pro-dwarf that someone my height, in a government building, should be beheaded by the public lavatory system. Hey, Graham,' said Kit, 'suppose you had to pay to have certain conversations, would you stump up a quid to be able to discuss the weather?'

'Touché,' he replied; and then, addressing himself to Joe, said, 'Kid sisters, born to put you down. Oh, what?' he jerked back to Kit, '—what, buy conversations at the supermarket, you saying? Two for the price of one? Buy "New Labour and Tory: what's the difference?"—and get a free go at "If there's another interest rate rise, I may end up defaulting on the mortgage"—?'

Joe dipped his head very slightly.

'That's it,' said Kit, 'except, I think if you wanted to have a *really* boring conversation—would it be cheap because it was so boring, or would that make it an indulgence, such that it needed to be extra expensive?'

'Oh, boring, it ought to be expensive, definitely,' said Graham.

'So, a conversation about the weather in England—'

'Luxury item. Cellophane and ribbons.' He took a deep breath, and said, 'If you'd shelled out big time for a conversation about the weather, you'd want to *save it up for a rainy day*.'

He was so pleased with himself that Kit clapped, which made him want to bow. He put his empty glass down on the table with the care due a full one, then tilted over his own belly.

'Oh yes, sorry,' said Kit. She pushed a few coins across at him. 'I forgot. I had to put the change in my pocket so I could carry the glasses. Sorry.'

'We're all right,' said Graham, refusing the money. 'What's a few pence?' he said. 'We're all right—about things like that.' There was a slight hiatus before he said, 'So, what's up with you two? I have to get in the old look-out-for-your-little-sister bit, right?'

'Graham,' said Kit in flattening tones. She didn't want Joe to have to sit through any more of this.

'Here's a lad all shaven and shorn, that loves the maiden all forlorn?' said Graham.

'Please, please, please,' said Kit, holding her hands up. 'Apart from anything else, and it's a big *apart*, I am no way forlorn.'

'Raise a glass to that,' said Graham, and did so, to find it empty.

'I think we need to be off,' said Joe, looking to Kit for agreement.

She immediately stood up. 'Are you going to be okay?' she asked Graham.

'Only going to Botley,' he said, staring at them both. 'I'm staying with Henry. Jump on a bus.'

'Why don't I call him and ask him to pick you up?' said Kit. 'You have his number, right?'

'Not to worry.' He made a feeble attempt to stand.

Joe said to Kit, nodding at her for emphasis, 'Sit back down a minute, stay here. I'll go outside and call a cab. Kit and I need to go out to Botley anyway, Graham. We'll all go. We'll drop you off.'

Graham grunted.

'You can catch all the buses you like in the morning,' said Joe.

'Shaven and shorn,' said Graham. 'Just take a piss.' And he raised himself, this time successfully, to his feet.

At Henry's house, all three of them got out of the cab together.

'Striking moon, look at that,' said Graham; for there it was still, magnificently huge and clear.

As Joe leant back in through the passenger window to pay, Graham added, in a hushed voice, 'You okay really, Birdy?'

'Yes, yes,' she said, his coins stowed in her pocket.

'You'd think he was a hard nut from the look of him,' he said in a whisper.

'I know, but he's—I'm fine, Graham, I promise you,' said Kit.

Graham turned round to Joe. 'Look me up sometime,' he said. He scanned through his wallet, evidently wanting to hand over his card; but, much as he searched, he couldn't find one. 'Oh,' he said. 'Anyway,' he said, 'any questions about seed crushing, I'm your man. Want to come in and say hello to Henry?'

'I think not,' said Kit, and she hugged her woebegone seed-crusher connection. He felt squashy and comfortable, he was wonderful and tall, and in their own funny way, they did love each other. Ah well.

Joe and Kit set off along the street; Graham, within seconds, gone.

Kit sighed enormously. 'Thank you for being so nice.'

'Like I said before, I'm well practised in the wayward-brothers department, as you have too much reason to know. Anyway, there's something endearing about him.'

'I can tell you exactly what it is.'

'Yes?'

'It's the play between him recognising and not quite accepting that he's a failure, as he understands it.'

'Is it? I don't know. Perhaps that's what you like about me. Don't worry,' he said, as she responded to this remark with alarm. 'Anyway, I liked him.'

'I know. All the same—I can't believe just when we're shot of your zonko brother we get stuck with my rambling, half-drunk half-brother instead. You don't mind me saying that do you?' she asked.

'It's okay.' Joe smiled. 'It was a revelation, *Birdy*—with the radio-aerial legs.'

'It's different though, you know?—because Graham and I have very little to do with each other. I mean, I don't feel responsible for him, is what I mean; not like you and Humpty. I mean, I would if he fell over in front of me, but I don't just worry about him, generally speaking. Normally his main topic of conversation is about various meals he can remember having eaten since the last time you met. I guess actually I do worry about him from time to time, but what I'm saying is, I don't do anything about it.'

'That's the position, at my weakest, that I'd like to be able to take with Humpty.'

'Weakest or strongest?'

'Ah.' Joe brooded over her question, then said, 'You know, I do find myself thinking that it's only for my own sake, now, that I care much about whether Humpty's coping or not.'

'Really? That doesn't strike me as true.'

'No, I used to care about him in a different way. My—I don't know—my selfless concern for him, if I ever had any, has slowly been worn away.'

'You have to look out for yourself, too,' she said. What else was she to say? 'Hey,' she continued, mentally changing tack, 'I'm sorry Graham didn't ask you one single thing about yourself. Maybe he had fog-bound sex on some balcony last night and it left his brains frizzled.'

'That was so cold, out in the damp like that,' said Joe.

'Well, it was; but wasn't it also—' Kit couldn't finish her sentence.

'You were inspired,' said Joe, 'by my inspiring balcony?'

She pulled a pious expression. 'It was pretty good, by my standards. Although I admit that using the word "standards" in this context might be pitching it rather high. Oh God.' She didn't want to pursue this. 'Outside—' she said, 'doesn't it make you wonder why you ever do it inside? Do you know what I mean?'

'Sure,' he said.

'I love wood smoke,' she said.

'Is that what it was? You were certainly different.'

'So were you.'

He laughed. 'I wasn't worried the whole time you were going to jump up like a startled horse and run away.'

'A what?'

'That may not be such a good way of putting it,' he said. 'It's all right. What were you expecting? You're a funny person, you know. You—' he stuttered a second.

Kit's thoughts went aslant, to *The Soiled Dove* and the Honourable Plaistow Cunninghame—to how he had found Laura Merrivale more and more unappealing, the happier she'd become. 'You don't find inexperience attractive though, do you?' she asked quietly.

Joe smiled round at her with his eyes. 'Not so much that I'd miss it when it was gone. Please,' he said, 'don't look so troubled.'

Meta Cherry, Kit thought.

'Just—don't run away like a startled horse, that's all,' said Joe.

'Where are we going?' she asked.

He was guiding her in the opposite direction from town.

'I want to pick up Humpty's car. It's a few streets this way.'

'Oh. I thought you were just saying about coming to Botley because you were worried about Graham. I thought you were making it up.'

'No. I credit your brother with being able to handle a drunken cab ride on his own.'

'I have to say,' said Kit, 'I can't think when he last talked about himself in front of me in quite such an open way, even if I couldn't understand it. Usually he plays everybody's uncle kind of thing, or at least a not-so-gloomy bon viveur. I don't usually see him just on our own, you know? It's usually family, kind of thing. Didn't you think there seemed to be something pretty wrong? Could you tell? I don't know if I should say something to Saskia. What can I do, though? I wonder whether—his mother died last year, not nicely either, I believe, wasn't found for several days, and without them ever having been reconciled, her and Graham, I mean. Honestly, he's a sweetie pie really. He'd help anybody. If he met the Queen, he'd try and help.'

'Yes, he told me he could get me in on this double-flush loo cistern thing.'

'Don't, for goodness' sake.'

'I wasn't planning to.'

'It's bound to be a con. And anyway, they already exist, for God's sake. Michaela's a fan.'

'He didn't say they didn't exist. He said there'd be a market of millions while everyone converted.'

'That's what I mean, though. He'd say the same thing to the Queen, "Tip me the wink and I'll get you in on green cisterns".' Kit sighed again.

'Who's Saskia? His wife?'

'Yes. You know, they're my people, but they're people who—they have these little bookcases along their landings, but none inside the rooms.'

'Do you have any idea what your face looks like when you say that?'

'Sorry. Yes, at least they *have* books. Saskia's from Holland. Isn't Graham the type of person you can exactly imagine marrying a foreigner? She's tiny. She always gives me these completely enormous garments for Christmas, like I'm a *Guinness Book of World Records* giant. I slightly dread it every year. To her I'm completely vast, even though I'm actually,' Kit pulled her stomach in, 'reasonably slim. Once, she gave me these American pyjamas with a pair of bottoms that were so loose around the waist that even with elastic they fell off me straight onto the floor. And they had this label in them that said, "One size fits most".'

'I like the sound of them,' said Joe.

'They were flannel with bluebirds on,' said Kit, with much disdain.

'Here it is,' Joe said, of a small and dented car. 'I stole it about three months ago.'

'Really?'

'I got in a panic, thought Humpty was going to end up killing himself, let alone anyone else, so I lifted his keys one evening and parked it where he wouldn't find it. Every couple of weeks I move it from one out-of-the-way street to another so it doesn't get reported.'

'Hasn't Humpty reported it himself?'

'He's not exactly tight with the police,' said Joe, opening the tin-pot doors.

They dropped down onto the punctured seats. It was miserably chilly inside and smelled of mould.

'Joe,' said Kit, as the engine finally took. He seemed to have gone into a dream. 'Joe, you know in the movies,' she said, 'where an important character gets in a cab, hands the driver wads of dollars and says, "Just drive".'

'Yes. Usually a yellow cab in New York.'

'Exactly. Do you think we could do that for a little while? I love going in cars. I know it's arctic—'

'I've put the heater on—' he said.

'—and it's a waste of petrol and will increase our carbon footprint by several sizes and contribute to destroying the planet—'

'Put that way, how can I refuse?'

'—but it would be so lovely just to sit back and prowl along the streets going nowhere special, just for a little while.'

'You aren't starving?'

'I am, but I don't care. Are you?'

'I can survive.'

'Is that okay then?'

'Yes, if it's what you'd like. My pleasure.'

'Thank you.'

He turned right and drove out onto the ring road, and they drifted around the city in silence, occasionally overtaking a crawling lorry. A couple of times, on a gear shift, the engine made a guttering sound, at which Joe swore. But apart from that, neither of them spoke.

They did an entire circuit like this, mainly sticking to the slow lane. Only when they reached the north side of town for the second time did he ask, 'Enough?'

'Yes. Thank you.'

He took the exit ramp and began to head back into Oxford. 'So, Charles Field's notes,' said Joe, breaking in on Kit's empty-headedness, 'what exactly's the plan now with the Grimwood question? You have anywhere else new to go with *Oliver Twist*, or are all avenues exhausted?'

'Probably,' said Kit in a small voice.

He glanced sideways at her. 'I do agree with you that it's a lot of similarities,' he said, 'although, back then, how different were two violent prostitute-murders going to be?'

'Yes, but Eliza's murder wasn't some regulation, ten-a-penny type affair,' said Kit, pulling herself together—not that there was any point them discussing it if all they were going to do was repeat themselves. 'I told you, it registered in the public consciousness as so extreme that when a *Telegraph* journalist tried to explain the Ripper killings *half a century* later, it was Eliza's murder he came up with by way of comparison.' Kit crossed her arms and looked out of the side window at the straggling periphery of the city, annoyed when Joe seemed to reply with a noise part way between a hum and a cough.

'What?' she said.

He frowned.

'What?' she said again, impatiently.

'Kit?'

'Yes?'

He hesitated, evidently trying to work something out before he spoke, then cursed under his breath as they were forced to slow to meet the tail end of the stalled inbound traffic.

'*What*?' said Kit.

'All right, don't bite my head off. You said Dickens wrote *Oliver Twist*—started it in—started it when?'

He shifted down through the unreliable gears.

'February, 1837.'

'And Eliza was killed?'

'May.'

'May, 1838?'

'May 26th, 1838. That's correct.'

'Okay. And Dickens wrote the book in instalments, but, you said, didn't plan it out well in advance, right?' They were categorically in a jam now, shunting a few metres at a time.

'Well done,' said Kit sarcastically, 'you were really paying attention.' Then she clasped her forehead with both hands and whispered, 'Oh God, oh God. Joe! Dear God.'

'Right, good,' he said, allowing himself to sound pleased. 'So tell me, when was *Oliver Twist* completed, the writing of it?'

'I'm so stupid, I'm not sure,' said Kit. She lowered her hands again, but with her fists clenched tight. 'But I—it must have been—latish in 1838? But, yes, when did Dickens actually compose Nancy's death scene? Not before May, surely? Shit. How on earth can I not have—'

'Hey,' said Joe, 'it happens. Don't worry. What we do know is that the murder is near the end of the book, yes?'

Kit shook her head distractedly and whispered, 'Fuck.'

'Any time,' replied Joe, in a comically debonair voice. The traffic mysteriously eased and they speeded up again.

'I'm crazy,' Kit said. 'I mean, God, Joe, I wonder. This way round it would all make sense, wouldn't it? I mean, wouldn't it explain everything? If *Dickens* copied from *Eliza*—

you're saying—if he wrote Nancy's murder after Eliza—*after-wards*, then for starters, none of the coincidences have to be coincidences any more: they'd be on purpose. Oh, wow.'

'Yes, while the slight differences would probably make sense as adjustments to fit with the novel's pre-existing plot.'

'Exactly. Although, I mean, if Dickens based Nancy's death on Eliza's, pretty much right after it happened, what a grue-some thing to do. Fucking hell. But at the same time—how can I not have seen this? If you're right—but you *must* be.' Kit thumped her legs with her fists. 'If you're right, Joe, then it has to be admitted that Eliza's death would have been like a gift to Dickens, or at any rate, extraordinarily perfect for his needs.'

'That is a bit disturbing.'

'Yes. Because, by the summer of 1838, he's already estab-lished Sikes as a robber, pimp and insanely violent bully, with a room he shares with his benighted prostitute girl-friend, who's afraid of being killed. All that would be there already. Then once Eliza has been done in—if this chronology's right—well, Dickens would find himself provided with just an amazing template for how his own set-up might play out in real life.'

'What's more,' said Joe, 'unless the dates prove not to fit, but as you've inadvertently been indicating all this time, it would seem he really followed the details incredibly closely.'

'You're telling me. I mean, a half-dressed girl on her knees—Nancy starts her death scene half dressed in bed, and so did Eliza, exactly the same—defence wounds, implicitly Eliza begged for mercy, possible self-sacrifice before the man she loved, because her silence implied not wanting him to be caught. Exactly that happens with Nancy. Eliza had her knees "crouched" under her, fell over backwards, Nancy the same. The rug: Sikes throws it over the corpse then plucks it off again because it's worse to imagine than to see. And Hubbard gave evidence that it was he who pulled the bedding back off Eliza's corpse. And there's this shocking moment at the inquest where they describe the police—it was the police who pulled up the blinds to let the dawn sun in on the scene. What does Dickens do? He has this great play on the light, with Sikes sitting there until the sun rises, and its beams bounce off the pools of blood on the floor.'

'Even Bull's-eye's bloody feet,' said Joe, 'if Dickens read that letter in *The Times* about Eliza's dog—'

'Yes, yes, Dickens ninety-nine per cent certainly would have seen that. And, what do you know? He has a dog in his story already; so, fine, *his* dog can positively wade through the stuff and get its feet completely drenched. And Joe,' said Kit urgently, 'everything I told you before about Hubbard going off his head, the unburied corpse putrefying, and him escaping a vengeful mob out of a window at the back of the prison—wouldn't it figure if Dickens riffed off all of that for Sikes: why don't they bury that ugly thing? Honestly,' she cried, hunching forwards into her seat belt, 'how can I not have seen this? How can I have gone at it backwards all this time? I was *so* close. I'm so *stupid*.'

'Don't do yourself down, please, that's ridiculous,' said Joe. 'You're the one who refused to give up on it all. You just went all the way to London because it was still bothering you.'

'Speaking of—' Kit shook herself. She put a hand to

the clock on the dashboard. 'Joe, would you mind terribly if—'

'Not at all.'

'I—haven't said what, yet.'

'I know.' He grinned. 'It doesn't matter. The answer is, "not at all".'

'It's just, if we were to drive straight on into town,' she said, 'my college is still open, our library I mean; we could make it with about—probably, twenty minutes to spare? I could smuggle you in and we could quickly check *Oliver Twist*'s publication history, plus look at Dickens's letters?—try, if at all possible, to pin down the dates? I have to know, Joe. I won't be able to sleep, otherwise. I can't stand it. Obviously, if there was a single sentence anywhere in which Dickens connected Nancy to Eliza, it would have been noticed. But we might find something, some tiny, overlooked detail, and we should certainly be able to find out if the chronology works. You must be exhausted, and I've completely screwed up your evening, but would you mind?'

'Oh, I'll cope,' he said, 'You haven't screwed up my evening, and at this point I'd like to know, myself. We'll find somewhere to dump the car and run.'

In town, Joe found legal parking, by a miracle, and though they didn't run, they did walk extremely fast, their spirits high.

'Thank God for Graham's crisps,' he said. 'Why haven't you fainted?'

'I haven't felt like it,' replied Kit flippantly.

When they got to her college, she took him by the hand and drew him in, waving at the porter on duty. They stepped lightly round the first quad and she put her key-card through the swiper at the bottom of the library staircase, causing the mechanism on the old oak door to click, so that she was able to push it open.

'Magic,' said Kit.

They crept up the ancient stairs to the rows of ancient, carved bookcases. 'Lucky what we want's the most basic stuff imaginable,' she whispered, taking Joe to the literature section. There were various other students in there, papers spread far and wide across the pews and tables where they were settled.

Kit pulled an annotated copy of *Twist* off the shelves, which she slung in front of Joe, then took the earliest volume of Dickens's letters for herself.

'That's it?' he said.

In reply, she hissed, 'Go!'

So there they sat, opposite each other along a narrow table, in concentrated silence, reading against the clock.

Joe flicked back and forth between various notes and appendices to the novel. Kit scrambled through clumps of pages in the large tome in front of her. She felt sick with anticipation, and her fingers trembled as she hunted.

With five minutes to go, she sat back, slowly raising her eyes to meet Joe's steady gaze.

'Yes?' she whispered.

'You first,' he said.

She smiled rapturously at him. 'I've *got* it. You, too?' Her hands were freely shaking now, rather as they had that morning, except with excitement. 'Between the letters and the footnotes, it's pretty much all here,' she said.

'Tell me.'

'Well,' she breathed, 'the actual first publication date of Nancy's death scene was November 9th, 1838. You have that as well? *After* Eliza: that's definitive. But listen to this, Joe. Back in March of that year, Dickens sent a letter to this guy called Frederick Yates about an unauthorised stage version of the novel. It was the first play version anybody attempted to mount, and the instalments were only half way through, so obviously the people staging it needed to come up with a conclusion to the plot. So Dickens writes to Yates and says that, hey, there's no fear they will somehow reveal the correct ending, because—listen to what he says, Joe, late March, 1838,' Kit opened the volume at the relevant page, 'he says, "I am quite satisfied that nobody can have heard what I mean to do with the different characters in the end, inasmuch as at present I don't quite know, myself".'

'Excellent.'

'Yes,' she whispered, 'yes, in March, Dickens had been publishing instalments for a year, but he hadn't yet quite figured out everyone's ending. Then, as we know, two months later, on the night of May 26th, Eliza is killed. Now, bear in mind that the inquest and investigation and so on were being reported in the press on an almost daily basis for at least the following month. I can tell you in parenthesis, for example, that *The Times* had a report near the end of June that Hubbard's brother had just auctioned off the complete contents of the house in Waterloo, including Eliza's blood-stained bed sheets.'

'That's nasty.'

'I know,' murmured Kit, 'although typical for the times.

Anyway, blow me down, on July 10th,' she flipped through the book to the second page she needed, 'i.e., a couple of weeks after *that*, what did Dickens write to his publisher, Richard Bentley? I should mention that they were hoping at this point to have Dickens finish the manuscript by September, so the pressure was really on.' Kit looked positively beatific at what she had to say next. 'So, yes, July 10th, Dickens writes to say, look, don't worry about *Oliver Twist* any more, because, basically *at last*, I guess, "I have planned the tale to the close". Yes? Meaning, before Eliza's murder Dickens hadn't planned out the characters' endings, but right afterwards, he had. 15th July, he started to work on the last third of the novel. And on—' she turned the book's pages, '2nd October, he tells a friend he's finally done it and killed Nancy. Quoting exactly: "Nancy is no more."'

Joe leant across the table and solemnly shook Kit's hand.

'It works *beautifully*,' he said. 'You know how old he was then, Dickens, in October, 1838? He was twenty-six.'

'Nearly as old as you,' replied Kit, grinning. She kept Joe's hand in her own, and remained like that for a few moments as she quietly enjoyed the triumph of these discoveries.

'It really does all fit,' she said, sitting back again. She was barely bothering to whisper any more. It was time to go, anyway. 'N.B., Dickens, across his career, caused grave offence by copying real people into his books. What I mean is, he does have form in this respect. Looking at it dispassionately,' she said, 'everything we've put together may not constitute hard proof—' the lights blinked on and off; Kit released Joe's hand and they stood up to join the select and motley procession of students being forced to leave—'but if you accept that Dickens would have known about Eliza's death when it happened, probably in considerable and even minute detail; and bearing in mind the enormous number of points at which the real murder and the written one intersect; and given, too, that we now know that he hadn't planned his characters' endings before Eliza's killing, but had within *two weeks* of her story running its course in the press—how easy would it be to defend him *against* the charge that he was copying from life? And the answer to that, friends, is, I just don't see a convincing defence.'

They stepped into the night air of the quad.

'I agree that this would seem to qualify as beyond all reasonable doubt.'

'Yes, or put another way,' said Kit, slinging her bag over her shoulder, 'suppose merely that Dickens wanted to avoid all possibility that his writing might seem to echo Eliza's murder, was he not unbelievably careless?'

'No shit.'

'You know what,' she said—she was suddenly thinking of the dance club, of the first time she'd gone, before Joe had introduced himself to her at the bus stop—'the inquest accounts of Eliza dead in her bedroom, that gives her in what one might call "ghost position". That's what Charles Field was faced with; but no matter how hard he tried, he couldn't place the other body back into this scene, her partner, the figure of the murderer. Dickens, though, picturing the same scene, could. And—that's what he decided to do. Let's get out of here,' said Kit. So they did.

They left the car where it was and walked all the way back to Joe's place. 'I'll shift it in the morning,' he said. He took

Kit's hand as they tramped the frosty pavements, then tucked it, with his own, into his coat pocket.

'Do starlings migrate?' she asked.

'Yes.'

'I never thought of that before.'

'Picture starlings as classy little Russians who like to come to England for a visit.'

'Mid-sized Russian passerines.'

'I knew there was a reason I liked you.'

'Not that I'm brilliant in bed?'

'You don't know how hopeful I am.'

She half smiled, half didn't; let the comment—much though she had solicited it—slip away.

'Starlings come to boring old England from Russia,' said Joe, 'the same way an English person might go and visit boring old Holland.'

'Please just don't ever say that to Saskia,' said Kit.

'Oh, excuse me.'

'Not at all. *I'm* not from Holland. You can say what you like to me. After all, Saskia gives me bluebird pyjamas that fall off on the floor.'

'I still think they sound great.'

As they walked up the stairs to Joe's flat, Kit's stomach audibly growled, so that they both laughed.

'Let me put the heating on,' said Joe, unlocking the door. 'Oh yes,' he said, distracted. He gestured at a large brown envelope on the chair by the coats. 'Buddy asked me to give you that.'

'What is it? It's—?'

'I assume it's his war letters.'

'Oh piss. He remembered.'

'He said, "Now you're chums with someone who appreciates history, Joe—"'

'Yes, I see.'

'And, yes, he's coming to tea next Friday. I said I'd ask you.'

'Gee thanks. No but seriously, I accept.'

'Is that all right?'

'Yes. Anything you like. You don't think I owe you—both? Yes!'

'I said four o'clockish, if that's good. Thank you.' Joe helped Kit off with her coat.

'Don't thank me. I'll be here. Joe?'

He was hanging up his own coat over hers, but turned back because of a tremor in her voice.

And Kit—Kit? She felt a terrible shock of desire, was overwhelmed, slightly lifted one hand towards him, tried to speak but couldn't, tried to breathe, stretched her quivering hand out further and—

Key in the door, Humpty came in, sauntered in, '—had some message, but when he saw it was me—told me to tell you he'd tell you another time, yes? I think he's gone off me, old Buddykins. Oh. Hello, Kit. You look ill.'

It was the second time Kit had seen Joe flinch. With difficulty, he dredged up a response. 'He's probably gone off you because you threw up on his landing.'

Humpty shrugged. 'In my world,' he said, 'everyone's vomiting something.'

The three of them stood in uncomfortable proximity, Kit and Joe effectively barring Humpty's way.

'Cup of tea?' said Joe mockingly.

'No thanks.'

'Actually, I might go,' said Kit. She stooped to pick up Buddy's envelope.

'Oh, come on,' said Humpty. 'Don't run away. I'm not going to be sick on *you*. I have got headlice, though; had a date with a girl from up the U-Bend, single mother. Hey, Joe, I did what you said, pastures new, and now I've got fucking headlice. I keep seeing lone magpies,' he said, 'even in Milan, through gritted fucks.' He slung his coat across the hall chair. 'The magpie, it's this shitty bird that goes about by itself of—of its normal processes, is it? Or, they usually go in pairs? The odds are stacked in your favour or not, for seeing *two* of them, I mean? Magpies. So I keep seeing "one for sorrow", I'm completely screwed? Or, what, the odds are against me anyway?'

'Pass,' said Joe.

Humpty wiped his nose on the back of his hand, then took a deep breath. 'Are magpies these, you know, evil, lonely little shits, or what?' he asked, sounding, now, agitated. 'I'm saying, the odds are stacked against? Or you see just one and you're *really* really screwed, because the magpie normally never flies alone?'

'Humpty,' said Joe, flattening himself against the wall, 'enough, all right? Enough. Go in the kitchen. I'll fix you up something to eat, you can tell me about Milan.'

'This is serious orthin—this—a serious *orth*inologi—Joe, you know what they're on about down The Forfeit?'

'No.'

'Oil Man's Finger Bingo.' Humpty laughed emptily, and

then hissed the answer a second time, '*Oil Man's Finger Bingo*. I hear you were down there with some tall old git?'

Joe turned to Kit, his face closed and angry. She had extracted her coat and was already putting it back on again.

'Yes, well, see you,' she said, giving Humpty a formulaic wave as, ushered out by his brother, she left the flat.

'He's back,' she whispered on the stairs.

'Kit,' said Joe, also quietly, 'we should—this is too much. I thought he was back tomorrow. I'm sorry I haven't fed you.'

'No less I haven't fed you,' she replied.

'No, but I'm sorry. He's not in a good way. They treat him like a mascot, Dean, their tame nutter. But something's going on—Milan. I don't know. I'm so sick of it,' he said, 'so sick of it. I worry he's going to get himself killed, and then I dream about killing him myself.' They reached the front door. Joe leant against the wall, the force seeping out of him, and shut his eyes, pale and disturbed. 'A bottle factory isn't going to do it,' he said, not unkindly, 'but,' his eyes flew open again, 'I've got to get him out of here. I don't know what else to do. I can't just wish this away.'

'It isn't only drugs?' said Kit at a venture.

Joe made a gesture as though he hardly knew where to begin.

'We have friends, back home, my family knows a family where the son is—Graham knows them better than I do, Anthony. I mean, he's done time in prison under the Mental Health Act, or, I don't know how it works but, I do have a small idea how draining it is for everyone else if—'

Joe said, 'Yes. That's okay. That's fine.'

'I didn't mean to—' Kit searched for how to express

herself, 'compare or anything, whether Humpty is, as it were—I mean, I'm just saying because of what you said.'

'Go ahead.'

'No, that was all.'

'Kit,' said Joe, 'I'd like to see more of you.'

In an attempt to lift his mood, she replied saucily, 'I thought you'd seen pretty much everything already.'

'I'm absolutely certain I haven't,' he said.

There was the sound of a crash upstairs.

'I guess I'd better be off.'

Joe took hold of her and kissed her goodbye as though this might be the last time, so hard she almost struggled against it, the side of her lip made sore.

And indeed, as she stepped out over the threshold into the ever-colder night, away from all the turmoil of his house, she felt she could as well have been boarding a train for Baden-Baden, or Moscow, or Finisterre.

'In here,' Michaela yelled. 'You didn't stay over—again?'

Kit pictured herself filling up the bucket from the housekeeping cupboard with icy water and pouring it on Michaela's head. She stood, tensed, in the kitchen doorway. 'So what?' she said, her teeth clenched tightly together.

'Nothing to say to each other?' said Michaela.

Kit rubbed her arms, trying to warm herself up. 'He was unavoidably detained,' she remarked blackly.

'Right, right,' said Michaela, 'his brother. I know, you told me. But it's crap. I'm sure it's crap.'

'Is that so?' said Kit. 'You just know it?'

'It's *so* so,' said Michaela, with a toss of the hair.

'So-so?'

'No, it's so "so". It so is *so.*'

'I mean, if you don't talk English, I can't understand you.'

'Go stuff yourself then,' said Michaela. 'But, Kit, look, listen to yer old mucker, please, okay? I mean, God, if I looked like you, fuck me, I'd *use* it. And you knock around with these people like you're a—Kit, why do you think you like him, seriously? Why?—*because he makes out like he likes you.* I'm not saying it's the worst thing ever. Lots of people behave like that, especially girls, I hate to say. All right. But if that's what it is, then the issue becomes, *why* does he like you, and how much really? Are you listening to me? Because, without wishing to be truly offensive, I can tell that he's taking you for a ride. How much do you really know about him?'

'Like what?'

'You see?' said Michaela, jabbing at the table. 'That answers my question *right there*. What, he's the strong, silent type, you're going to say? Man of mystery crap bollocks?'

'Honestly, Michaela—'

'Because, pardon me, but did you know he's leaving?'

'What do you mean?'

'Oxford.'

'What?'

'You heard. He's leaving.'

Kit, without having any reason to, immediately believed this. 'No he isn't,' she said.

'I think you'll find he is. I asked a friend about him in the maths department. He said, "Oh yes, I know Joe Leppard. He's quitting at Christmas. He's been poached to work on this government project thing. It's all happened last minute and now they're having to find someone to step into his shoes".'

'That can't be right,' said Kit.

'Just listen,' said Michaela. 'Listen to me, Kit. Live-and-learn only works if you don't end up in the bloody gutter. I bet—I mean, I bet you aren't the only girl he has on the go. He's not that special or anything, but I *just bet*. When they don't say much, you make it all up for them. I know this. I know a piss artist when I see one. You don't believe me, but the good-looking ones are—they're—Kit, men are *twats*,' said Michaela, weeping, 'they're *cunts*,' she said—she cried, 'Have you *still* not figured it out that I'm fucking *pregnant?*'

CHAPTER 7

'By whom?'

'An irrelevance, she says.'

'Maybe to her.' Joe unwrapped a Battenberg cake from the Co-op. 'He is the father.'

'Of a teaspoonful of ashes, it'll be, soon enough, I'm afraid.' Kit sighed, pulled a chair out and sat down at Joe's kitchen table. 'In all the time I've known her, she's—well, it doesn't matter. But, Joe, she's asked me if I'll go with her next week to some clinic in London, next Friday, in fact. I feel quite ill about it, but she's several weeks gone already. She could go longer, but yuk, it's all so unpleasant. I was reading this thing just the other day about subsequent prematurity, amongst mothers who abort?'

Joe, laying out the tea things, glanced at Kit from time to time as she spoke. When she had arrived at his door, the sight of him, his presence, had made her blush, and he had leant round carefully and kissed her on the cheek.

'I think it's because I'm not really a close friend of hers. I mean I sort of am, but not really; or by circumstances more, which in a way is more like family, isn't it, who you're stuck with?' Kit began to play with the knife Joe had placed by her tea plate. 'Of course, she and I do have a bit of history now, or witness, I suppose; but what I mean is, because I'm not tied into her social loop, I think that's why it's me she's asked, basically—so the whole thing can just go away when it's over. No one she seriously cares about will know, sort of thing. Frankly, I can't think of anything I'd like to do less, especially on a Friday, you know? And she acted like I should have worked it all out already. But how could I? She's not sticking out or anything. God, Joe,' Kit put the knife back down, 'I promised her I wouldn't tell anyone and now I've just gone and told it all to you, oh dear. What am I doing?'

'Come on,' he said, 'I don't count. Who am I going to tell? You haven't told anyone else, have you?'

'No, no. God, no. No, and I wouldn't have told you unless I trusted you, I just—trusted you without stopping to think about it. Thank you, by the way. I know this is completely unimportant by comparison, but the business of her picking on me all the time, what I told you last week, I'm guessing now, well—that I was simply the most convenient person she could get cross with, so to speak.'

'Doesn't she have a boyfriend, in the Amazon, you said?'

'I know, I know. I said to her, "What about Greg?" And she said, "Greg? Who cares? I thought you didn't believe in him, anyway. And anyway, he's probably having it away with some kind of tropical rainforest gorilla". And she said— about the putative father, the father not-to-be, in case you're interested—she said that although he's beneath contempt, well, guess what, she despises him massively anyway.'

Joe grimaced.

'But this *morning*,' Kit couldn't keep the sorrow out of her voice, 'this morning, after all, she said she wasn't so sure what she was doing. All week we've been having these dreadful breakfasts and she suddenly said she wasn't quite sure she'd made up her mind to do it, and I said, she must just let me know, I would drop anything if she needed me. And she just said, "Well, mustn't grumble." Mustn't grumble! So I don't really know what's going on at this point. You know, she talks about population control, for environmental reasons. She says, "Tell me where's the cake for the Third World: this is a nation of seventy million Marie Antoinettes." And then—'

Kit trailed away, remembering a conversation she'd had with Michaela the previous Tuesday evening; not a conversation so much as a one-sided outburst, during which Kit had started to wonder whether she perhaps had a duty to intervene—though how?—because Michaela had said, 'Listen to me,' increasingly desperate, 'you don't understand, I went in with my sister when she had her baby. Her husband was still in Germany. The whole thing was *sick*. Honest to goodness, she screamed so much she was hoarse for three days, and after the actual birth I had to go out and get her cough syrup and pad things and crap knows, things for leaking breasts, and she'd got torn down there, ripped up, and, and—he came out early so she hadn't got all the stuff she needed, she'd been so laid-back about it. That's why Andrew was in Germany, because the baby wasn't due for three more weeks. So I went to the shops and everywhere was packed. And the whole time, that afternoon, it was like nowhere was the same place it was before, and I had this—this horrendous vision that every person in the crowd had, themselves, also been through this absolute horror of being *born*, and that, give or take a bit of medication, all of them, every single human being pressing in on me, each one of them had started their life in the beginning with their mother screaming and screaming like it's the end of the entire world. I saw all these people with their mothers' screams attached to them, I can't explain it, like the most horrendous horror movie ever made. I mean,' Michaela had started trembling, 'isn't it wrong?—that we can go around and *do* this insane thing?—of making other human beings, from scratch? Don't you think? Honestly? Because I think it's appalling. We're all appalling. Everyone's *appalling*.'

'Are you all right?' said Joe. He sat down opposite Kit.

'Sorry,' she said. She blinked. 'I was just—it's so dark already. I don't like it when the clocks go back. It's November, I can't believe it. Joe,' Kit needlessly cleared her throat, 'you said last week that you wanted to talk to me about something. I mean, did we have that conversation?'

'No rush,' he said. 'It can wait.'

Kit's heart sank. Had Michaela been right? Was he really leaving town: *The End?* Farr, Christine Iris, she said to herself, has this *everything* been, after all, so very little?

With difficulty, she focused on the moment, tea, Buddy—food arranged on the table, cake, biscuits: ten to four.

'Have you got round to telling your tutor, finally, about the Eliza stuff?' said Joe.

'No, not yet, no. I haven't seen him.' She could have stopped right there. Joe was trying to distract her, she felt sure. She did stop, mournfully, but then started again. 'There is a sting in the tail to that whole story.'

'That I don't know about?'

'You, my dear?' she said, putting on a funny voice. 'You know nothing.'

'So tell me.'

She glanced up at him. He smiled back. Life was so stupid, she thought. 'It's, yes—well.' Yes, well. 'Joe,' she said, 'you really want me to blab on?'

'Hard to say. Does this instalment involve dismal deeds, dramatic upsets, disaster and death?'

'As it happens,' she replied, 'yes.'

'Well then, go right ahead.'

She couldn't help a very small smile of her own. 'Okay. Well, in brief, you know there were loads of unsanctioned stage adaptations of *Oliver Twist*, during when it was coming out and everything—remember me saying?'

'Yes.'

'I'm not sure the exact timetable, but did I mention that it didn't take long for all dramatic versions to be banned by the Lord Chamberlain because of the violent effect on the audiences of Nancy's death scene?'

'No.'

'Well, they were; the plays were banned, even though the killing scene was usually done offstage, as far as I can tell, every surviving script I can lay my hands on. The audiences still got madly worked-up about it, so that was that: no more stage versions. And by the way, Dickens was infuriated by these adaptations. But nevertheless— and this is the thing—it's as though the idea of doing Nancy's murder as a performance got somehow lodged in his soul. Because, if you fast forward a couple of decades, by the early 1860s Dickens had come up with this idea of

233

making masses of money by giving live readings in theatres of the most affecting scenes from his novels, and he particularly wanted to do Sikes murdering Nancy. His friends went to enormous lengths to persuade him it was just too dreadful, and he mustn't.'

'I can imagine.'

'And for about five years, *five years*, they succeeded. But the compulsion was too much for him. He was overtaken by it, and he *did* come to enact the scene—though it was billed as a reading, presumably to accommodate the fact that acting it was still illegal—in the end, he did it, on the public stage, repeatedly. And the consequence was shock on the part of his audiences, plus a devastating toll on his health. His stage script is actually worse than the original book version, and you have to consider that he was playing both Sikes and Nancy somehow, he was kind of killing himself. Forgive me, but since you asked, I have to read you out this thing.'

Joe laughed, gratified to have got her going.

So be it, she thought. She looked through her bag for her notebook with growing panic. 'I can't find—oh God—'

'Try your jacket pocket,' he said.

And there it was.

Kit blew out slowly. 'What would I have done if—'

'I don't like to think.'

'Fine.' She was thumbing through the pages. 'But, oh yes, listen to this. This is another thing. Here's a typical 1838 review of the novel: "We have but one objection to urge against the whole—that it introduces us to a description of life which, however faithfully portrayed, is indescribably repulsive and demoralising." That was standard, even if—' Kit ran a finger down to the bottom of the page, 'even if Queen Victoria found it "excessively interesting", so she said. But what was Dickens's answer to this objection? The thing is, he believed that what was truly immoral was people of the sniffy persuasion *failing* to acknowledge that these lives of repulsive deprivation underpinned their own social order. Where has Buddy got off to, do you think?'

'He'll be here in a minute.'

'I'll stop if he arrives.'

'Don't worry.'

'Well,' she turned a few pages, 'what I meant to read you wasn't that, it was this contemporary description of Dickens's performance, listen: "Gradually warming with excitement he flung aside his book and acted the scene", wait, yes, here, "shrieked the terrified pleadings of the girl, growled the brutal savagery of the murderer". And I mean, Dickens added in gestures, right? "The raised hands, the bent-back head—" Why did it enthral him to such an extent? While he was on tour, he wrote jokingly to people like Wilkie Collins that he was going to "murder Nancy" again in the evening; or to another friend, "I commit my murder again on Tuesday, the 2nd of March". Other times he'd say things along the lines of, you know, tonight, once again, I'm going to be killed by Mr Sikes. He said it both ways. And he was so frenziedly convincing that he felt hated by his audiences, like—yes, here, "it is quite a new sensation to be execrated with that unanimity". He'd be plunged into terrible glooms afterwards, which could last for hours, feeling as though he might be about to be arrested. On top of which, the effect on his health of repeatedly pulling this off was so severe that he had to have a doctor on hand for every performance. He would swoon away and have to be revived before he could continue the show. People begged him to stop. His mate Forster wrote that doing Sikes and Nancy "exacted the most terrible physical exertion from him", and even Dickens admitted that he was tearing himself to pieces. And in the end, the day did come when he was so shattered by it, he had to quit half way through his latest run of shows, greatly against his will—a few weeks after which, when he was still in a desperate state and unable to recover, he had a violent fit and shortly afterwards died.'

'He died?'

'Yes. Fancy that, right?'

'He *died?*'

'Yes. That's how Dickens died, aged fifty-eight. One report says that two days beforehand he was found wandering round his garden by himself, yet again acting out Sikes killing Nancy. And a lot of the people who were closest to him ascribed his death, the single most important cause, to his insisting on performing the murder. Wilkie Collins apparently said it contributed more to killing Dickens than all his other work added together. So,' Kit closed her notebook, 'so this, my friend, this is the sting in the tail. If you accept the theory that Dickens was given courage by Eliza Grimwood's murder to construct an uncannily similar and equally horrific death for Nancy—that, far from gracelessly chucking a spot of grotesque melodrama into a poorly thought-out plot, he was in fact moved to lift the event near-wholesale from the lives of the very people whose degradation he was at pains to invoke—if you accept this, if you accept that the real killing in any degree whatsoever inspired the extremity of the written one, then by extension, Eliza's unknown murderer can be understood to have had a hand in the death of Dickens himself.'

'That's a pretty startling conclusion,' said Joe.

'Thanks. Did I make sense?'

'Yes.'

'Thank you.'

'Please tell me you're going to run this past your tutor eventually?'

'Oh sure,' she said, 'when I've hammered out a few more of the details.'

'What about Orson? You could impress him with a potted version, surely?'

Kit was touched by the concern Joe seemed to be expressing. 'Orson?' she replied. 'Didn't I say? No, sorry. It's so weird, it's as though he never really existed. But he's gone, back to the States. The course director rang me up. I couldn't tell if it was Orson's health or someone in his family or what, but he's gone. And we still had over fifty quid's worth of tutorials lined up, which is extremely sad. You're reminding me I should email him and find out if he's okay. I was meaning to. I've been so busy. I felt bad for a couple of days thinking about when he tried to talk to me and how I pretty much ran away. But oh well, what do I know? Not a lot. And the real reason I haven't emailed him is that I embarrassingly haven't yet read his manuscript, although where was I supposed to find the time? I worked out, if it's two minutes per page, it would take me *twenty hours* to get through it. Isn't that exactly the sort of reading one ought to do in a café? I had this thought recently, that the feel of any given city is going to be determined for an individual largely by the quality of its strangers, don't you think? I mean, presumably wherever you go you'll make a few friends, quite possibly not unlike yourself. But it's the people you don't know who give you—' There was a knock at the door.

Joe rose to his feet, and said, with a touch of anxiety, 'You do remember Buddy will probably be imagining you've had a chance to check out this diary of his, or whatever it is?'

Buddy looked crushed in the bright lights of the kitchen.

'Do you think we need to get the chimneys swept?' Joe asked him. 'I laid a fire a couple of days ago, then wasn't sure I dared light it.'

'I remember last time they swept the chimneys here,' said Buddy, 'thirty, forty-odd rooks showed up. Set up a right old rumpus.'

'When was that?'

'A while back. Ten years?'

'Ah.'

'The downpipe from the gutter's loose by my bathroom,' said Buddy. 'I'd fix it, but I'm getting a bit past it these days.'

'You're hardly past it,' said Joe; and then, to Kit, 'Buddy's a pillar of the bowls club on the Marston Ferry Road.'

'Oh, a toothpick,' said Buddy, tucking himself in at the table. 'No, it's a shame you have to be *old* when you're old.'

'Maybe tomorrow or Sunday I can look at it for you?'

said Joe. He boiled the kettle and they helped themselves to the good food he'd spread out on the table.

Kit kept quiet as their conversation turned to Frank, his virtues, and, tenderly, his failings; to building management; to the French people downstairs.

'And another thing: he couldn't write, you know,' said Buddy, interrupting himself.

'Really?'

'Illiterate. It's more common than you think. Didn't mean he was any less than he was.' He turned to Kit, visibly connecting one thought to another. 'You've not had a pop at my letters, then?'

At Joe's suddenly controlled expression, Kit allowed herself a smile. 'They're—' she grinned at them both, 'Buddy, what can I say? They're absolutely fascinating.'

Joe's shoulders dropped with relief.

Kit pulled a naughty face at him. 'They're amazing,' she said. 'I read them last night till three o'clock in the morning. I haven't quite finished them yet, but blimey.'

'Bloody unbelievable what they went through,' said Buddy gruffly.

'I know,' she replied.

Joe glanced from Buddy to Kit and back. 'This is—the First World War?' he asked.

'Yes, the Macedonian Front,' said Kit, 'push to retake Serbia, defeat the Bulgarians, or "Bulgars" as they said back then; win over the Greeks, whose king was vacillating and probably servicing the Germans and so on. As for the people down in Salonika, fat lot of help, knifed the British soldiers who went in with money for supplies. But the fighting conditions, God, were unbelievably bad—dreadful: typhoid, dysentery, sand flies, poisonous snakes, malignant malaria, heat so intense they could barely move. And then in the winters it was wolves, floods, boils, trench foot, and such cold that some nights half their horses would freeze to death.' Kit made a gesture to Buddy, a motion asking him if he wished to take over the talking. But he preferred to hear someone else explain; basked, really, in Kit's outpouring. And so, for his pleasure, she continued.

'—and he's very surprising about Christianity,' she said, after a while. 'He says it's pure bunk to call the average Tommy a Christian. He says, they're the best men in the world, immensely tough and uncomplaining, but also completely immoral, in that in their death throes they were most likely to ask him not for spiritual solace but for a cigarette. He gets quite depressed about this and says, "I hate the Anglicans", even though he is one; and that the funeral service in the *Book of Common Prayer* just doesn't begin to serve when you're in a mud slide on the side of a mountain burying a man who has a wife and five children at home, and whose intestines have just been ripped to pieces because a bullet happened to hit his ammunition pouch. Added to which, worse than that, the—' Kit halted because Joe's mobile was ringing in his pocket.

He pulled it out, listened to a voice that sounded to be apologising, and then spoke simply to confirm a plan, it seemed, that had just been proposed to him.

Buddy and Kit sat in silence, the mood at the table deteriorating fast as, for all his intentness, Joe grew palpably distressed.

'Shit,' he muttered as he rang off. 'Buddy,' he leant over and patted the old man's arm, 'I'm so sorry, but Humpty's—'

'Right you are,' said Buddy.

'You two please carry on.' Joe got up from the table and started to walk towards his bedroom.

'Time I was off anyway,' said Buddy. 'Oh, Joe?' Buddy swallowed down the rest of his cup of tea. Kit could see that Joe was frustrated by this—he was trying to get out of there. 'Could you,' Buddy rested his cup neatly beside his plate, 'lend me a couple of matches?'

'Not a problem.' Joe stalked back over to a drawer and got out a multipack of matchboxes. 'Help yourself.'

'I can just—I only need—'

'Please, take a box, Buddy, or, just do what you like.' Joe went out of the kitchen.

Buddy, raising his voice, called, 'Right-o, I owe you a box of matches, then.' He sniffed. 'Lower than the lizards,' he said. 'I've no time for that lad any more, none. Joe's too soft on him. Other night, he was sick outside my door. I heard this commotion, thought we were being burgled. And it's not just drink,' he said. 'He's all right, but he's not right up here. He's a bit touched, in old money.' He tapped the matchbox against his skull.

'Humpty? I know,' said Kit.

'Joe's a wonderful boy, but, saying that, he's too good to him. It won't do in the end. Tell you what, though, put Humpty in the army, that'd soon sort him out.' Buddy stood up at last, 'I'll be off then. Nice talking to you. Regards to Joe. Keep the letters as long as you want.'

Kit was almost amused by the crazy idea of sticking Humpty in uniform. 'We'll have the other half of our conversation soon, yes?' she said. 'I'd love to finish reading these. Apart from anything else, I now feel like I need to make it to the end of the war.'

Buddy gave a deep nod, then shuffled off. He was more crumpled-seeming even than he had been when he arrived.

'Gone?' said Joe, walking back in as the front door clicked shut—like stage comedy, Kit thought, standing up herself.

'Yes, just,' she said.

'Kit, I'm sorry, but I think I'm going to have to jump on my bike, go looking.'

'For Humpty? Where?' she said. 'Should I come? I mean, can I meet you somewhere?'

'You don't have to,' he said. 'If you'd prefer to keep out of it, I understand. It's not going to be any fun. That was Pauly. I—I don't know what to say.'

'Where will you look?'

Joe stepped out into the hallway. 'He thinks I may find him at The Chequers, in Jericho? Apparently it's been mentioned. I don't know, but I'm going to go and see. You know it?'

Kit nodded. 'Can you tell me what this is about?' she asked, unable to help herself; but at Joe's reaction, she said, 'No, no, sorry. That's okay. You just go.'

'By the way,' he said in a different voice, 'you'd read masses,' pulling on his coat and glancing brightly at her.

'I didn't want to let you down.' She twinkled back at him. 'Besides, they were genuinely interesting. I'm sorry if I went on a bit. You know, you always could have stopped me.' She put a hand to the wall, and watched as Joe checked through his pockets to see he had everything he needed.

'Well,' he replied, only partly concentrating now, 'I'm sure you made Buddy's day—week, probably. Month.'

'A pleasure,' said Kit, 'and since you'd invited him anyway—'

'Ah, but no,' Joe stooped to tuck his trouser leg into his sock, 'the truth is, he invited us first, but I told him to come upstairs. If you go to tea with Buddy it all tastes of washing-up liquid.' Joe opened the flat door, then lingered to look at Kit again, until she felt unequal to his gaze.

'He invited me too?' she said.

'He did.'

'Is that a, more or less,' she stepped forwards, 'I don't know why I care, but, a back-handed—blessing?'

'I dare say.'

'You go. I just need the loo. And then I'll probably follow along to The Chequers?'

'You don't have to, Kit, Christ knows.'

Again straying onto thin ice, she said, 'Your hand—'

'I don't intend to use it for dastardly purposes.' He took a piece of junk mail off the hall chair, pulled a pen out of his coat pocket and scribbled down his mobile number, it looked like. 'If I'm not there, call me. I have no idea where I'll try after that.'

'You go,' she said. 'That's fine. Don't mind me.'

And so he went, and Kit was left standing all alone.

She recognised no one at The Chequers, close to full as it was. Joe must have been and gone again. On her walk over there, Kit had been forced by a couple sharing an umbrella to edge into a bush that overhung a fence, so that her right sleeve was now sodden. She tried to shiver off the chilly drizzle that had fallen relentlessly the whole way. After a moment's pause to take stock, she went up to the bar and bought herself a half, then sat at the only free table, small and clunky—it had three stools ranged round it in a manner to suggest that they had only just been vacated. Lucky to get a table. Joe had told her to phone him, but what if he was caught up in a—what, an *incident*?

She was too late: she had arrived too late. She decided to drink her drink and simply calm down for a minute. The two people nearest her, women, were catching up on news of a sister, a grandchild; news of work. One of them was a cleaner.

'Does your mum—she still go to the bingo, then?'

'She's got this ulcer on her leg, so it's been a couple of months.'

'How old is she?'

'Yes—she's eighty-five.'

'Denny still living with her?'

'That's right.'

A young man walked past and swiped one of Kit's spare stools. Useless to protest, and who could say she needed it?

'—holiday in three years. Weekends, though. September, Mary stopped in with her.'

Why did I come here, anyway? Kit thought. Why, through the rain and the cold? She pushed her wet hair back, drank fast and kept looking at the door, until a second young man asked about the remaining free stool. 'You wanting this?'

To answer 'no' would constitute a—'Would you be wanting this?' he repeated—sad admission, Kit felt. In reply, therefore, she stood up, attempting to look haughty, and headed for the door, and would have walked right out, except that as she reached it, one of the barmen came in from outside—blundered in, blocking her way as he said loudly, though not shouting, just loudly, 'Man down, boss. I don't know if you want to call—I think—might—' Kit was already an obstacle to—'want to fetch—' people who were trying to cram past her the other way, round her and the barman and out.

She unlodged herself and went in their train: what a day, what was she being caught up in now?—all of them, her included, making for the alley to the side of the pub; she, in the tail end—had been leaving anyway. The rain was worse. Kit, at the back, caught just in time a glimpse, through the upright bodies ahead of her, of a single figure dropping, smeared with blood, gobs of it, red on a white shirt, dropping defencelessly to the ground; heard, in a moment of common arrest, so it seemed, the sickeningly soft thud as it hit the wet tarmac. A second man was being dragged away backwards from the blow he had just delivered, the scarlet on his fists diluting in the rain; against his will he was being dragged back struggling and yelling, 'Bastard', and, 'You fucking wait', over the noise—Kit turned—of a van door being slid open. She watched as he was bundled in, sandwiched between the driver and another man who climbed in after him. He grinned and made a telephone sign through the windscreen to someone still on the pavement, *call me*—before being driven, with a gratuitous wheel screech, away.

A latecomer jostled Kit against the young man in front of her—'Sorry,' she murmured—who wiped the wet off his face and remarked, 'He's a dog's back leg, that one.'

'A what?' she said.

'Shouldn't have stood back up again. Should have stayed down,' he said. 'A total fucking cock-up, less muscles than a fart.'

Kit looked along the street and jumped—and felt a wish to protest her innocence—as she saw Joe swerve up on his bike. He flung it aside, scattering a puddle, and pushed through the small crowd to the front. The mass murmuring of interest and derision dimmed a little and then revived. How, Kit thought desperately, could it not have occurred to her, not have occurred to her, not have struck her, she had been so sure she was too late—how could she—fool, *fool*, and *three*, and *four*—not have seen, understood, that the young man laid out in the alley was—it *was*—she bent down, looked through an assembly of knees at the blood-stained figure, registered the dark, curly hair, a useless hand: Humpty.

She stood up again in slow motion, feeling old, with vomit rising in her throat, gazed blankly at the assorted watchers, and became aware of an impulse to explain to them that she belonged to this scene. Another murmur arose. In Joe's wake swung a sinister and hideous, caramel-coloured Rover. It floated forth out of the rain, rumbling like a pleasure boat, with Donald at the helm. His off-white eyeballs swivelled as he drove the vehicle by inches down the alley, causing the crowd to swear in annoyance as it was forced to shunt those self-same inches this way and that, reforming itself into a differently shaped blot.

Two young men stooped to help Joe shift Humpty's resist-less carcass onto the plasticated back seat of the car. There was wet and blood everywhere. Kit pushed forwards, opened the front passenger door and bent in. Donald, chatting on his mobile, nodded at her to take the seat beside him. 'Ta, bye,' he said and dropped the phone into his lap, before asking cheerily, 'All right back there?' checking Humpty in the rear-view mirror. 'Got caught with the wrong girl— finally,' he said to Kit, patting his phone. 'She got done first, had her arm broken. Not sure about this one,' he indicated Humpty, 'what a fucking nutcase. I tell you what, though, she had it coming, always fooling around, trying to get blokes interested. We was at school together,' he said.

Joe walked round the car and got into the back beside Humpty. Before he had even closed his door, Donald had begun to reverse, on a curve so that he could swing out into the street, swearing, 'Fuck, fuck, fuck', as his rear bumper grazed a bollard. Someone, perhaps warningly, hit the front passenger window with the side of their fist. 'Fuck!' said Donald again, and then, '*What?*'—because Humpty was hissing, 'Wind scream, wi-wind—' He gathered himself, 'Wind *screen* wipers,' and then his head sagged down and his eyes drifted. Joe slung an arm across him to stop him falling off the seat.

Donald flicked on the wipers. The rain seemed even heavier once you were out of it.

'Better?' he said.

Joe said, 'He gets sick if he can't see out.'

'You think he's going to throw up, you shove his head out the window, all right?' said Donald. 'I'm telling you now. You know he took a pop at Neil yesterday? Smacked him. He's off his head, I'm telling you.'

At last they got out clear into the street, and away.

They drove for quarter of an hour without speaking, but only when they had slipped through the Link Road junction and were cruising past the Marston Ferry Bowls Club did Kit allow herself, by a small margin, to relax.

She angled round in her seat to look back properly at Humpty. He was a wreck of blood and dirt, on his face, his jacket and shirt front, in his hair. She felt as though the opposite of the truth was true, and that she somehow meant it when the words came quietly out of her, 'They were not unkind to the parts they liked'—his fine, bloodied face, curls soaked with blood, his eyes deranged, his white, filthy shirt front.

Donald said, 'Anyway, whatever they done he's probably be safer off if they *did* brain damage him, this one, to tell you the truth, if it shuts him up. Can't keep his bloody mouth shut.'

He shot a glance at Kit.

'Fair do's,' he said. He pulled a cassette out of the glove compartment, Andy Williams, and slotted it into the car's ancient tape player. The music started up midway through a track, 'Moon River', the slushy orchestral backing making Kit want to titter.

She sobered again fast, though. Donald's driving was extremely poor, especially given the rain, and he most certainly wasn't sober. It occurred to her that they might be—not just Humpty, but all of them—about to die, who could say? She didn't protest because she didn't feel like protesting. She slouched down, tipped her head back and allowed herself to enjoy, for the second time in as many weeks, the simple business of being in a car. Andy Williams, she found herself reflecting, was probably dead already.

'Look,' said Donald, jamming his left arm sideways so that his elbow brushed her nose, 'look—' the vision now behind them, 'there,' he pointed backwards, 'bloke with a fox on a lead.'

'Where?'

'Back there.'

Where? Kit pulled herself straight again and looked, bewildered, out of the window.

'Ah, there you go,' said Donald. 'Sharp eyes see, blind eyes see nothing.' And he clicked his tongue softly twice.

Joe got out of the car into the rain without a word and went over to a selection of wheelchairs, misassembled like used shopping trolleys under the A&E portico. The downpour was relentless, beating noisily down on the roof of the car.

How on earth do I come to be *here*? Kit thought, surprised after the fact at how events had overtaken her. She had been musing on the fate of Joe's bicycle, abandoned at the pub; had been fretting, too, at the idea that the barman might unnecessarily have summoned an ambulance. She had also been concerned by Donald saying that he didn't want vomit in the car, because—'There's blood all over the back,' she said to him, as though the person slumped there was gone.

But blood, it seemed, was in a different category to vomit.

'No problem,' said Donald. He was still gripping the steering wheel. He looked like a coin-operated driver waiting for coins. 'This car—my mum lost a baby on the back seat once, down Cowley Shale.'

Kit had a spasmodic thought about—that she must try to be a better friend to Michaela, because—but she couldn't stay with it: Donald was getting out, pulling his collar up against the rain, helping Joe manhandle Humpty into a rackety, collapsible wheelchair.

'All right then, mate?' said Donald, almost shouting.

Humpty didn't respond. Joe began, in cumbersome fashion, to push the wheelchair single-handed, holding Humpty round the shoulders with his other arm to stop him tumbling out again. Kit stepped out into the wet herself, and followed, uselessly offering her assistance. Two paramedics walked past them, overtaking them without interest.

'I'll be off then,' said Donald.

Kit turned, hand raised in acknowledgement, but found that he already had his back to them.

She ran the couple of steps to catch up with Joe, confused that he hadn't thanked Donald for driving them there. 'Do you think he had something to do with it?' she asked breathlessly.

'You don't get,' said Joe.

'Get what?'

They passed over the threshold of A&E, and shook themselves, dripping into a density of warmth. They were inside.

'Kit—'

'What?' she said.

'He—' Joe dropped his voice to a whisper, sounding more upset than she'd ever heard him—'it's worse than you realise.'

*

250

Joe dealt with reception. Kit instinctively hung back, hot and dazed—found herself staring at a door marked 'Dirty Utility: No Unauthorised Access'. She snapped to only when Joe and Humpty were led off to a small, three-walled cubicle. She trailed after them as they made their ungainly way past a woman who, leaning at an angle against a counter, appeared to be weeping. Her dud orange hair, which hung across her face and hands, had evidently had its true colour sluiced out with peroxide. Kit hovered, then asked, 'Are you all right?'

Through hair and hands, not to mention snot like water, the woman snarled back, '*Yes?*'

After a shortish wait a nurse arrived, or at least a man dressed in a light blue, easy-wash uniform. Kit stood a few steps outside the cubicle, feeling disengaged.

'I'm afraid he's a bit of a mess,' Joe said.

The man pulled a face, as to say, 'you're telling me'.

A bit of a mess, thought Kit. Humpty's a bit of a mess. He's a bit of a mess. The hospital smell was in her throat. She put a hand out to steady herself against the corridor wall, remembered doing this at Joe's place, realised that she must—must, if for no other—to stop herself fainting, didn't want—

She succeeded in keeping herself present. The nurse pulled on exam gloves, latex free, dragged from a dispenser, then bent forwards to speak to Humpty. 'Hello? I'm Saleem? Hello? Humty? Hello, good sir. I want you to answer couple of questions, okay? Do you know where you are—as of now?'

Humpty muttered unintelligibly.

'Do you know what day it is?

Another noise, still unintelligible, but different.

'Do you know who is prime minister, Humty?'

Kit thought: *the state funeral for the prime minister's legs*.

Saleem looked up at her. He had been making notes in biro on his exam glove, in the triangle between his thumb and first finger. 'Next question,' he said to Kit, who steeled herself, 'should be, "Prime minister any good?"' After a tight, luminous smile, he reverted to his job, checking blood pressure, pulse, temperature.

'We'll get him a bed in a minute, okay?—have him checked. I'm not hundred per cent worried, but quite rightly to come in, okay?'

Kit tipped forwards to filch a peep at the grades of consciousness listed on the form Saleem had been completing, which went from 'alert', through 'drowsy', through 'acutely agitated and confused', to 'responds only to pain'. Humpty scored as 'drowsy', qualified by, 'responds to voice'. What kind of a response, though?

'All right, mister, we got you,' said Saleem. 'Hang in there. We'll get you sorted soon as we can.'

'Thanks,' said Joe, though barely sounding as though he meant it.

It felt like a long time before they were taken, by a different nurse, in a darker uniform, to a new cubicle, which had a concertinaed front curtain, a sink and a trolley bed.

Kit stood just inside this retreat and abandoned herself to information overload: clocks, security camera warnings, LCD screen, pin boards, white boards, scribbled multi-coloured acronyms, plastic phials, plastic aprons, plastic disposal bags, cardboard sick bowls, contaminated sharps incinerator buckets, pulse rates, respiratory rates, urine output, blood pressure, wrist bands, next of kin, shouting, questions, history, belongings disclaimer—in case of loss or damage—wires, electrics, blinks, beeps, laughter, vilely heated odours, alcohol wash, pink spray, disinfectant, stasis.

Joe had taken the sole chair at Humpty's bedside. Kit, stuck on her feet, pictured herself collapsing through one of the concertina curtains opposite into somebody else's disaster. She was still on the edge of the dizzy symptoms of brain slippage, so she moved right into the bay and sat down abruptly on the floor, back against the sink unit.

A small woman with pigtails strolled in, looked at Humpty's notes, sized up the tableau, addressed herself to Kit, 'Girlfriend?'

Kit felt flummoxed. It wasn't a word she ever applied to herself.

'I'm his brother,' said Joe.

The woman switched all her attention his way. 'Name?'

'Joe,' said Joe. 'Oh, Humpty? Yes, sorry, he's called Edward. Humpty, usually.' He made a throw-away movement with his hand. 'When he was little he was fat.'

The woman leant over Humpty's bloodied form and shouted, 'Humpty, how you doing?'

He emitted a fraction of a whimper.

'Do you know what happened to you?' she asked loudly.

No response.

'Do you know where you are, Humpty?'

'He isn't really—' Joe didn't find the words.

The woman shone a torch into Humpty's eyes, said, 'One minute,' and walked out again.

'All the king's horses,' said Kit, licking the salty sweat from her upper lip.

'And all the king's men,' replied Joe, not bothering to look over at her. 'All the king's horses *and* all the king's men. And if only they'd remembered the legless dog that's strapped to a rollerskate. All the king's horses, all the king's men,' he said bleakly, 'and the fucking dog that's strapped to a fucking rollerskate.'

'You say that,' said Kit from her place down on the floor, 'but, realistically, the *horses?* Granted, the dog; but—that well-known egg-reconstruction specialist, the horse? Come on, give me a break.'

Humpty draped a hand over the side of the bed and groaned.

'All the king's nurses,' said Joe.

Time sagged as they waited. 'What about the girl?' Kit asked, breaking their silence. She couldn't, from her present vantage point, see anything much of Humpty, or much more of Joe than his feet.

'Not our problem,' said Joe's voice.

'Donald said her arm got broken.'

'Yes.'

'Might she be in here somewhere, in Minor Injuries or something?'

'No, she's not here.'

'For definite?'

'She's been taken down to Kent.'

'Kent?'

'Kit—' Joe's disembodied voice became edgy, 'she's not

our problem, okay? What do you want? You want the police involved? It's not that sort of situation.' He stopped, then added bitingly, 'But of course, you're party to all this now, aren't you, assault. Perhaps you'd like to go to the police yourself?' He paused. '*No?* Because you might want to consider,' he did now tilt forwards in such a way as to be able to look at her, 'if you're worried about justice being served, here it is: served. You may find it a little unsophisticated,' how unkind he sounded, 'but it's done now. As for the girl, fuck her,' he sat back again, 'she's her own problem. Anything we could conceivably do would only—' the woman with pigtails returned, 'make things worse,' Joe finished quietly.

'Right,' said the woman, 'sorry about that. Start again. I'm Dr Curtis.' She closed the curtain fully, so that for the first time they were cocooned in their own little pool of penetrating light.

'Get you a chair in a minute,' she said brusquely to Kit. She took a long draw of breath and turned to Joe. 'Okay, so what's happened here?'

He stood up, and with concentrated inattentiveness, replied, 'I gather he fell off a ladder.'

So conspicuous was the lack of any reaction to this absurdity, that he was drawn into adding, 'Onto irregularly positioned cobble stones.'

'This being Oxford, after all?' Dr Curtis put a sour drag on her words.

'Exactly.'

'Only human in history to break his fall with his knuckles?'

'He's a one-off,' said Joe, now matching the tone she had adopted.

Dr Curtis shook her head and bent to check Humpty's hands more closely—moved his legs and arms one by one, then said, as though to herself, 'Alcohol'—it wasn't a question—'plus?'

'Plus I don't know,' said Joe, 'but pretty certainly, yes. Working assumption: yes.'

Despite her demeanour, Dr Curtis was impressively gentle as she undid Humpty's upper clothing. She looked him over, tapped his chest, listened to it with her stethoscope.

'So,' she said, straightening up again after getting her results, 'he managed to fall on the left and the right of his ribcage both at once?'

'That's correct.'

'See it happen?' she asked, flinging a glance down at Kit. Joe looked at Kit also, who shook her head.

'No,' said Joe.

Kit, now she was part of it, climbed to her feet.

'He may have broken one,' said Dr Curtis, gliding a finger along Humpty's bruised ribs. 'Help me get his trousers off then,' she said.

She and Joe did this together. Kit gazed with calm curiosity at the pitifully lean white body laid out before her.

'Managed to protect his privates anyway,' said Dr Curtis bluntly, before pulling up the light bedding. 'I don't like rowdy boys,' she murmured, but very much as though she didn't hate them either. 'Don't think we're going to get urine right now,' she said. She unhitched Humpty's notes from the wall; began to add notes, and to stick on little stickers. Then she took blood into a set of phials with different coloured lids.

At this, Kit felt herself sway. To her the scene wasn't

registering precisely as an examination in a bay in A&E. In her general state of faintness the light was too sparkly, even as her vision was blacking at the edges. The picture before her seemed more akin to a photograph on the move than to life—was more like an uncertain photograph showing a doctor, a battered boy and his brother; their exchanges an ungraspable caption that would be cut later, presumably, and replaced with something pithy, like, 'Friday, First Fight of the Evening'.

'Well,' said Dr Curtis, once more flitting her fingers over Humpty's bruised frame, 'he'll be in the queue for an X-ray. Not too bad so far,' she checked the time on her watch. 'Shouldn't be that long. You all right?' she asked Joe. He had Humpty's blood lightly spattered across him.

'Yes, thank you.'

'Do I remember you?' she asked.

'Yes.'

'Thought so. Wasn't that long back?'

'Not that long. July.'

'Okay. You want to step outside here with me?'

Joe nodded grimly, then pointed Kit to the chair, before walking out. She lifted a hand to wipe the sweat from her forehead, and was about to walk round the bed and sit down, when the curtain twitched aside again and Dr Curtis stuck her head back in. She indicated the sink and the paper towel dispenser, and said, 'You might want to clean some the blood off of his face. Use gloves.'

She disappeared again before Kit could ask anything, or protest, or simply mention that she was feeling sick.

*

The blood was remarkably difficult to lift if there was any thought of being careful. Kit took off her coat and jumper and rested them on the back of the chair. It was unbearably hot. She pulled the chair to the top of the bed and tried to do the job sitting down, but this felt as unnatural to her as sitting down to iron would have, or to wash up saucepans. After a false start, she decided to try to loosen the blood by dripping water on first, which made the mess slippy, she found, and more offensive. It smelled disturbing, and this smell mixed horribly with the bleach-type odours coming off the floor and fixtures, let alone the medicated stink of the bedding.

Her timid but persistent efforts roused Humpty so far as to attempt her name.

'Yes?'

'Kid?'

'Yes?'

'Someby once said—' He failed mid-sentence.

'Somebody once said—yes? The Sandman? Who? Wee Willie Winkie, was it?'

'Edison,' said Humpty. He hadn't opened his eyes.

'Oh.'

Kit now had a map of the injuries to his face, and was steering around and between them with a clutch of sodden paper towels, creating a butcher's archipelago of the damage. The wounds weren't individually as extreme as Humpty's blood loss had, to her inexperienced eye, implied; but his saturated hair she didn't attempt to clean, and who could say what further damage lay there? She wondered whether the matted blood would suffocate his headlice. 'Said what?'

'What?'

'Edison, you said—said what?'

Humpty opened his eyes a slit and then closed them again, speaking effortfully. 'Once said—Edison, "I fear anything—"' he groaned again and shifted a little; Kit leant in to listen because his voice was sinking—'you and Joe,' he muttered, '"I fear anything, that works first time".' Without obvious emotion he began to cry, tears that, as they trickled down his temples, stained pink.

'But—' Kit was confused, 'I wouldn't exactly say, Joe and me—do we *work*? What does that mean? Did we work first time?'

'Yes,' mumbled Humpty, 'you didn't.'

What was he talking about? 'Hey,' she said, trying to push this snarl from her mind, 'hey, Humpty, "the state funeral for the prime minister's legs".'

'You can,' he whispered.

'What?'

'Come.'

'Really?'

'Welcome.'

'Really? You could have fooled me.'

'Yes,' he said, glancing at her again through slitted eyes, 'I could.'

Kit felt an unexpected press of tears herself, pitying her own disordered lightness.

She did the best job possible with his face, then stripped the disgusting gloves off her hands and disposed of all the waste as instructions instructed. Then she sat back down and considered again the uncared-for body before her.

Some minutes passed before it came to her to wonder exactly how hard it would be to cut off Humpty's head using a single-bladed, Spanish-style switch knife. Her resulting reverie absorbed her completely until Joe returned, looking haunted and desperate, followed by Dr Curtis, though they didn't appear to have come together. Kit remained fixed in the chair.

'I was just told by someone outside that you want to rule out a punctured lung?' said Joe. 'And any skull fractures?'

Dr Curtis stared hard at Humpty's notes again, speaking as she read, 'What it seems is that—yes. Although I doubt it.' She looked up. 'In regard to the pneumothorax—punctured lung—he'd likely be breathless and in a lot more pain; but given we don't know what he's been taking—'

'Dulling his reactions?'

'Exactly. We need to take a look, rule everything out. It's also a reason to keep him in overnight, to be honest, get his sats back to normal. I'm sure the registrar will agree when he sees him. Give him a couple of stitches, keep him under observation. All being well, he should be in a lot better state in the morning.'

'Right,' said Joe.

She put the notes back. 'So,' she said, 'shouldn't be too long before an X-ray. There's been an RTA on the ring road so there's a bit of a queue now. Should get the green light after that—bad way to put it, sorry.' She rubbed her forehead wearily, then left.

'Thank you.' Joe leant back against the partition wall and stared down at his brother.

At first it had been a relief to Kit that they'd been talking only about the architecture of Humpty's body; that he'd been being treated as possibly broken only in the straightforward sense of a cracked bottle, or a pencil snapped under heel—not that bottles and pencils could be mended. And Humpty's bones weren't dry but wet, Kit reflected; weren't white but red—at the thought of which, of slick, wet, live bones, her imagination seemed to dislocate further.

'Doesn't he look amazing,' she whispered, her vision still a little too bright.

Icily, Joe replied, 'You find this interesting? It entertains you?'

'No,' she exclaimed. 'No—no.'

'Because, you know what I think?' he said, his voice ragged, 'I think this is boring. I think it's extremely boring. This,' he pointed at Humpty, 'this is violence, Kit. *This* is what it looks like. And it doesn't entertain me at all. I'm exceptionally, profoundly and terminally *bored* by it.'

He stared towards her with exhausted eyes, and she saw that he, as she was, was tensed as for a blow.

'To real life,' she said, lofting an imaginary glass.

'My cup overfloweth,' he replied, very slightly tipping a glass of his own.

There was a fraught silence between them when in walked the registrar talking crisply of CT scans, chest X-rays, head trauma, intracranial bleeds—Kit, staring round dumbly at the man, couldn't take yet more visceral chit chat, couldn't stand it. She picked up her things and edged out of their bay, out of Majors, out down the corridor and away, any residual sense that she belonged to what had happened unravelling with every step.

She found a waiting room in a side area next to reception, and for the next twenty minutes sat there, as people do, and simply waited.

Then, with her dizziness adequately quelled, she stood up and left.

Kit hesitated under the A&E portico, staring round until she made out a bus stand beyond the car park, whereupon she took a deep, cold breath and walked out into the rain, over the black, twinkling tarmac, to the long rank of shelters. There were various timetables. She found the right one, read it, perched on a fold-out seat. She had just missed the buses that must have scooped up everyone else, but she found it pleasant to be out there alone in the night, only notionally in transit. The cold was a relief. Pretty quickly it made her feel a lot better, and it sharpened up her thoughts, too. She began in her mind to try to put together, out of all his bruised parts, not Humpty, but Joe.

What had he said going in? 'It's worse than you realise.' But he hadn't explained. Was she supposed to understand this now? He had looked so terribly lonely.

How long she attempted to think Joe through, she couldn't have said. It felt like a long time. But it was perhaps not so many minutes later that he appeared beside her, like a wraith.

'I've been sent away,' he said.

Kit mumbled a noise of sympathy.

'The registrar doesn't seem that worried, after all,' he said.

She nodded.

'They're going to keep him in, though.' He folded out the seat next to Kit's, and they sat there like that, silently, in the night.

In the end, a bus did come, but the driver turned the engine off. 'Five minutes,' he said, getting out to have a cigarette. He let them climb on board, the air inside in an instant disgustingly hot again. They sat near the back.

'If I hadn't found you, would you just have left on this bus without telling me?' Joe asked.

Kit looked down and shrugged. 'I gather you're leaving town,' she said. 'Were you just going to do that without telling me?'

Angrily, he asked, 'Where did you hear that?'

'Michaela.'

'Christ, I hate Oxford,' he said. 'I hate this place.'

'So it's true, is it?' She looked round at him. 'Is it? Since when did you know?'

'Kit—*Christ*,' he said. She looked back down again. '*Christ*, woman. You're asking the wrong question. You know that? What you should be asking is, "Joe, how come you've delayed deciding all this time, despite everthing?"' He gave a short, wincing laugh. '*You*, of all people.'

At a loss, she said, 'You haven't decided, then?'

'Not officially,' he replied, almost spitting. 'No. But since we're on the subject, allow me to inform you that I have to give them my answer by Monday.'

'Oh,' she said, her voice very small indeed.

A couple more people got on, followed by the driver. Joe went up and bought tickets. The bus pulled out and sped downhill. Kit stared at the spent raindrops as the wind propelled them sideways along the window panes. She felt light-headed and incapable. 'Was this what you wanted to talk about?' she asked. 'This was it?'

'I wanted to talk to you about Humpty.'

'Then, please do,' she said, 'anything. I'm listening.'

Joe spread his hands out over his knees. 'I don't know that there's much point.'

'No, please,' she said, 'please.'

'Kit,' he turned to her, turned away again, struggled with himself.

Hand hidden, Kit crossed her fingers. She continued to think, *please*, *please*, *please*, in silence.

'What you don't understand,' he burst out, then moderated the volume at which he was speaking, 'what you don't understand,' he said, 'is that he's not the same person he used to be.' There was another long pause before he could make himself continue. 'You know he read history here at Oxford?'

'Really? That's—'

'Until he got thrown out.'

'Okay.'

'Look, I'm explaining to you, all right? I'm explaining.'

'Yes.'

'Fine. He was thrown out, wandered around a bit, found himself a job as a kitchen porter at Christ Church for a while, eventually wound up in rehab in a place outside Chipping Norton, skimming over the details.'

'As a kitchen porter? That's pretty funny.'

'I know. He was a kitchen porter, then he lived on the scrounge for a while, had a job delivering the *Yellow Pages*. He knew where he could get food, a free bath, places to sleep. Anyway, after rehab the question was, what was he going to do now? We grew up outside Devizes. My father was an auctioneer, but in the end he got himself, in effect, blacklisted, so he claims, and was forced to quit.'

'By?'

'The Masons.'

'You're kidding. They can do that?'

'I don't know. That's his story, because he refused to join. Probably just an excuse. You may have deduced that I don't get on with my father. Anyway, after Devizes, Dad went in on an antiques dealership in a place outside York. So that's where they live now, my parents. But there was no way Humpty was going to agree to go up and live in Yorkshire. Meanwhile, I'd just got a job here, and it all seemed to make sense when Dad set up the flat as a property investment. Humpty started on a furniture-making course at the college in Headington; his choice, furniture, a brand-new start and so on, putting the past behind him; but also therapeutic in a way, you can imagine the rationale behind it.'

'Okay,' said Kit, not wanting Joe to stop.

'And, lo and behold, now my father had me and Humpty

living together, putting me in a position where I was forced to look after him. But that's another story,' he said, sounding bitter. 'Anyway, the furniture: it transpired he had a gift for it—*has*,' said Joe, militantly. 'I mean, we grew up around antiques, right? He'd been tinkering with that kind of work since he was a boy, so a lot of what he needed to know was second nature to him from the off, especially making the legs look right. My father has this saying that if you know what you're looking at, the wrong legs on a piece of furniture comes over just as wrong as badly shaped legs on a woman. So, yes, Humpty studied restoration techniques, went on, you know, got qualified over time, more qualified and then hyper-qualified—but then just hyper, because, while all this was happening, he fell in with this gang of lads he met initially through college and—it was okay at first, or at least, I didn't see how it was playing out. He got work. He became part of their thing, their set-up, and he was in work. But he also started getting back into drugs again, as was inevitable, you might say; Christ knows what, recreationally and all under control, he said, weekends, whatever came his way. But I had this sense after a while that they were actually encouraging him. That's what I couldn't understand, Kit. It even seemed that his boss was supplying him. Why, though? It didn't make sense. How good was his work going to be if he was out of it half the time? Anyway, three or four months ago he started sleeping in the work- shop most nights, not apparently eating. I haven't really been able to get through to him for a while now, haven't known who to turn to. I arranged minimally to meet him on Fridays, for fuck's sake, so I'd have some sense of how he was, and then I—'

Because Joe didn't continue, Kit said, 'You—?'

'You wanted me to explain?' he said, angry again. 'I'm *explaining*, okay? You want me to explain?'

'Yes. Sorry.'

'No, I'm sorry. Forgive me.' He took a deep breath. 'It's not you. I don't suppose you know anything about the antiques trade?'

'Not really, no.'

'The thing is,' he put a hand to his forehead, 'at the bottom end of it, the very lowest of the low, there are these scum who target old people, usually, the vulnerable, knock on their front doors, talk their way in, then con them into parting with their valuables for a fraction of what they're worth. They're known in the trade as "knockers".' Joe shook his head despairingly. 'Most antiques is a bit shady. I'd say ninety-nine per cent of it is lightweight fraud at a minimum.'

'Your father?'

'Oh, absolutely. Yes, a fine example. But I've been very stupid, really stupid. I didn't ask enough questions. In particular, I didn't realise that Humpty's lot was operating right at the bottom end of this scale. And even then, Kit, it would somehow be different if he was just in their workshop, stuck the far side of the U-Bend, tarting up dubious pieces of furniture.'

'I don't know where this U-Bend place is.'

'No, of course you don't. It's on one of the estates. But, Kit, what I've discovered—I didn't—it transpires that in return for supplying him with God alone knows what, Humpty's boss now has him out there, my brother, working as a knocker, essentially stealing from little old ladies. That's what he's been doing, my own brother. I can hardly express to you how utterly I despise even the thought of it. He says I'm ignorant and don't understand how the world works, but—fuck.'

'Why would they want Humpty, of all people, to do it?'

'Oh, because of the way he sounds, right? His accent? I mean, he went to Oxford. He's capable of charm, and absolute bullshit, and he knows exactly what he's talking about. You've only ever met him on a Friday evening. As long as they make sure he's just about holding it together on the job, I can see that he'd be perfect. And I think in the most disenfranchised part of his mind, it probably gives him a buzz to walk into someone's home uninvited and persuade them to hand over their most valuable possessions.' Joe tightened his hands around the rail of the seat in front of him. 'But it's not just what this is doing to his soul, Kit, if he still has one. He could end up in jail. How do you think he'd survive that? Fucking Jesus Christ. I mean, I thought these people were giving him a second chance. I can't—'

Across another of his despairing pauses, she asked, 'How did you find out?'

'Pauly.'

'Ah, right. And where does Dean Purcell fit in?'

Joe flexed his right hand. 'Let's just say that where a person is inclined to smuggle small antiques, silver and so on, they're well advised to rope in someone who knows how to disassemble cars and put them back together again. In

Italy, there's this guy in Milan—well, it doesn't matter.'

'You mean it?' she said. 'You're seriously telling me Humpty's in with, kind of fraudster-type burglarish *smugglers*, kind of deal?'

'I'm not telling you anything,' said Joe in thin tones, 'except that, if this gang ever goes down and Humpty's still with them, I don't see how he can fail to go down too. And what I haven't explained to you, the sting in the tail,' he said mirthlessly, 'is that, not only is the guy who runs this racket, Humpty's boss, a vicious prick, but the girl Humpty's fallen for, whose knickers he tastefully described to you the other day, she's related to this fucker: she's married to one of his cousins.'

A bit of a mess. *A bit of a mess.* They were growling along in the darkness, only four passengers on the bus, one of them up front chatting to the driver; almost a whole bus at their service, in the chill and the dark and the rain.

'Of course, if this were in a movie, it would all be fine, wouldn't it,' said Joe.

Kit mentally skipped this remark, nerved herself, and pressed a little further. 'Where does your job offer fit in?'

'I'm sorry you heard about it from someone else,' he said. 'Don't worry.'

'What it is is: Humpty's had this long-standing offer of work from a guy who used to teach him here. I like him a lot. He's one of those people whose help really isn't self-serving. He knows what he's doing, you know? I suspect he has a bit of a past himself. Whatever, he moved to this place in Gloucestershire, an old farm with outbuildings, lots of space. Humpty could live there, everything. It would be ideal, in that it's work, it's someone who respects Humpty's abilities, who'd know what he was dealing with, and it's right away from here. But that's also why Humpty has dreaded and resisted it, being stuck out in the countryside. I've been trying for ages to persuade him, long before I knew what was really going on. Then, of all things, the day after I first saw you, the very next day, I get this call asking me if I'd like to join a team for a year working on a project at GCHQ. They gave me six weeks to decide. I thought, this is a godsend, something that might finally get us back on a better footing again. I'm not naïve, but what else was there? And he agreed, Kit. He finally gave in, said that if I took GCHQ and was near at hand, he'd do it.'

'I wonder if he's been getting into fights on purpose, in a way, to provoke a crisis.'

'I've wondered that too.'

'So you got this call?'

'Yes, and I cleaned up the flat—took me three days; it's never looked so spick and span, you may have noticed—got a couple of rental agents in to look at it, no problem. I'm telling you everything now. They said they could get tenants in a week if I wanted: terrific. And through all of this, from the minute the phone call came in, I tried to put you out of my mind. I thought I'd better show up for Beginners the following Thursday, given I'd asked you; but when you didn't come, I thought, that's it, good, it's over. Then the next day I didn't know you wouldn't go back for Intermediate instead, and I thought, fuck it. But I didn't want to stand you up if you went. So *again* I went.

And this time, there you were, except you were late, by which point I was so fed up that I asked you to dance backwards, thinking you'd turn me down and that would finish it. But you didn't, Kit. You agreed. You did it. I had every reason to accept the job and no very good reason not to—until, against all good sense, I found myself thinking that, Christ, maybe I had just discovered one sitting opposite me in a little dive of a café in East Oxford, crying into her cup of tea. I couldn't tell you what was going on because—how could I say any of this to you when we'd scarcely met?'

'No.'

'You kept telling me you didn't want to think.'

They got off the bus. The rain had at last more or less stopped, but they still walked quickly, to maintain their warmth.

'And what is the GCHQ project?' Kit asked. 'You didn't say.'

'I don't fully know yet,' replied Joe, speaking, she noticed, in an ordinary way; and at this she realised just how disturbed he had sounded before. 'And I wouldn't be allowed to say if I did,' he added. 'It'll last a year, that's all. I can take a sabbatical here if I want, that's in the bag. The whole thing has come up very last minute, but the connections would be to everyone's advantage.'

'Give me a hint,' she said.

'No, no, you don't understand, I'm not *allowed* to say—anything. We're talking security vetting; the works. I mean, they employ mathematicians, yes? And my specialisation is in the right general area. That's it.'

'For code breaking? What, I don't know—encryption?' She watched for a flicker on his face, but he didn't react.

With a sudden diffuse sense of relief, she laughed. 'That would be so fantastic, Joe, if the reason I didn't know what you did could be the Official Secrets Act rather than because I'm just too dumb to understand it. It would be much more glamorous, anyway.' She leapt over a large puddle.

'Glamorous, I rather think not,' he said. 'Oxford to Cheltenham, that's, out of the frying pan, into the, what?— toxic waste incinerator.'

'Joe,' said Kit, 'I don't really know the answer to this. May I ask you something silly?' She considered not proceeding, but carried on anyway and said, 'Why did you think you might like me, in the first place?'

He sounded wistful as he replied, 'Because you were funny, and sharp, and easily upset, and because the things that pleased you pleased you so much.'

'You please me,' she said.

Joe buried his hands in his coat pockets.

'Cheltenham isn't so far,' she said. 'It isn't the moon.'

'No, it isn't the moon.'

'You love Humpty, don't you.'

He gave her a look, and then, as though putting to her something she still hadn't understood, replied, 'We're brothers.'

'I had a conversation with him just now,' she said, 'well, sort of; when that woman took you outside. I think he was telling me that I was okay now or something. He said I could go with you to the state funeral for the prime minister's legs.'

'He talked?'

'Yes.'

'Why on earth didn't you say?'

'I'm sorry?'

'You do realise they wouldn't have been half so worried about head trauma if you'd told them he was talking?'

'I—no. I didn't think—I don't know about these things. He didn't talk, he mumbled. I'm sorry. Joe, I didn't know.'

'Forget it,' he said wearily.

'I'm sorry.'

'It doesn't matter. Forget it. You know, Kit, not everyone would take it as a compliment, being approved of by Humpty.'

'Did I say I was complimented?'

'You sounded mildly chuffed.'

'Well, I suppose I was,' she said.

'Well, there you are.'

She didn't take in very much after that, until she found herself walking into Joe's kitchen.

It was cold inside. Kit was struck anew by the blood spattered across him, but he didn't seem bothered by it. He did wash his hands, though.

'What do you want? Food? Shit—' he picked up and ate some of the remains of the Battenberg cake that sat, even now, on the table.

'A cup of tea would be a mercy,' said Kit.

This must be what it's like in the aftermath of a shock, she thought—cups of tea, and normality not seeming normal. She stared at the smooth, clean work surfaces and shuddered.

'I wonder why Buddy never mentioned his letters to me,' said Joe, pointing at them.

'I don't know.'

'Perhaps because you're a girl, that made him more comfortable about it.'

'What, giving me stuff on funk holes, trench foot, lice shirts, Bulgarian rapists—' Kit cast around in her mind, 'malignant malaria, spineless Anglicans and the blast patterns made when the Germans drop their bombs on your ammunition stores?'

'Perhaps you *were* the right person.'

'Who knows? But you should read them, definitely.'

'What's a funk hole?' said Joe.

'Oh, a shallow dug-out you dived into at short notice when under unexpected fire. The troops got moved around the whole time and would adopt other people's funk holes in vacated positions. You know what? When they didn't have enough soldiers to man the trenches properly, because the casualties were so extreme, do you know what they did? The men would run up and down, crouching, and let off bursts of fire every few minutes, to make it seem as though there were two or three times more of them than there really were.'

Not sitting, but leaning against the counters opposite each other, they picked away at the food left on the table, and nattered. It was almost as though Joe had said nothing to Kit since the hospital. She desperately wanted time; felt she couldn't process what she'd been told, baldly standing there in front of him.

Perhaps Joe also felt strange, she thought. At any rate, he sounded tense as he said, 'May I ask you something?'

'Go ahead.'

'Eliza Grimwood, when you first encountered the case, what made you look at it so closely?'

She couldn't imagine why he was asking. 'I just had an instinct,' she said. 'I had a feeling about it. And then, as you know, it rapidly turned into a puzzle.'

'That's it? You became puzzled; wanted to get a few facts straight?'

'Joe,' she said helplessly, 'the times I've asked you before about your work, as soon as you've started to answer, my mind has kind of seized up and gone blank.'

'I know,' he said. 'That's a depressingly familiar reaction, from my perspective.'

'But if I sat down and paid attention?'

'I'm sure I could get you to understand it in outline.'

'That's what I was trying to say.'

The kettle began to boil, then clicked off, but Joe didn't move.

'What time does Humpty need fetching tomorrow?' Kit asked.

'I have to call in the morning and find out.'

'Not too early, I hope.'

He glanced piercingly at her. 'You think you'll still be here in the morning?'

'Is that—would that—would that—?'

'As you wish,' he replied.

Would it be all right? She couldn't tell. 'Yes. I mean, yes, maybe,' she said diffidently. 'I'm very tired. For once I'd be pretty surprised if I didn't sleep. You look as though you will, for sure. And I was wondering, anyway, I mean, before

275

all this—Humpty—I was going to say, whether you'd like to go to the fireworks tomorrow? You said you liked fireworks. Have you remembered it's Bonfire Night tomorrow? I mean, the Saturday displays are all tomorrow and the weather's supposed to be clear; I checked.'

A painful look passed over Joe's face. He pulled himself together, turned away and flicked the kettle on again, got a couple of mugs out. Kit watched him while she continued to speak. 'Of course it might not be possible if Humpty needs looking after,' she said, 'although, if he's walking wounded or whatever, he could come too. We could decide at the last minute. It's just, I love fireworks.'

Joe put their tea on the table, pulled out one of the chairs and sat down.

Kit remained on her feet. She was speaking, now, principally to cover his silence. She had the feeling that something was very wrong, but she didn't know what. 'My theory is that the English set them off too late at night,' she said. 'We have such amazing sunsets this corner of the year, early November. Can you imagine if all our Bonfire Night fireworks were set off against skies that were red and purple instead of boring old black? In India, the Independence Day celebrations in Delhi, they let their fireworks off at dusk, these brilliant flares with little parachutes on, so that they take much longer to fall. It looks utterly fantastic seeing the flares drifting down against a more pearly grey and orange kind of sky, you can't imagine.'

Woodenly, Joe said, 'So you've been to India; and Egypt. Where else?'

'Oh.' What were they on about? 'A few places?' she said. 'I love travelling, but I quite get a bit down-hearted after a while taking in everything all on my own. Joe, why are you looking at me like that?' She could hear the agitation in her voice.

He hunched his shoulders desolately, then laid his head in his hands on the table.

'Joe? Joe? What is it?' she cried. 'Joe?'

With a break in his voice, he said, 'I've been waiting all this time—all this—all this *fucking* time for you to ask me to do something—anything: I needed to know you wanted me enough to—' He sat back up and stared gauntly at her. 'I thought, I'll just stick to Fridays, and if she never once says—in *six weeks*—if you never once said to me, "Let's get together, let's do something, can we meet some other day, come to my place, I'll call you", *anything*—then I'd know that you, you didn't really—just *once*—was all I needed. Just once.'

'What do you mean?' She was appalled. 'What,' she said, 'this is some sort of Grimm's fairy tale where I have to pass *tests?*'—angrily throwing her arms out sideways to reject the notion, and smashing—there was a terrible noise— smashing the glass in the picture of the reading girl: it cracked across several ways so that the whole pane slipped, fell out and shattered on the floor. 'No!' Kit clasped her hand— painful as it was, uncut, though the tiles at her feet were strewn now with glittering shards. She re-ran the scene in her mind, throwing her arms out but not smashing the picture.

Except, dreadfully, she had. Here was a blizzard of fragments at her feet. 'Oh no,' she breathed. 'I didn't mean it. I'm so, so sorry. I'll clear it up.'

'Forget it,' said Joe.

'I'll go now,' she said.

'Don't go.'

'I'll pay,' she said, staring at the pattern of slivers flung across the floor.

'Don't be silly.'

Again she—if only; so careless, so humiliating, pathetic. 'Anyway,' she said miserably, 'anyway, who knows *what* they want?'

'I do,' he said.

Kit found herself, for the second time that night, on the edge of tears. 'Look, I just *did* suggest something. I suggested fireworks. I said about fireworks, didn't I? For your information, that equals meeting up on a Saturday, in case you hadn't noticed.'

Joe glanced at his watch, then said, 'If you remain where you are for about three more minutes, it'll become Saturday without anybody trying.'

'Joe—' Her legs felt weak beneath her. She pulled out a chair and sat down.

'What I was trying to ask you just now,' he said more gently, 'I need you to answer this, Kit. You told me—you said, the first time you came here, about facts and truths in literature, that they were understood to have a particular kind of difference in the period you're studying.'

'Yes.'

'So tell me,' he said, 'with Eliza, you've been trying to get the facts as straight as possible. You've been wanting to solve a puzzle, you say—yes? But what *about* truths? That's what I was wanting you to explain. What have you learned— from this ivory horror show, as you once put it—that you would describe as a truth? Can you answer me that? By the way, I would very much like to go to the fireworks.'

Kit retreated far inside herself. A truth? A *truth?* This wasn't something she had properly considered. Her head felt empty; her eyes were brimful of tears. If she had even acknowledged to herself the existence of this question, it was only to the extent that she had been aware, occasionally, of avoiding it—and yet, as she sat and revolved the matter in her mind, she realised that there was a truth she had started, finally, to grasp, at an indefinable moment somewhere between the library table, a dance hall, a balcony and a hospital bus stop; a truth, she thought falteringly, an understanding, that desire was—was one of the most ferocious things a person could feel; and that, if you thought to wed desire to love, then you had to love the person and desire them for all of what they were, their whole human self.

She didn't immediately speak because, as this thought came to her, she was also thinking that she must reply with great care—which she didn't do either. What truth had she learned? Impetuously, she started to say, 'That everyone is—'

She stopped.

'Everyone is—?'

Kit was too shy to tell Joe something so simple; but there he sat before her, *real*.

She made an imploring gesture with the hand that had smashed the picture.

'What?' he said. The vision of her struggling caused his face to slant into a smile.

Kit gazed back at him, overwhelmed by a kind of anguish.

Instead of words, she rose once more to her feet. Without caring, she trod through the litter of glass shards, round the table, walking as a scoundrel might walk the plank. And for the first time, so she realised as he seized her, she kissed Joe passionately, passionately, for himself.

POSTSCRIPT

One holiday, aged about eleven, I found myself quartered in a room with a spellbinding windowsill, on which were wedged not only yellowing paperback adventures by Desmond Bagley and Nevil Shute, but also a desiccated copy of Josephine Tey's 1950s bestseller, *The Daughter of Time*. Its plot concerns a detective, confined to bed in hospital, who attempts via intermediaries to disprove the common notion that Richard III was responsible for the murder of the Princes in the Tower. This implausibly compelling tale evidently remained in the back of my mind for all the years that followed, as it was the first book I turned to when it occurred to me that I, too, could take a genuine mystery, which I had stumbled on while messing about in the Bodleian, and give it to a fictional character to solve.

It is perhaps worth noting that the nineteenth-century material cited in this book is all real. The sources of details and quotations are generally indicated where they appear on the page, but in Chapter 7 there are exceptions to this rule. The review of *Oliver Twist* that warns readers of its being, in places, 'indescribably repulsive and demoralising', can be found in the *Atlas* newspaper, 17th November, 1838. The account of Dickens's public reading, in which, 'gradually warming with excitement he flung aside his book', is given by Edmund Yates in *Tinsley's Magazine* (iv), 1869. The story of Dickens acting out 'Sikes and Nancy' by himself two days before his death, is reported by John Hollingshead in his essay on Dickens in, *According to my Lights*, Chatto & Windus, 1900. The text of 'Sikes and Nancy' can be found in Philip Collins's, *Charles Dickens: The Public Readings*, Oxford, 1975; while for an elegant modern analysis of how this reading affected Dickens's health, see Helen Small's essay on the subject in, *The practice and representation of reading in England*, eds. Raven, Small and Tadmor, Cambridge, 1996. Meanwhile, as suggested in Chapter 6, Charles Field's daily log of his investigation into Eliza Grimwood's murder really can be found tucked away in a box in the Public Record Office in Kew, catalogue reference, MEPO 3/40.

All the passages in this book taken from *Oliver Twist* itself are given in their earliest known form, i.e., as they first appeared in print in 1838. In subsequent editions of the novel, Dickens felt moved to tinker with the scenes of Nancy's murder, making the language slightly less dreadful. He also cut down on his references to Bull's-eye's bloody feet.